Providence
Times Three

Robert Underhill

Also by Robert Underhill

Strawberry Moon
Cathead Bay
Death of the Mystery Novel

Providence
Times Three

Robert Underhill

Northport, Michigan

Providence Times Three
copyright © 2008 by Robert Underhill
ISBN 10: 0-9798526-2-5
ISBN 13: 978-0-9798526-2-6
Library of Congress Number 2008941720

Delicti Press
Northport, Michigan
editor@delictipress.com

This is a work of fiction. Names, characters, places and
incidents are either products of the author's imagination,
or are used fictitiously. Any resemblance to persons living
or dead is purely coincidental.

Publisher's Cataloging-in-Publication
Underhill, Robert
  Providence Times Three / Robert Underhill—1st ed.
  p.cm.
ISBN 13: 978-0-9798526-2-6
    1. Surgery residents—Chicago—Fiction. 2. Murder—
    Fiction. 3. Chicago—Fiction. 1. Title
    813',54—dc22

Acknowledgments

My thanks to Reed Omary M.D. of Nothwestern University Feinberg School of Medicine for a clinical refresher, without which the patients in this novel would have been at risk.

For their close readings of the manuscript and very helpful ideas, I thank Trudy Carpenter, Kathleen Snedeker, Nancy Tefertiller and my wife, Trudy.

1

What the . . . ? Alarm? Telephone? It's the phone. Who would be . . . ? My God! I spin upright, confused for the moment by the strange room. I've slept late and they're calling me from the hospital!

Before I pick up the phone, I try speaking, "Testing one-two-one-two." I pick it up expecting to hear the voice of the Chief of Surgery asking angrily where the hell I am.

"Hello," I croak.

"Well done. No, actually, only fair."

It's only Jeff and not the hospital. I do now what I should have done right off and look at the clock. 5:10 a.m. I haven't overslept after all. Now the question changes to why he's calling me at this ridiculous hour?

"Don't tell me you're calling to grade my early morning phone skills."

"I'm doing what any best friend would do, making sure you've got a good alibi."

"Alibi?"

"Any minute now, the police will call you. I don't want you to slip up and admit you were out driving Pete's van near Northwestern Hospital around nine last night."

Jeff helped me move into my new apartment yesterday afternoon. It's on Fullerton in Chicago's Lincoln Park where the street parking is next to impossible and the traffic too heavy to double-park. We ended up carrying all my stuff two blocks and then up two flights of stairs. After Jeff left, I worked on into the night arranging my paltry possessions before I set the alarm and collapsed fully clothed onto the naked mattress.

Jeff is waiting for my comeback, but I can't think of anything except, "Huh?"

"OK, I'll cut the cute stuff. Last night a hit-and-run driver clipped Mason Atkins as he was crossing Fairbanks Street and killed him."

"Killed . . . you mean he's dead?"

"Like very dead."

Nine o'clock last night. I had still been working away emptying boxes, and I'd noticed out the curtain less window that it was snowing very hard. Jeff gives me the details as he knows them, and I picture the scene in my mind. Atkins was killed on Fairbanks, a block and a half from Northwestern Hospital, at the height of snow storm. Nine o'clock, a dark deserted street except for one witness. Atkins lived in one of the hugely expensive "Gold Coast" apartments within walking distance of the hospital—only three streets to cross on the way home—one too many it turns out.

"The guy didn't stop?" I ask the obvious.

"Probably in Kansas by now."

I know hearing that someone you know has died should bring on feelings of sympathy, even sorrow, but I can't help it: I feel nothing but joy.

"By the way," Jeff adds, "I noted that you weren't appropriately surprised that I'd think you'd need an alibi. Everyone at the hospital will think you need one. I, of course, being a good friend didn't even inquire if you were cruising around the hospital in Pete's van last night. Concern is all that . . . "

"OK, enough BS. If that's all you've got to say, I'm hanging up. Goodbye, good friend."

"A little gratitude is all . . ."

"Goodbye."

The alibi bit Jeff kidded about is because no one has a

better motive for erasing Mason Atkins than I. He is—I can hardly believe it—he *was* the Chairman of the Department of Surgery at Northwestern University and the Chief of Surgery at Northwestern Hospital. For reasons known only to him, he has "loaned" me, a second-year Northwestern surgery resident, to a pigsty of a hospital called Northpark General for the past five months. I swear to you I'm not boasting when I say I know more about medicine than ninety-five percent of Northpark's surgical staff. I don't mean I've had more experience. God knows they've taken out a helluva lot more gall bladders, because that's all they do is take out everybody's gall bladder—the old fashioned way. So, as it sinks in that Jeff isn't joking, and Dr. Mason Atkins is now but a shade, I'm experiencing what one must feel like after hearing that an unknown relative has died and left you a parking structure on Chicago's "Magnificent Mile"—hearing it while gulping down a quart of Red Bull.

I should have been able to find a solution to my dilemma short of depending upon an accident. In many good training programs, residents are given assignments at smaller hospitals. Usually this is done to provide the resident with more, or unique clinical experience. But that would be for one or two months at most, not five going on six. So at the beginning of the third month, I called Dr. Atkins and sort of reminded him I was still at Northpark General. His very short, acidic reply was, "I know damn well where my residents are, Brahms. I don't need you to remind me."

A mixture of shock and anger kept me from demanding a better explanation. His tone, plus the fact of my exile, made it clear to me that I had been banished for cause. Damned if I can figure out what the cause is.

Add it up: my five-month exile to Northpark plus its rat's nest quality and you get my feelings. There's more.

And, maybe this is the worst part—guilt by passive participation. What I mean is I feel guilty knowing that the patients who are treated at this place are getting third-rate medical care and they don't know it. On rounds I have to stand and hear a botched, simple appendectomy requiring a two-pint transfusion described to the patient as "more severe than we expected" followed by "We got it just in the nick of time." The patient expresses gratitude and the bozo surgeon accepts it with noble grace.

In order to avoid guilt, I would have to tell each patient as he or she checked-in to quickly get themselves the hell out of Northpark and into one of the city's many good hospitals. I don't do this. Why? Because—I hate to admit it—I'm more concerned about what would happen to me, knowing Atkins's attitude toward me, than what might happen to the patient. It hurts to face this, but there it is, guilt by passive participation.

The other thing I could do is quit. I don't do this either. That would mean leaving the Northwestern surgery program—one of the country's best. Not something I'd consider—not if my life depended on it—not yet anyway. Jeff suggested I appeal to the American College of Surgeons, the accrediting body for surgical training programs. Going over your Chief's head when you have years more to work under him, is not ideal, especially when you're going to need his letters of recommendation for possible advanced training and board certification.

So, my non-solution has been to endure and hope that whatever burr Atkins has under his saddle will work its way out. Now do you understand my present joy?

I feel confident that Ralph Springer, the staff physician who'll probably take over now as Interim Chief, will quickly rectify my plight. The question before me as I sit here on the side of my bed is, do I call Springer in spite of knowing he'll have his hands full this morning with what he'd consider more important matters, or do I go on in to Northpark and suffer one more day? I start dialing.

When I get Dr. Springer on the line, it's clear he's preoccupied, but it's also gratifying to know that he has my situation in mind.

"Are you scheduled for surgery today?"

"Not today."

"How about your patients?"

"Everything's under control. They could all go home today, in fact."

"Then come on in here. I'll call that hospital and deal with them."

"Thank you, sir."

"No need to thank me, David . . . I'm . . . I'll talk to you later."

Was he about to say, "I'm sorry"? I'd like to think so.

I get a piece of cold pizza from the refrigerator, the remainder of the one Jeff and I'd bought yesterday, and eat it as I walk the two blocks to where my friend Peter Graham's new minivan is parked. At the last minute I'd reluctantly had to ask to borrow it. Earlier, I'd arranged with my old friend, Mike Moran, to use his beat-up old Dodge Caravan, but when I went to him to get the keys, he told me he was sorry but something had come up unexpectedly and he had to use it. So, I was forced to ask Peter. When moving furniture, I'd rather the vehicle is not spanking new.

A muddy sky hangs low over Chicago this morning. It's mid-April. After several warm, sunny days we were surprised last night with five inches of snow. Tired after a long winter of shoveling and thinking hopefully, "It will melt soon anyway," no one is making the effort to clear their section of sidewalk this morning. Fickle spring, teasing the way a father might, returning home from a trip and holding the present you know he has for you behind his back.

The snow doesn't bother me this morning. I'm immune to frustration. My spring has arrived as sure as if I were walking under a sunny sky surrounded by warbling birds perched in flowering trees. I smile and give a hearty greeting to a guy I pass, not caring if I'll get a reply. My joy bubbles up into laughter that I have no wish to control. All this because Mason Atkins has been horribly killed. Well, not because he was killed horribly, or even that he was killed, but rather it's because he's gone ... gone forever. "Divine Providence", if you're so inclined to believe.

I'm anticipating one problem returning to Northwestern Hospital. Shortly before Atkins exiled me last fall, I'd started psychoanalysis. When I'd first arrived at Northpark, I'd informed them in a matter-of-fact way of the three mid-day appointments I had to keep each week. They accepted it without question as if I'd said the appointment was for dialysis. Come to think of it, they probably didn't know the difference. I'm sure the same request to keep these appointments won't get the same reception at Northwestern.

If you've never been to the new hospital, you're in for a surprise. It's as plush as Chicago's finest boutique hotel. As you walk through the door, it hits you; this can't be a hospital, it must be the Ritz-Carlton. Behind the mahogany information desk, a dazzling explosion of matched mahogany panels soars to the ceiling of the three-story lobby. Multiple groupings of tapestry-covered sofas and chairs are scattered about the half-acre waiting area. Or maybe this is an up-market fat farm, you think, where the only medical procedures offered are lipo-suction and botox injections. The docs working here readily admit to feeling embarrassment when colleagues from other hospitals visit. It's like having your buddies come over to your house and find out that your mother irons your undershorts.

I'm happily surprised to find everyone is very friendly this morning as I walk onto the surgical floor: attending staff, fellow residents, nurses and ward clerks. It's not the kind of welcome given to one who has just been released from prison after serving his time; it's more like mine had been a false arrest. Jeff was right, several of the residents kid me about needing an alibi for last night. Something else, I sense that's it's again OK to be a friend of mine and not just an acquaintance. A few of the residents dared all along to be seen as allies, but human nature cautioned others against guilt by association even though I'd committed no crime. A social taint, no matter how unjust, is a very hard stain to remove. Understand, I wasn't as philosophical about this feature of human nature while it was happening to me; I was pissed.

Jack Plamondon, a third-year resident on the general surgery service, is very happy to hear of my return; he can now move on to Children's Memorial Hospital and pediatric surgery, his chosen field. On the other hand, my friend Mike Moran, now the senior resident on general surgery, is equally unhappy when I tell him I need to have time off for my appointments with my psychoanalyst.

"You don't need a damned analyst, Brahms. Nobody on this service has time for personal problems. If you want to waste your money though, you'll have to do it after four o'clock on the days we're not operating. What time is your appointment today?"

"Eleven-thirty."

"OK, keep it, but that's it."

No wiggle room there, but I got off easy. Mike Moran is a good guy, but he also possesses a famously explosive temper. He's been a long time friend and mentor, my "big brother" in my college fraternity and an upperclassman in medical school and this residency. Usually it's been "tough love', but he's always been at hand with valuable advice when I most needed it.

So why am I in psychoanalysis? Mike Moran doesn't know the reason. Neither do my parents. In addition to the analyst, Dr. Mordecai Steiner, only three people know: my best friend, Jeff, Ann Collette, the head ER nurse, and Dr. Vincent Collette, her husband. Back in September, before I was shipped off to the Museum of Medical Mismanagement, I was on duty in the ER here at Northwestern. I was asked to go to one of the treatment rooms where an accident case, a young teenage boy, had just been taken. As I approached, Ann was standing next to the gurney blocking my view of all but the patient's head. She looked over her shoulder when she heard me enter the room and stepped aside and raised the boy's arm. His index finger was literally hanging by a thread of skin.

I passed out, crashed into the gurney and almost knocked Ann down. My head hit the control handle on the bed giving me a two-inch gash. Ann immediately knew she had three problems to administer to: the boy's injury, my laceration and my reputation; it is not good to be known as a surgery resident who faints at the sight of blood. She got me into the adjacent room with a butterfly bandage on my cut and put out the story that the IV stand had fallen over and hit me. She notified the hand specialist, who took the boy to the OR to reattach his finger, and then she doubled back to talk to me.

"David, I've seen you handle gunshots, stabbings, multiple fractures and terrible burns without flinching; what was there about this injury that got to you?"

"Damned if I know."

"I saw the look on your face. Horror. Pure horror."

"I haven't a clue. I'm still shaky."

The plastic surgeon, whom Ann called to close my wound, couldn't figure out how the IV stand could have caused my particular lesion. I knew him pretty well, so I told him the truth and asked him to keep it to himself. The next time Ann and I were on duty together in the ER, she pulled me aside and told me she had discussed my ER incident with her husband, who is a professor in the Psychiatry Department. It was his judgment that I should talk about my unusual reaction with someone while my feelings were still fresh in my mind and before I did what we all tend to do, rationalize, minimize and then forget, passing up a chance to understand and uproot a problem before it becomes entrenched and left to derail us later on.

I agreed. My compliance, however, was mostly because of my wish to please Ann. I was grateful for the genuine interest she'd shown and the actions she'd taken to spare me embarrassment. So that's how I got to Dr. Steiner. The first few sessions with him were very fruitful, bringing to light an incident from my early adolescence involving my father. It wasn't something I'd completely forgotten, but I hadn't come close, until then, to associating it with what had happened in the ER. It fully explained my collapse there.

It was shortly after the ER incident that Dr. Mason Atkins sent me off to Northpark.

2

At eleven-ten I come out of the hospital and get into a cab, which has just dropped off a woman and child at the entrance. I don't use cabs much, but I take one this morning so I'll get to my analytic appointment and back to the ward again as quickly as possible. I settle back for the few minutes it takes to drive to 122 S. Michigan and take that time to let the fact of my good fortune sink in. Even the approaching forty-five minutes with Steiner can't dim my glow, and I have no doubt that he will attempt to do just that. Since Atkins banished me to Northpark, I've been complaining to Steiner about the deliberate, unwarranted, sadistic and personal nature of that S.O.B Atkins's intention to thwart and hurt me professionally. Steiner has tried to get me to consider, instead, what lies behind my conviction that my chief was out to defeat me. Steiner wants me to reflect upon the antecedents of my attitude, which he insists were born in the rotten relationship I'd had with another doctor, my father, Dr. Luther Brahms. True, there's no denying the problem that lies there. Try as I might, I could never get on the good side of my old man. Steiner believes if I could come to terms with the disapproval I experienced from my father, I'd stop blaming Atkins for my problems. Well, I just don't buy it. Lousy relationship or not with dear old Dad, Atkins is— was—really out to stick it to me. I can't get Steiner to acknowledge this. No doubt a big reason I've kept coming here to see him is my stubborn need to convince him he's wrong. Another reason is lying up there on his couch at this very moment.

Already knowing today's session will be a waste, I enter the building where nearly all of Chicago's analysts have their offices. Steiner will attempt to mine the same old vein, but I'm feeling too high to participate. Today I'm an introspection no-show.

Waiting for the elevator, I begin to wonder for the first time why nearly all of Chicago's analysts are in the same building. A herding instinct? But animals huddle together for protection. Do analysts experience the world as hostile? A fleeting thought.

I get off at the 14th floor and cross the hall to Steiner's door, rereading the sign, "Mordecai Steiner, M.D.", as I have done each time I've come. Am I afraid he might have moved?

You can always tell an analyst's office door. Only a small discreet sign with the name, no more than that, no indication of what goes on behind the door. Internal Medicine? Ophthalmology? No, just a doc in there named Steiner, waiting for you to land on his couch like a cerebral spider waiting for a *mishugina* fly. Well, that simile definitely doesn't apply this morning. I am nobody's fucking fly today. I stride into the small, dimly-lit waiting room with the authority of a field marshal and drop aggressively into one of the two chairs and pick up the same damn New Yorker I've been looking through for the past month. We patients are about due for a new magazine—one to look through for the next month. Perhaps Steiner thinks one should actually read the articles, but I'm never in the mood when I'm sitting here— ads and cartoons, *no mas*.

To enter Steiner's inner consulting room from the waiting room, you walk through a small hallway where you can hang your coat. Its real purpose is for privacy; two doors lie between those pouring out their secrets and those who might overhear. Listening with anticipation, I hear the muted click of the inner door being opened. One of the three peak moments of my week is about to occur—I will see the patient who has the appointment before mine. She has to walk past me as she leaves. The door into the waiting room opens and there she is. She is unbelievably attractive to me. It's as if those who designed her had access to my mental blueprint for the perfect woman.

We have advanced to the point of as much intimacy as is possible with our analyst looking on from the open doorway. This means that I smile my most mature and friendly smile this morning and say, "How's it going?" in a tone intended to tell her what a helluva guy I am. She returns a friendly smile and says, "Hi." Do I hear something new in her tone? Is our relationship deepening?

For a moment I'm lost in the intoxicating fragrance she has left in her wake, then I become aware of Steiner standing there, observing me. He says, "Good morning." His deep, slow, lugubrious voice reminds me of Boris Karloff's. Looks like him too, which is scary. Some might say his usual expression is neutral, but that would only be if you are the kind of person who tastes a vintage Chambertin and pronounces it "OK" instead of identifying the complex hints of berry, vanilla, cinnamon, leather, tobacco and witch hazel. (I've never had any wine in that league, but I do read Wine Spectator at my dentist's.)

Today, Steiner's is definitely not a neutral expression. I discern: 1) amusement over my helpless passion for the other patient, 2) his silent, condescending judgment that any hopes that I have in that direction are misguided and 3) that he is sorry he had to end his session with her and now has to endure the next forty-five minutes with me.

I don't care. Nothing can bother me today. Dr. Mason

Atkins is dead. I'm eager to dump on Steiner the fact that this chance of fate has done more for my well-being than the hundred or so sessions and the small fortune—even at a very reduced fee—I've squandered on him. I don't intend to phrase it just like that. Actually, I feel some guilt about any discrediting thoughts. After all, he doesn't make me come here, and his behavior has been a model of serious professional dedication. And, yes, I have learned things about myself and about how we *Homo sapiens* think and act. However, the problem that brought me here in the first place was resolved long ago and this delving into the past in order to understand my feelings about Atkins can't compare to the exuberance I experience from his death.

Steiner closes the door, follows me into the room and goes to his chair, which is close behind the head of the leather couch. The couch, I've learned, is a standard model for psychoanalysts. There are no arms and no back. One end slopes up at a slight angle to an attached cushion. Upon this is placed a fresh paper tissue for each patient, which is too bad. I'd rather have my head touch the same material as the beautiful head that lay there a few minutes ago.

I lie down and wait for the familiar squeak of Steiner's chair easing back into the reclining position. The couch is still warm from the woman's body and I will my own to absorb it. I look up at the holes in the acoustic-tile ceiling and compulsively locate and put together the ones that look to me like the Pillsbury doughboy. This done, I stare down over the toes of my shoes at the curious picture that hangs there on the wall. It is representational enough to suggest people involved in some kind of ritual, or, then again, it might be that they're playing marbles or rugby. The picture irritates me. It seizes my attention and I waste several dollars worth of my time each session wrestling with its meaning. I have accused Steiner of placing it there for assorted, devious reasons: to keep patients occupied while he has a chance to clip his fingernails, to collect responses for a book he intends to write, entitled *The Crazy Things People Say*, or that his granddaughter painted it in her kindergarten art class and he is being the good granddad even if it does waste his patients' money. You're getting an idea why I think he would rather still be seeing the previous patient.

Usually I lie on the couch for most of a minute thinking of where I will start. Today I know where I'll begin. I'm only searching for the right words.

"Doctor Mason Fucking Atkins was killed by a van," I blurt out.

"A van?"

His response baffles me. The operative words here are "Atkins" and "killed" but he has focused on the car's model. He senses my confusion.

"I mean, I heard on the radio that he was killed, but there was no mention of a van."

"Yeah, there was a witness who saw a dark-colored van hit Atkins and take off. The guy who saw it was a block away and couldn't make out any other details—make, license number."

My thoughts come back to myself.

"Doctor Springer, who has taken over as Interim Department Chief, told me to return immediately downtown to Northwestern Hospital to the general surgery service. There was an admission contained in his words—as much of an admission as he dare make—that Atkins's loaning me to fucking Northpark for the last five months was wrong. He said, 'I'm sorry.' At least I think he was about to say it."

"The general surgery service?"

Steiner does that a lot—repeats what I've just said. They must learn that in a class.

"Right. I've lost five months already, but with Springer in command I'll start making up for lost time." I pause and feel the relief of knowing the barrier blocking my advancement has fallen.

"And this never would have happened unless Doctor Atkins had been killed?"

"Absolutely."

Steiner lets it lie, but I know he doesn't think any problem I have with my self-image could be resolved by a moment of bad visibility on a dark Chicago street. I can't leave it alone, however, and bait him a bit on the subject of real change versus psychic change. He doesn't take the bait, but comments in a way that I know will be his final statement on that topic today.

"To paraphrase Freud, 'A cigar may carry much symbolic meaning, but one can also smoke it with satisfaction.'"

OK, so to humor Steiner I make an effort to let the current situation evoke what it will from the past, a half-hearted effort at best, which dries up before long. Glancing at my watch, I see that there are five more minutes to go in the session. I tell Steiner that now that I'm back downtown, I've been told that I won't be able to keep the same appointment times. He replies that he has one opening in the afternoon and will try to work out other times for me.

I don't want to think about the past any longer but I have to fill time and my mood makes me daring—my mood and my knowledge that I won't be coming at my former appointment times. This carries the huge significance that I'll no longer be able to sit and watch the beautiful fellow patient walk by.

"It's on my mind, so I should say it, right? So here it is, I want to meet the woman who has the appointment before mine. I also think you don't want me to."

"Yes?"

I snort a short laugh. "She could be that once-in-a-lifetime perfect mate for me."

"Yes?"

"So that's it. What's her name and telephone number?" I laugh again knowing that what I ask is forbidden and there isn't a snowball's chance that he'll reply. A few moments pass.

Steiner says in an even voice, "You said that I don't want you to meet her."

So I say without censoring, "You don't think I'm good enough for her. It would be like the butler's son asking the lord of the manor if he can marry his daughter." I laugh out loud. "A daughter whose name he doesn't even know."

There is a smile in Steiner's voice as if he is enjoying what he says next.

"What do you make of the fact that you have made me this woman's father?"

"Hmm. I guess I did, didn't I."

"But not yours apparently." After a few beats he adds, "Our time is up today."

3

I leave Steiner's office, take the elevator down to the lobby and am fastening my coat before I face up to the meaning of the final words of the session. They mean that my issue with fathers—good and bad—has not ended with Mason Atkins's death. I'll have to think about that more, but my immediate concern is getting back to Northwestern Hospital as quickly as I can. I step out of the building into that wind tunnel called Michigan Avenue. Through tears brought on by the raw, icy blast I scan the next cohort of traffic for a vacant taxi.

On my way back to the hospital, I think only of never seeing my dream woman again. As it is, she's only a face glimpsed on a passing train, but I've been able to see that train pass three days a week. Perhaps it's this repeated stimulation without any real satisfaction that has stoked my obsession with her.

I check in on my ward to let them know I'm back and that I'm going to the cafeteria for some lunch. I spot Peter Graham sitting alone at a table. He's one of those who openly remained my friend. It was his van I used to haul my furniture to my new apartment. He waves to me to join him. I go through the line and get a tuna sandwich and coffee and take it to his table.

"Good to have you back, old buddy," he says. "I notice that you're not wearing a black armband for our late chief."

"Terrible tragedy, but my mourning apparel is at the cleaners. By the way, did Jeff give you your keys? He said he'd see you this morning. I parked it where you usually do in the structure."

"Yeah, I got the keys. Your move go OK?"

"Let's say that all my things are in the door."

"Know what you mean. By the way, Dave, I did some checking a while ago and found out that no one from our program ever rotated through Northpark General before you were shanghaied there. That was a shitty thing Atkins did to you."

"Yeah, I know no one else has been so favored. You checked it out? Why?"

"Curious. No, it was more than that. I wanted to know if he was as big a bastard as I thought."

We concentrate on our food for a bit before he turns to me with a mock-serious expression.

"I hope you have a good alibi for the time he was killed. After all, I can think of no one with a stronger motive for knocking him off."

Here it is again. I wonder if Jeff put him up to it. I study his face. No, he thinks the joke is original.

"Never thought of that," I say. "But you're right, hit-and-run is a crime."

"Maybe more than that. I was in the ER last night when Atkins was brought in. He was D.O.A.—skull fracture— but when I heard about it, naturally I came around. One of the cops, the one who was first on the accident scene, started talking to me. You know how it is; a person needs to unload. The cop told me he knew the witness who'd reported the accident. The guy owns a business on the cop's beat, that deli two blocks from here in the luxury condo tower. The cop said that when he first arrived, this witness told him in a confidential between-you-and-me kind of way that it looked to him like the van had swerved deliberately to hit Atkins."

I had been picturing the scene as Peter spoke and I

say, "Yeah, but the streets were very slippery. Hitting the brakes could cause a skid that might look like a deliberate swipe at Atkins."

Peter gives me a look with feigned suspicion. "If I were the investigating officer, I might hear what you just said as very defensive."

"OK, but if I did do it, remember you're an accessory for loaning me your van."

As the days pass, Mike Moran's statement proves correct. I am so immersed in the intense stimulation—over-stimulation—of the demands on both the wards and the OR that the only other concern to penetrate my consciousness is occasional hunger.

Although Dr. Steiner finally manages to work his patients around to make two late afternoon appointments possible, I have really lost interest in the process and mildly resent having to depart from my demanding new present to "free associate" about my past. I don't want to hurt his feelings, but it can't go on much longer. If only he'd admit I'm right about Atkins.

Not a small part of my loss of interest, I realize, is due to not seeing the beautiful fellow patient. Now, as I sit and watch different patients depart through the waiting room before each of my new appointments—one an adolescent boy with an attitude and the other a middle-aged woman with too much makeup and a diamond big enough to cause tennis elbow—I experience a sense of tragic loss. As they say, it's only when someone is gone that you realize how important they were. Hadn't fortune brought this wonderful creature into my path, only to have my passivity let her slip beyond my grasp?

The only way I can think of arranging to see her again is to hang around in the lobby of Steiner's building at the time I know she'll be leaving her appointment. "Hi, haven't

seen you for a while. I'm David Brahms, a surgery resident
at Northwestern. I had to change my appointment times
with Steiner. Don't you think it's weird the way you can see
someone for so long and never really get a chance to meet ? If
you have a few minutes, we could go and get a coffee."

Does that sound as if it would work? I'm not sure and
I'll only get one chance. That uncertainty is not what is
holding me back. The big problem is that I can't get the
damn time off to be there in that lobby.

I feel I should say something about this idea of the
"only woman in the whole world." This notion, of course, is
way out of date. It's a poetic, sentimental concept from the
time when guys wrote sentimental poems to women they
mooned over, because other sentimental poems told them
that they should. It was the ideal of medieval romance
reborn in the literature of the Victorian age and repeated
in the movies of my parents' generation. I'm embarrassed
that here I am a solid citizen of Chicago, that hip center of
advanced technology and hot and now life styles, yet
possess this Victorian core. It's as if the editor of *Gourmet*
magazine had a secret craving for Jello salad. For this
reason I haven't mentioned my obsession with this woman
to any of my friends . . . until today in the hospital cafeteria
to my friend, Jeff Richards.

I say as casually as I can, while stirring a little sugar
into my coffee, "There is this woman who used to have the
appointment before mine at Dr. Steiner's. I never got to
meet her or talk to her, but there is something about her
that makes me think she is the perfect woman for me."

"Really?" Jeff allows as he reaches down the table for
an abandoned *Tribune*.

He didn't look disgusted and say "Puke" so I'm
encouraged. I continue, "I know it's stupid, but maybe it's
true that she is the only perfect . . . "

"You're right . . . it's stupid," he mumbles as he's looking for the sport pages. "I felt that way once when I was in junior high. What a fucking mistake that was. It turned out that the only 'perfect' thing about it was the match of the benzene rings on our hormones. Those few months when I was suffering that delusion almost ruined my life. That is, it almost turned me off women."

Standing, Jeff brings his big-boned, six-feet-three to attention and makes a loud announcement to a 4 a.m. hospital cafeteria peopled by two cafeteria workers, two OR nurses and us.

"I want to publicly testify to my enduring gratitude for my escape from the clutches of Emily Boynton." Then he sits down and opens the *Trib*.

I have my answer. I have to face up to having an unspeakable affliction, probably not even as acceptable to my friends as a flesh-devouring venereal disease. That doesn't change the fact that I have it. I have a bad case of LOVE AT FIRST SIGHT. This pain I feel in my chest must be love. If it were pericarditis, I'd have a fever.

I decide that if I subject this amorphous emotion to scientific analysis, I might restore my standing as a rationalist. If I'm successful I can even write a scientific paper, modern man's triumph over the supernatural. So, that's what I occupy myself with the next several days every time I have a free moment. Which means that I'm able to think about it for a total of fourteen minutes.

I have an excellent specimen here to investigate, an uncontaminated case, since mine is love based on sight alone. I know nothing about the object of my love except her appearance. I hear an objection. I do know she is seeing a psychoanalyst. I will cite this contaminant in my paper for the sake of completeness, but between us I think it is irrelevant. Any kind of person may seek the services of an analyst for any number of reasons. So that doesn't really tell me anything. Now back to her appearance.

She's lovely . . . no, that's not specific. She's about five-six—maybe seven. Her hair is very dark with perhaps an auburn highlight. This would be best determined in the sunlight. I believe her eyes are a greenish-hazel. Again better light than the forty-watt bulb in Steiner's waiting room would help decide that. Her complexion is an olive hue, mysterious by the soft light.

So far, what have we got? Not much. I have probably seen a million women, give or take, with these features without falling head over heels. So what else? Her movement. It's unique. It's a composite of such subtle and complex elements that it will be a push to describe it convincingly enough to satisfy the editors of a scientific journal. Her movements are graceful yet quick. Her stride is long and purposeful as if on her way to a meeting where she will make the final judgment on the *New Yorker*'s next cover. She carries her head erect, because she hesitates to meet the gaze of no one. And she meets one's gaze with a look—that look—it's one of openness, but not naiveté, rather that of an exquisitely sensitive person who has known pain at the hands of others, but still believes true friendship is possible and is willing to give you the benefit of the doubt. OK, maybe that's a lot to see, but damn it all, I swear I'm right. Her smile. I have only experienced it in that limited context I've described, and only for two seconds each time, which means I have only been able to observe the tip of a vast reservoir of sweetness. Only a thorough and genetically natural sweetness could cause the muscles around her mouth and eyes to move into that exact configuration.

I have only seen her in the clothes of cold seasons, hence I can only guess at what lies beneath wool jackets and sweaters, but I can say with confidence that she is slim and athletic.

I have not made a judgment, thus far in this analysis,

about beauty. I read recently of a study undertaken to define "beauty" in women. This research team showed hundreds of pictures of women's faces from various cultural groups to men and women from all the groups and asked them to pick out the most beautiful faces. The investigators found that the same pictures were singled out by all of the groups. In other words, there is universal agreement, no doubt genetically determined, among the members of our species about who is a beautiful woman. I flatly state that my dream woman's picture would end up in everyone's "beautiful" pile.

OK, concede for the moment that her appearance is really unusually special. Still, why should I have this uncontrolled mental-chemical thing happening to me? As I've stated, I have lived a number of years in a setting rife with cool females and this never happened before. Jeff Richards contends that my condition is common in junior high. Is, therefore, mine a case of retarded development? After a short time will I spontaneously recover as Jeff successfully did? Right now that isn't the outcome I desire, but I'm suffering and the time might come when I want to be put out of my misery by any means.

To further my scientific analysis, I ask myself what goes on inside the person "falling in love." Maybe everyone doesn't think his or her loved one is the only person in the whole world, but they do in their own minds make the loved person into something more special than their friends experience that person to be. I remember when my soon-to-be brother-in-law was obviously smashed over my older sister. I thought he was indeed out of his mind. I knew the truth about her. Understand, she was a decent person who had treated me kindly . . . on the whole. But to look at her the way he did? Come on. Everyone has heard it said that a man picks someone who reminds him of his mother. Not a chance. The dark lady of the waiting room looks nothing like my mother. Psychoanalysts are quick to say, "Ah ha, that means she is the opposite of your mother." To be fair, I've never heard an analyst say that, but it wouldn't surprise me. Well, she's not the opposite of my mother, either, just to get that out of the way.

Today standing gowned and gloved for an eternity while the OR team is completing a tardy prep, I get to thinking about this puzzle. It comes to me that there is something very narcissistic about falling in love. One creates a perfect being in one's mind and then has that perfect person choose you out of all the rest of mankind for a mate. Talk about egotism, I laugh out loud at the thought of it and the anesthesiologist, who is all thumbs this morning having just dropped the same bottle for the third time and is certain that I'm laughing at him, shoots me an angry glance.

Tonight I'm making penne with olive oil, garlic and rapini for dinner. I turn the greens over in the pan with a wooden spatula, while continuing to explore the connection between narcissism and falling in love. Suddenly, I find myself wondering if the perfect woman isn't in fact a perfect female edition of oneself; the woman one would want to be if one were a woman. This is beginning to sound and feel sort of kinky, so I retreat from these thoughts and settle back into the ignorance of simply being hopelessly, helplessly in love—enough questions asked. Or rather, one question remains; how will I meet her?

4

Once a month the Surgery Department holds an M&M conference. M&M is not candy in this case: the letters stand for morbidity and mortality. It's where the department's dirty linen is hung out to dry. Not dirty in the sense of wrongdoing, but a presentation of and examination of errors that have occurred in clinical judgment. It's a big deal and most of us residents attend if we can.

This morning Mike Moran is the presenter. Mike is a muscular, kinetic kind of guy, who always appears to be about to initiate some action: swing a bat, lunge through a starting gate or throw a punch. This morning he has taken a stance in the front of the room like a football captain about to make a half-time locker room speech telling the team it had better get its ass in gear, or answer to him personally after the game. He starts to speak, stops and glares until everyone gets quiet and then he begins again. We all know something about the case he is going to present. The incident occurred last fall, just before I was shipped out to Northpark General. Normally, an incident of this kind would have been scheduled for M&M review much sooner, but because a lawsuit resulted, it was delayed until after the court's decision. That came down a week ago—the hospital lost. Mike begins telling us of the night last fall when he was one of the residents covering the OR. At 3:10 a.m. he was called to the ER to consult with a first-year resident on duty there about an auto accident case. The ER resident suspected that the twenty-one-year-old woman he'd just examined had suffered a ruptured spleen. The woman's abdomen was difficult to palpate, because the muscles were in spasm, a sign of irritation of the abdominal lining and possibly caused by bleeding from a damaged spleen. Her hemoglobin and hematocrit were normal, but her heart rate was very fast and her blood pressure was 90 over 56—much too low.

It was a clinical picture of rapid bleeding into the abdomen. Immediate surgery had to be performed to save the woman's life. Mike ordered a unit of plasma to be started and a blood cross-match to be done. He told the frightened woman they would operate and everything would be fine. He turned away from the gurney to head for the OR to scrub, when a nurse walked up to tell him two men were demanding to speak to him. Immediately he was confronted by a guy in his mid-twenties and an older man dressed in black. The younger one identified himself as the woman's fiancé and informed Mike that under no circumstances could the woman receive a blood transfusion as it was against the tenets of her religion. She was a Jehovah's Witness.

This was something Mike had heard of, but not something he could credit as rational. He turned back to the woman and asked her if it was her decision to not allow a blood transfusion. She looked at the two men standing on each side of Mike before answering, then nodded weakly.

At that moment, the woman's parents arrived in the ER and brushed past the nurses and onto the scene. After they had identified themselves, Mike told them of the situation. Both parents were furious, shouting that Mike should not listen to these "two nuts" or to their daughter, who had been brainwashed by them.

The older man in black then spoke. He said he was the woman's pastor and that she had signed a "contract" when she joined their congregation, one stipulation of which was the ban against accepting a transfusion of blood.

Now, emerged the Mike Moran of my experience. He told the nurse to call security and have everyone removed from the ER and to have the patient transported immediately to the OR. There he removed the woman's spleen, while administering five pints of blood. He saved her life, but the fiancé and the church sued the hospital and the hospital lost.

The bottom line and the lesson we are to carry away from this morning's presentation: you cannot go against a person's wishes—even it means they will die. Before he sat down, Mike summarized his own interpretation of this lesson. "You do what you know you must do and let the pieces fall where they may."

That's my Mike, headstrong and impulsive, but . . . well . . . Mike. I agree with him, but I wonder if I would have reacted with such decisive saber strokes.

As we're about to hear the next case, I see Jeff come into the lecture room and look around. He sees me and comes to the vacant seat next to me. He leans over toward me.

"The June and July on-call schedule is out. Do you know if you're on call over the Fourth of July weekend?"

"No, I haven't seen the schedule yet."

"I didn't think you would have." He looks around to see if he is disturbing anyone. "It happens that you're free and so am I and I have a plan for restoring our exercise-starved bodies to youthful health."

"We're going to paint your apartment."

"Even better than that if you can believe it. My older brother and his wife have a vacation cottage up in northern Michigan on the Leelanau Peninsula."

"We're going to paint your brother's cottage?"

"Listen to me. There is this outfit that puts on bicycle tours. It's a great place to ride: beautiful scenery, good, low-trafficked country roads, plus—tah tah—there'll be plenty of neat women we can invite to share our free beds."

"They'll be too tired and very sweaty."

"They'll be too tired to resist and the cottage has a shower."

"I don't have a bike."

"My brother said we're welcome to use their bikes."

"Isn't that a long way to go just to ride bikes?" I ask.

"That's where the free cottage is and that's where the bikes are."

"OK, but why the bike tour thing? That must cost something. These are public roads, right?"

"The tour is where the chicks are."

"Ohhh."

"You're a little slow, Brahms, but not entirely hopeless.
"

That evening, as I'm getting out my keys to enter my apartment building, Mrs. Heilman, on her way out, holds the door open for me. She is a friendly, tiny widow in her early sixties who lives on my floor.

"Oh, Doctor Brahms I'm happy I ran into you. Are you free this evening?"

This takes me by surprise, so I can think of nothing to say except the truth, that I am free, even though I had sort of pictured a quiet time at home brooding.

"My daughter is in town with the Ambrosia Quartette. They're playing at the Newberry Library. I have an extra ticket if you like chamber music."

What can I say after admitting that I'm free, besides I do like chamber music . . . if well played. Back when I was moving into my apartment and had a heavy box of books in my arms, she stopped me and introduced herself as my neighbor. She followed that by saying she had a daughter who was a musician. I become nervous when daughters are mentioned in the first fifteen seconds, especially by a mother who does this even though she can see that I'm holding a heavy box of books.

The Ambrosia Quartette? I take the ticket realizing that now I'll have to make an appearance. This audience will be sparse and my absence obvious. I climb the stairs studying the ticket in my hand. Should I ask someone to go with me? Whom can I ask? I begin flipping through a mental address book of women I'd dated recently until I recognize that I have no wish to be with any woman but one.

I check my answering machine. No calls. The apartment doesn't feel like home yet. What needs to be done? Maybe I miss the El train roaring by. It only cleared the windows of my old apartment by a couple of feet— shook the dishes, stopped conversations. Strangely, the place came to feel like home and, as you'd expect, it *was* cheap. But, friends insisted that I move. Jeff claimed he had to take Xanax before he could come over.

The menu tonight was to be Tabasco-slathered, canned baked beans with a cut-up "no fat" hotdog over toast. But after washing out some socks and undershorts for tomorrow, I realize there's barely time to make it to the concert, so I change quickly and hurry to the Fullerton El station planning to grab a sandwich downtown after the concert.

It is a fine spring evening, one of those that makes one believe there really are "new beginnings." A decent-sized crowd is entering the Newberry. I should find out who Newberry was; he or she did Chicagoans a big favor by endowing this place. I notice there is an exhibition of antique maps, which I'd like to see, but the crowd is larger than I'd anticipated and I'd better find a seat. I go into the room where the performance is to be held and look around for Mrs. Heilman, but I don't see her. The program contains three baroque standards and an equal number of pieces that are unknown to me. I see Mrs. Heilman come out of a room at one side and take a seat saved for her in the front row. Following her are the four musicians. They take their places, acknowledge the applause and get right down to business.

Ambrosia, the food of the gods. It takes chutzpah to call one's group the Ambrosia Quartette. It creates an initial "Oh, yeah?" in the listener which the musicians, then, have to overcome. Three women and one guy make up the quartette, the guy plays the viola. I try to guess which of the women is the daughter. The cellist is a big rough and ready kind of gal, who clamps her legs around the instrument much as an Aussie sheep shearer would. I imagine wool flying off with each vigorous stroke of the bow. I eliminate her. That leaves the two violinists. She must be the one playing the first violin part; I see a resemblance. She's maybe late twenties and attractive in an academic sort of way. I sit back and listen. In the end, the quartette convinces me they have a right to their name.

After the concert, I walk over to Mrs. Heilman and tell her how much I enjoyed the concert and she makes me wait until her daughter comes out of the green room so she can introduce me. Her name is Emily. There is an excitement in Mrs. Heilman that I have seen in mothers who are hopeful that they've found a man for a daughter about whom they have begun to despair. Emily emerges carrying her violin case and smiles and shakes my hand. Her grip is unexpectedly firm and I find myself thinking a violinist should be more careful with her fingers. I compliment her on the performance, wondering how I can comfortably disengage from mother and daughter, when a tall John Cleese look-a-like joins us. I recognize him as the violist. He also turns out to be Emily's husband and I gratefully shake his hand as if he had just returned my lost wallet. His name is Eric.

To celebrate the occasion, Mrs. Heilman is treating them to "a bite to eat" at a nearby restaurant and invites me to be her guest. I'm hungry and they appear to be good table companions so I accept.

The instruments are stowed in a van parked at the library and we start out along Walton Street on this balmy evening. I learn, as we walk along, that the musicians returned only this morning from Ann Arbor, where they played a concert at the university's spring music festival. They are buoyant with success after all those thousands of hours of practice and doubt. Their laughter says it has been worth it, but a couple of Eric's quips suggest that his long apprenticeship on the edge of poverty has established that condition as the default reality and the present recognition and applause as only a temporary one that might crash at any moment. By the way, I recognize it's my months with Dr. Steiner that have sharpened my awareness to that kind of content in a quip. But, happily for me and for them, Eric apparently has also adopted the attitude that since success may prove ephemeral he's going to enjoy the hell out of it while it's at hand. So I anticipate a good time. I'm surprised when I discover that Mrs. Heilman has picked Le Colonial on Rush Street for this "bite to eat." One doesn't "bite" one's food at this fine room; one savors.

In the entrance foyer we encounter a group coming out. Peter Graham, my fellow surgery resident, is one of its members. We greet each other and then as a second thought Peter draws me aside.

"David, do me a favor. There's a guy sitting at that table in the corner. The guy with the big hair."

I look over his shoulder and immediately pick out the person he means. He's somewhere in his sixties with a great head of wavy silver hair like one might see on a

tanned, Italian industrialist attending the Cannes Film
Festival, a stunning young woman fastened to his arm. In
this instance, she's sitting across the table from him.

"What about him?" I ask.

"Just watch him and let me know tomorrow what you
think of him."

"Why?"

"I'll tell you tomorrow."

I want to press him for an explanation, but his group is
moving out and mine is on the way to a table.

It so happens that the chair left for me when I get to
the table is the one facing the subject of my assignment. I
take another glance at him while I'm opening my napkin
and putting it on my lap. He didn't get his tan in Chicago,
that's for sure. He is animated, laughing overmuch at
something he has just said in a way that might be intended
more for those around him to see and appreciate than for
his impressive young dinner companion, born I would
judge about the same year the guy got his first face lift. I
put him out of mind for the moment and immerse myself
in the conversation at my table.

I become aware of the man again when I catch some
movement in my peripheral vision. The waiter and the
maitre d' who seated us are standing at the guy's table. The
maitre d' is shaking his head emphatically. The waiter
pours a small amount of red wine into an empty glass and
hands it to the maitre d' to taste. My interpretation of his
gestures says the wine is good—very good. At the same
time, the waiter is opening another bottle.

A sample of this new wine is poured for the customer,
who says something, while sadly shaking his head.

The face of the maitre d' becomes flushed, but my
silver-maned object of study is smiling a tolerant smile,
like that of Sir Neville Mariner listening to an argument
that hip-hop is superior to J.S. Bach.

If I've figured it correctly, Mr. Handsome has rejected two bottles of wine. I'm too far away to read the label, but I can see simple, sedate, black lettering on a white background. This just might be one of the biggies. Like a sensitive film director, who knows when to resolve the crisis, the guy smilingly asks for another entirely different wine. How do I know this? Because the maitre d' and the waiter leave, and the waiter returns with a black-labeled bottle. The guy's lovely companion has enjoyed the performance. Her expression says that she knows her man is very experienced in both life and love.

"What are you looking at?" asks Eric.

"Guy over there just refused two bottles of wine. Never seen that before."

"Great, I wonder if the restaurant will sell us the rejects at a discount?" Clearly the comment of a guy who still thinks like a poor musician.

5

The next morning I arrive at the hospital to find that a special assembly of the entire Surgery Department has been called. It's scheduled for ten o-clock. Busy on the ward with the changing of dressings, fluid intake and output charts and such, I don't cross paths with any of the surgical staff until the announcement over the PA reminds everyone of the special meeting.

Peter Graham sees me before I go into the lecture room where the meeting is being held. He stops me and puts the question.

"Well, what did you think?"

"You mean about the guy at the restaurant? Unless I missed something, and I must have or it's too easy, I make him out as a garden-variety narcissist. What's the story?"

Peter smiles. "You'll see." With that, he puts his hand on my shoulder and guides me into the room.

I see that Jeff has saved a seat next to him, so I make my way over and ask how things are going. I have paid no attention to those who are on the stage at the end of the room, because I expect a lineup of the usual suspects. It is Jeff's focused attention and the fact that he hasn't heard a thing I've said that cause me to follow his gaze to the front of the room.

"Jesus!" I gasp.

"I see you've fallen right in with the opinion of the powers that be at the university. However, I know better; I've been told by a reliable source that he's uncircumcised."

I don't know what the hell Jeff is talking about, but I dismiss it because, I'm trying to understand what the guy with the big hair at the restaurant last night is doing on the podium looking so pleased with himself.

I lean toward Jeff. "Who's the guy up there in the silk suit?"

"That's our new Chief, the new Chairman of the Surgery Department, our new lord and master, Doctor Dickson Conway—Dickie to his friends and the rumor is that surgery residents are not among those honored few."

"They sure didn't lose any time finding a replacement for Atkins. This guy must have been standing in the wings." I add, "Hey, maybe he's the one who killed Atkins to get his job."

Ralph Springer steps up to the lectern, taps the microphone and begins the introduction. He is smiling and trying to sound as pleased as his message claims he is. I don't have perfect pitch, but my acquaintance with Springer tells me the note is off key. He is very disappointed, maybe even sad having to make this introduction. He tells us how fortunate the university and the hospital are that Dr. Conway could be persuaded to leave his post with the National Institutes of Health, where he was Associate Director of a division called the National Center for Research Resources. Springer says that Conway's special experience at the NIH will strengthen an area of our program that must be brought in line with the demands of today's medicine.

I'm wondering what that area might be, when Jeff whispers, "He means Dickie has contacts to get research grants."

Of course, that would be Dickie's specialty—he has contacts.

Dickson Conway's acceptance of the introduction and the obligatory applause is beautiful to behold. Just a *soupçon* of humility to show you he knows the form, but not enough to cause you to make the mistake of thinking you had any chance of being considered an equal. He makes what he deems to be a charming reference to the "pulchritude" of the departmental females he has met so far and pays lip service to the excellence of the medical staff. This latter is done in a masterful choice of words, hesitations and body language that communicates his intention to get rid of those he considers to be dead wood ASAP. Next, he cuts to the chase with a preview of the emphasis his chairmanship will place on research.

I remember Jeff's quip about contacts and I understand the university's choice of Dickson Conway. Someone in the upper echelon wants more research coming out of the Surgery Department and more grant money with which to do it. Teaching doesn't impress alumni donors as much as media headlines. "Solar Powered Elbow Installed by Northwestern University Surgeons Helps Ailing Cubs Pitcher Win Pennant."

Conway continues, "I'm keeping this meeting brief this morning, because I want to get to work right away, but I will be setting up meetings with each of you to discuss how your interests can be wedded to the department's new goals. Thank you."

Conway jumps down off the podium, eschewing the stairs and dashes out the door like a man with a mission. Poor Ralph Springer uses the stairs trying not to look too much like a sycophant hurrying to keep up. At the doorway he casts a backward glance at all of us that pleads for sympathy.

"Marry your interests to the department's new goals," I repeat.

"There's no doubt about who's going to wear the pants in that marriage," Jeff tacks on.

Today is Thursday and I have an appointment with Dr. Steiner in the late afternoon. The teenager with the attitude exits the inner office and snarls as he walks past me. All on its own, my foot makes a slight move toward tripping him. Steiner is at the door watching. His sad look says we still have much more work to do.

The first thing I talk about when I'm on the couch is Dickson Conway's appointment as chief, but Steiner seems disinterested.

"The word around the hospital is that a homicide detective has questioned some of the people in the hospital administration about Dr. Atkins. Peter Graham had told me earlier that the cops were viewing the hit-and-run as a homicide. This seems to confirm it. Every time anyone mentions Atkins's death, the "joking" suggestion is invariably made that I need to work on a good alibi for the time it happened. They've got me wondering if maybe I did do it. You know what I'm saying? Possibly during a trance—a fugue state—I killed him without remembering it. I did fall into a deep sleep that night, exhausted after carrying furniture up and down two flights of stairs. Maybe in an altered state of consciousness I let my unconscious wishes take over and I drove downtown and ran over him."

"You're serious?" Steiner says this in the voice Jeff might use if I were to ask him to skip an evening with one of his nurses to go with me to see *Casablanca* at the Gene Siskel Center.

"Yes, I'm serious. I have a history. After all, I did lose consciousness that day last fall in the emergency room."

"What you're postulating is that you got up from your bed and drove downtown to arrive at precisely that moment when Dr. Atkins was crossing the street to his apartment building. After running him down, you drove home and found the same parking place you had vacated earlier to still be empty—in your neighborhood a miracle worthy of a report to the Vatican."

Steiner is having his bit of fun. You can't blame the guy; a psychoanalyst's work must be very dull. If his other patients rattle on about the same self-centered nonsense as I do, it has to be a long, long day, only listening, while never being allowed to get in a word about his own life.

"What about my fainting in the ER; wasn't that a psychic thing?"

"I'm sure you remember from your medical school psychiatry lectures that an amnesic fugue state, required for this midnight ride you propose, is a psychological horse of an entirely different color than fainting."

"I think I missed that lecture."

He says nothing, so I add, "Well, it was something that bothered me. I assume from what you've just said that I am safe to forget it." No answer. "Good," I say.

It crosses my mind to ask if the beautiful patient has said anything about not seeing me in the waiting room. I bury that question.

I change the subject. "I've heard nothing about returning to Northpark General, so it looks like Dr. Conway is for my staying put."

No comment from Steiner.

"There's no doubt that he's in love with himself, but maybe he's not such a bad guy after all."

Nothing but horse droppings. If I can't get into more worthwhile material, Steiner is liable to cut his own throat. But, I can't; more thoughts about the beautiful woman come to mind and nothing else seems important. Either I've got to make an active move to meet her, or I should quit coming here.

I make a couple more stabs at thinking of things to say and then give up and wait for the session to end.

We are at the bedside of a patient on rounds the next morning, when a nurse comes up and motions me aside.

"There was a call for you. You're wanted at the Surgery Office."

"You mean, now?"

"Yeah, the secretary said, 'Right now. There's someone here who wants to talk to him.'"

Someone? What's this all about? I go back to the bedside, wait the few minutes it takes for the staff doctor to finish his examination and to move on to the next patient, and then I leave the group and walk over to the Galter Pavilion.

Mrs. Tobin, the Chief of Surgery's secretary, looks up as I approach her desk. She has the expression of a person appraising another after having just heard unsavory news about them.

"There's a homicide detective here who wants to talk to you. He left, but said he'd be back in a few minutes. You can wait for him in the office across the hall."

My impulse is to ask her what the guy wants. "Thanks, Mrs. Tobin. Has he been interviewing any of the other guys?"

"Not to my knowledge. He asked specifically for you."

It's about ten minutes before a stocky man of medium height wearing a black windbreaker comes into the room and closes the door.

Lieutenant Mario Gemiano has just entered my life. He is one of those few people you'll ever meet who possesses what you'd call a huge personality. He commands the same kind of attention as that of a cannon ball whizzing toward your nose. His approach is quiet, but then a cannon ball's probably is too. His stocky body supports a head that could have come off a bust of the Emperor Tiberius.

"So you're Brahms." I hear the voice of my grade school

principal that first time I was sent to his office, and I relive my same muffled, squeaky answer.

"Yes, sir."

He sits quietly, appraising my appearance and my reply. I can see that his summation doesn't place me in a category with his heroes or even his poker buddies.

"Where were you, Brahms, on the night of April nineteenth."

"April nineteenth?"

"Yes, the night your former chief, Mason Atkins, was deliberately run over."

"Deliberately run over?" I've become a parrot.

Gemiano waits for my answer.

"Ah, I was at my new apartment. I'd just moved in that day. At nine o'clock, I was emptying boxes of books."

"What's that? How do you know it was books? Why not pots and pans?"

"Well, I only have two pots . . . or are they pans."

Gemiano looks at me with ignited interest, as if he just realized I was a space alien.

I hurry on, "I looked out the window and I noticed how hard it was snowing . . . great big flakes."

"You say at nine. Why was it that you were noticing all these things at precisely nine?"

"You see I still had a lot of unpacking to do and I looked at the clock to see how late it was getting to be . . .that's when I looked out . . . out of the window . . . it was books I was unpacking when I looked . . . out."

"You know, Brahms, I didn't ask you what you were doing at nine o'clock."

"You didn't?"

"No, I didn't but I know why nine o'clock is on your mind."?"

Where the hell are we? I feel like Alice in Wonderland.

We sit looking at each other for maybe a full minute.

"I understand a friend helped you with this move. Was he still there when you were unpacking these books?"

"No, Jeff, Jeff Richards, went home much earlier—seven, something like that."

"Then you were alone?"

"Yes."

"The rest of the night, alone?"

"Yes."

Again we sit looking at each other for another minute.

"You hated Mason Atkins," Gemiano states flatly.

"Well, no . . . I admit I didn't like . . . "

"Didn't like my eye, you hated him. He was screwing up your life. What did you do to make him treat you like that?"

"I . . . I don't know."

"You don't know what you did to make him screw up your life?"

"No."

"Then, you admit you thought he was ruining your life?"

Did I just admit that? We sit looking at each other again.

"OK, I admit I hated . . ."

"The bastard."

Finally, my brain gets itself together and decides to say no more. I think the Lieutenant recognizes this.

"One can understand why you ran him down."

"I didn't run him down."

Gemiano stands up. "That's all for now, Brahms."

"It was just a fishing trip, old buddy. A half-hearted one at that." Jeff has opened up his ham sandwich and is applying three more little plastic bags of mustard.

"Why do you say half-hearted? It sure as hell felt

whole-hearted to me."

"Look, if they're really serious they haul your ass to Police Headquarters. They can really scare the shit out of you there. All he was working with is motive, and yours is money-in-the-bank. But, that's all he has. From what you tell me, he did some of those Lieutenant Colombo dance steps to see if you'd trip over your own feet—and you did. But, what did he gain? It's no secret you hated Atkins. Furthermore, the bottom line is that they don't have any other suspects, or he wouldn't have played this charade with you."

I feel better, not splendid, but better. However, I can't get myself to believe Mario Gemiano would do anything dumb. When a great general like Napoleon seems to be making a stupid move, the wary opponent starts to sweat.

Foolishly I put Dickson Conway out of mind much like some legislators do global warming. But, it only takes a few days before the reports start to circulate about the meetings he's had with the senior residents. Most thought that nothing would change for them since they were so close to departing the program. Not so. The stamp of Conway's rule is to be on all of us. We are to march forward from our training and into the real world under the banner of RESEARCH. All of the senior residents are having an extra month of research and the writing of a publication-ready scientific paper added to their graduation requirement. This means delaying their leaving by a month. Outrageous! Very inconvenient for all of them, since they were going on to other commitments such as private practice or advanced training fellowships and they are expected to show up there as per their earlier agreements. Immediately we are coming together in groups to discuss whether or not Conway has the authority to do this. The conclusion is that since he's the chief he can do anything he damn well wants to in the program, but we also believe we'd be supported if a formal complaint were directed to the American College of Surgeons, the authority supervising training programs. No one, however, wants to be the person to file that complaint. Again, who dares to get on bad terms with one's chief when letters of recommendation will be needed in the future? We all think Conway's action to be totally high-handed and unfair. The senior residents are all very angry, but it ends there. Most get busy making their adjustments. Mike Moran is unable to do this. Because he can't show up July first, he'll lose a coveted fellowship in surgical oncology at Johns Hopkins. Mike is furious. The seniors have it bad, but it turns out it can get worse.

My appointment with Conway to learn of his plans for me is on a Friday morning. I go over to the Galter Pavilion to the Department of Surgery office and approach Mrs. Tobin's desk. I'm nervous. I'm nervous because I don't like the guy and I'm afraid it will show. I don't want him to even notice me. I want him to forget about me. Let me get on with trying to make up for the time I've already lost.

Mrs. Tobin checks with Conway then tells me to go in. Right away I notice that major changes have been made to the office décor of the Chief of Surgery. The walls are now plastered with photographs of Conway with various people. I'm not free to examine the pictures closely, but I'm certain the other people can only be celebrities. The desk looks like the one Atkins had, but the chair behind it certainly isn't. I'd bet it's the same massive, black leather throne I once saw in a film about Mussolini. Conway is in it, his magnificent hair set off nicely against the dark leather background.

Conway is not the same bon vivant I remember from the restaurant. He is now a field marshal, sparing a moment from the battlefield to deal with tedious, mundane affairs of state.

"Have a seat, Brahms." He waits until I'm down and then asks, "Are you by chance related to the composer?"

Here's a question I've heard often. I hate it because it's a downer however I handle it. I am related very distantly to the great man, but if I go through the true version, including the fact that I don't know a treble from a clef, I come out a disappointingly weak link to my famous ancestor. If I take the short and simple route and lie and say, no, I disappoint just the same.

"Distantly." I hope this will get me by.

"Really? How distantly?"

"Well, very distantly."

I can see his disappointment. He would like to have been able to brag that one of his residents was Johannes Brahms's favorite great, great, great grandson. I don't want disappointment to be his association whenever he sees me or hears my name, so I continue to talk—about Brahms—about anecdotes I've read about the great man. This has to come from things I'd read, because he had never been mentioned much in my family. I watch with despair as I see his disappointment turn into boredom and then into irritation. Finally he puts me out of my misery by raising his hand and switching the topic to the program he has devised for me. Contrary to his earlier stated intention that there would be a marriage of the residents' interests to his own goals, no mention is made now of my wishes in the vows I'm required to take. He tells me in a matter-of-fact tone that six months of research is being added to my residency.

Maybe I wasn't paying attention and I didn't hear that correctly. He must have meant to say six weeks.

"I'm sorry, sir, but you just said six months."

He looks puzzled, as if I had just pointed out that he was sitting down.

"Yes, Brahms, that's true; what's your point?"

"That's half a year, sir." I choke out.

"If you prefer to view it that way."

"But, sir, you see, I'm already delayed in my clinical rotations. I spent five months at Northpark General Hospital doing intern's work."

At this point, Conway opens the folder that is lying on his desk.

"I know all about that. I have Doctor Atkins's report here. He makes it clear that he did not consider you mature enough to continue the usual training program and hoped that given a year more of general ward work, you might be able to resume your surgical training. It was his judgment that a year would be required and only half that time has passed."

My mouth gapes. Immature? What the hell does that mean? I feel rising rage. Atkins had been planning to keep me in that medical wasteland for a whole fucking year! Some miraculous source of good judgment controls my tongue. I sit and stare at Dickie Conway. Again, to whom can I complain? If I appeal to the American College of Surgeons, Conway can point to his predecessor's documented assessment that I'm immature and perhaps not surgeon material at all.

He closes the folder. "Your research rotation will begin June first and you will be in my lab working with me. I have an interesting project in mind and expect some good work from you. After that . . . we'll see."

I stand up. "Thank you, sir. I look forward to working with you."

Part of me is observing this whole scene as if up in the corner of the ceiling looking down at the two of us. It's a scene from some movie, but something is missing. Oh, yeah, I'm not saluting and clicking my heels.

Much frustration can be siphoned off through a good sweat. At the start of our roller-blade outing this Sunday, I had been seething with anger about the cold-hearted tyranny of Atkins and Conway. By the time Jeff and I have skated north from downtown along the Lake Shore bike path to Lincoln Park, I have blown off my wild anger and I'm able to address my situation with something like calm objectivity. We collapse on a bench looking out at Lake Michigan.

I take a swig from my water bottle and say, "I have to be careful not to lump Atkins and Conway together. Conway can't have it in for me like Atkins did; he doesn't know me. He's only a narcissistic bully who is going to see to it that his name is in lights no matter how many slaves die in the silver mines."

Jeff blinks, bewildered. "You've lost me. Slaves in the silver mines?"

"OK, it's a shaky metaphor. The point is, he is able— thanks to my pal Atkins—to rationalize using me in his lab while I 'mature'. He promised to give me a squeeze at the end of six months to see if I've ripened into a decent resident. Believe me, I know the only way I'll achieve that is through six months of ass kissing."

Two nice-looking women on bikes pass, diverting Jeff's attention. He grabs my water bottle, takes a long swallow then says, "As far as I'm concerned, Conway has a death wish. I mean, giving you a six-month sentence, when he must have heard the rumors that you're the one who ran over Atkins."

I don't respond to this, but I know Jeff pretty well and I can see that he's worried about something and I think I know what it is. Hearing what Conway has done to me has him worried about his own fate. He's now on the vascular surgery rotation and is worried Conway will yank him off for another one of his research projects.

I say, "You could suggest to your chief, Boyle, that you have a research project in mind that deals with vascular surgery, one that utilizes your current clinical data."

Jeff regards me with surprise at my clairvoyance.

"If you can get something underway immediately," I continue, "Conway would find it difficult to take you away from Boyle. After all, you'd be doing research."

Jeff brightens as if I had just informed him that a traffic judge he's about to face is his father's old college roommate.

"Right on, Dave. You're a good friend, and I know just the project. As a matter of fact, I've been collecting some data on my own already. Great idea."

Jeff is smiling, potential disaster averted. I seem to be on a problem-solving roll, so I direct my attention once again to my own situation.

"I may be wrong, but I'd swear Atkins hardly knew my name before last fall. As a matter of fact, he used to get me mixed up with an orthopedic resident named Bramley. Hell, he might not have even known I was in his program."

Jeff gets up off the bench. "Let's keep moving. I'm getting a little cold." The breeze coming off the lake, which had felt good at first, has become chilling.

"You know, that's not too far out, Dave. I mean his not knowing you. I heard that Atkins was at a cocktail party where he introduced himself to Vince Grauer. It was the day after Vince graduated after five years in the program. Surgery residents flew below Atkins's radar."

We are skating slowly, heading toward the Zoo.

"Then how in hell did he come to the conclusion that I was immature, so immature, in fact, that I needed 'a year more of general ward work'? And why send me to that cesspool where I couldn't learn a damned thing, because I already know more than most of the staff. What was it that happened last fall to bring me to his attention?"

"Wasn't it last fall that you went through that period of telling a lot of grade-school-level jokes? I remember the one about the guy who used one of his wife's tampons to . . . "

"OK, OK."

Jeff was right; an old friend's wife had forwarded a lot of bad jokes on e-mail. There is something about a really unfunny, bad-taste joke that compels one to pass it along. I broke out of it by ceasing to open anything she sent me. What was she thinking?

Reviewing that period in my mind reminds me of my fainting in the ER. Atkins must have got wind of that. The plastic surgery resident, to whom I'd confessed the truth about my fainting, must have told him. Atkins would be the kind of person who'd need to disassociate himself from such a wimpy resident, like the French general in the movie *Paths of Glory* who had a soldier shot because he broke down and couldn't leave the trench during a suicidal charge.

We take off our skates at the primate building and make our way to the Colobus monkeys in our stocking feet. Jeff and I have been regular visitors to this family of apes since medical school and we have given them names. The senior male, old Rufus, spots us as we come up to the window. We know that he recognizes us, but he has to play it cool as if to say humans are beneath his notice. Sissy, the young aunt to Pamela's new baby, sees us and flashes a seductive smile. She quickly grabs the baby from her sister and swings over to another branch, where she gives Jeff a look.

I nudge Jeff. "She's saying, 'Hey there big fella, see what a good mother I'd be.'"

Long-suffering Pamela climbs up and pulls her baby out of Sissy's grasp and barks a reprimand.

"Go get your own kid!" I say in my Pamela imitation. "I would if only Jeff could get a night off from the hospital," I reply for Sissy.

Jeff flashes an inverted lip kiss toward Sissy. "Brahms, I'm beginning to believe in love-at-first-sight."

"A guy could do a lot worse."

We skate the quarter mile to Clark Street and a diner, where we get a couple of bowls of chili. Dickson Conway is on my mind.

"You know, when I was listening to Conway I had this feeling that he and Atkins were alike in some way. They certainly don't look alike. But there's this gut feeling that they had something in common apart from being arrogant pricks. I said this to Doctor Steiner and he said I was correct: what they have in common is that I have transferred my unconscious anger with my father onto both of them."

Jeff jumps up and returns to the service counter where he gets a bottle of habanero hot sauce. Sitting down he begins transforming his chili into a bowl of fire, saying, "I don't mean to contradict your shrink—whom I admire, by the way, for hanging in there with someone as sick as you—but I did hear about something those two have in common—or had in common, other than your unconscious. They had been buddies for a long time, how long I don't know."

I think about this. Could I have tuned in to vibes about their friendship? I don't believe in clairvoyance. Maybe they hung out together so much they picked up each other's mannerisms.

"How did you find this out?" I ask.

"Grapevine."

"I wonder if it explains Conway getting Atkins's job so quickly. Maybe someone on the hospital's Board of Directors is an old buddy too."

"Like they say, it's who you know." He runs a spoonful of blazing chili around his mouth, swallows, pauses as he follows its scorching slide into his stomach, smiles through tears and adds, "So I'm counting on your becoming rich and influential."

"Now my life has purpose."

Of course I regale Dr. Steiner with the gross unfairness of my changed training schedule. I whine more in his office than outside of it, just as kids whine more around their parents than away from them. Outside of his office, I appear to have resigned myself to my fate. And, what Dickson Conway has me doing qualifies as fate. The so-called interesting project he said he would be working on with me has me alone in a small, windowless room feeding data into a computer all day. Most days I don't see him at all. In fact, most days I believe he isn't even in town; he's showboating at some meeting where he is invariably part of a panel discussion. Panel discussions that I've experienced consist of half a dozen hot dogs sitting up on a stage saying little of importance while using up an hour or more of your life stroking each other. OK, I'm bitter.

As I see it, there are two types of research, one expands our knowledge and the other expands someone's *curriculum vitae.* The ones with the most substance to contribute to the world can usually do it with one or two publications, as did Watson and Crick or Fleming or Harvey or Einstein. Beware the man or woman with forty published papers. Dickson Conway has fifty-five and counting. I'll bet you not one of them has influenced any other research of importance. My half-year here on the hamster wheel will kick out at least five more useless additions. And they will all get published in reputable journals because of his name. The emperor is sending us a piece of his clothes, so we had better display it in the window.

I said I was bitter. And I'm exaggerating. Not everyone with a long list of publications turns out crap, but I won't waffle when it comes to Conway. His dedication to research is as great as his appearances in the lab would indicate. Plus the data he has me entering has nothing to do with surgery. It deals with the cost effectiveness of various compositions of ward personnel. This is administrative research, not surgical research. Eventually I'll get these numbers compiled into tables, with which he can bore a sleepy post-lunch group at one of his out-of-town meetings. But, hey, who cares? Certainly not those who hired him. They turn to other business, no longer concerned with what they've put in motion. But you can bet they'll applaud him heartily at every opportunity. The last thing they want to hear is negative feedback.

I'm spending a year of my life as a slave in the silver mine, clinging to the same hope that enabled those poor Indian bastards in colonial Mexico to keep putting one foot in front of the other: someday I may be free.

I find myself having fantasies of a dark van clipping ole Dickie at one of his conferences.

6

The July Fourth weekend arrives and, while I wasn't excited about a bike tour when Jeff first mentioned it, I'm now very ready to get away for a few days from Chicago and the monk's cell where Conway has me imprisoned. I'm also hoping the break will provide some distance from the nagging knowledge that I may be alone on Lt. Gemiano's list of suspects. We take Jeff's car and make the six-hour drive, first south into Indiana and then all the way up into Michigan's Leelanau Peninsula.

On Saturday morning we unload the bikes from the car at the tour assembly point in the parking lot of the village of Leland's public athletic park. Jeff and I are late, because the key to the garage where the bikes are kept at the cottage wasn't where his brother said it would be. The phone hadn't been turned on yet for the summer and we couldn't get a signal on our cell phones to call Jeff's sister-in-law. Getting the cell phone to work meant we had to drive to the top of a nearby hill. Once we got into the garage, we found that the tires were flat and no pump in sight.

We arrive at the assembly point and spend the first few minutes finding someone who will loan us a pump. The guy says something about "pista" when he hands it to me. I soon find out that means it doesn't fit the valves on our mountain bikes. I'm just getting started on the second pump, when one of the tour leaders comes over and gives us a hurried, capsule version of the info he'd delivered earlier to the rest of the group. Finally, we're ready, except that I have wound up with the sister-in-law's bike. I'm six-one and she must be four-foot-nine. I've extended the seat post as far as it will go. It's like riding a unicycle.

There is a good crowd, maybe fifty or so, all with that eager "thank God winter is over and we can live out-of-doors once again as man was intended" kind of look. A sharing experience like this tends to lower the usual social barrier between people. Bonding is rapid, as Jeff had predicted. In other words, if you join in with the flow, you can make out like a *bandido*. And, surveying the crowd, I see plenty of passable candidates with whom one might enjoyably share a natural human urge.

Jeff is looking at me and smiling. He sees that I'm into the idea.

I smile back. "Nothing like restoring our exercise-starved bodies to youthful health."

The *Obergruppenführer* is a woman in her mid-forties and without a doubt a Marine drill sergeant, who spends her leaves taking skiing groups down the north face of the Eiger. She holds up her arm in a gesture dangerously resembling an infamous salute.

"We're heading out," she commands in a tone that says only the brave need follow.

Immediately before this, she had been talking to a group of three women at the head of the pack, all wearing the same type of black Lycra leotard riding garb you'd expect to see on serious racers. Their matching shirts bear the same flashy green, orange and pink design—members of a cycling club or maybe even a racing team. Some of us are going to do some damn serious cycling.

My gaze becomes fixed on one of these three women. She has her back to me, but the information my retina gathers forms a gestalt that is identified by the control center in my brain's optic cortex as an object whose presence should immediately be made known to the procreative center in my hypothalamus. "Now hear this!

Now hear this! Prepare to procreate!" With an efficiency to be envied by the military, I feel my groin swinging into action. I can't dignify my reaction more than this, because ninety-nine point nine percent of the data is originating from my focus on the woman's buns—her marvelous buns in shiny Lycra. What my peripheral vision picks up of the rest of her doesn't object.

She swings an unbelievably shapely leg over the bicycle seat as she turns to say something to one of her friends. My heart does a back flip. There is no mistaking the profile even with the helmet. She is the dark lady of the waiting room. I can't believe my luck. What a coincidence! After months of having her pass within inches of me, it is way over here on the other side of Lake Michigan that I finally have my chance to meet her. I have only to navigate through fifty eager bikers to accomplish it.

A tangle of bikes bearing bikers of every persuasion slowly funnels through the narrow driveway exiting the parking lot. My impatience to get to the head of the pack has me attempting to cut people off and squeeze through nonexistent spaces. At this stage of the ride everyone is fresh and no one is content to pull aside and let some pushy jerk pass. All I accomplish is to gather menacing looks. By the time I get out of the lot, my girl is out of sight.

Jeff manages to zigzag through the crowd and up to me.

"What the hell's got into you, do you need to make a pit stop or something?"

I already know Jeff's opinion about love at first sight, so I'm not about to give him the chance to call me stupid again.

"I hate crowds. Give me the open road."

"Yeah? Well, your rudeness has already eliminated at least a dozen very sharp ladies as possibilities for our evening entertainment."

I'm not interested in any possibility but one.

"C'mon," I say with challenge, "Let's put our backs into it—see how fast we can go. A show of virility is an irresistible aphrodisiac for women."

This causes Jeff to picture us speeding by choice females, smiling and making opening remarks that can be collected later when we stop for lunch. He shoots out ahead of me.

After leaving Leland, we cut across the peninsula. I think we do this so we won't miss an opportunity to climb every god damn hill. I feel queasy and want badly to take a granny-stop except that by now Jeff and I have passed so many other riders that I think we must be getting close to the dark lady and her friends—just up ahead around the next bend or over the next hill. So I keep pumping, until there comes a point where I know I'll have to stop or die. Just now, a knot of riders appears about half a mile ahead gathered around the sag-wagon under the shade of a roadside tree. Drawing closer I can make out the distinctive uniform she's wearing. The problem, I now realize, is that I don't want her to see me in my depleted condition. In addition to which, I'm sure I won't be able to speak and I might even throw-up on her spiffy biking shoes. I needn't have worried, because before Jeff and I can dismount, she remounts and speeds off with her two buddies.

I don't feel well and can only sip at the water offered me. Maybe I've made a mistake. Maybe she isn't the woman for me after all. Perhaps I need a mate that likes to go for walks . . . strolls. What's wrong with an evening over a chessboard?

The next stop is the village of Northport, where lunch will be ready in the city park. Surely she'll take enough of a break for me to have time to go up to her with whichever of my prepared introductions seems best suited to the moment. Jeff became chummy with a cute blonde during the pause for re-hydration, so he is content to pedal along slowly and schmooze her up. I tag along behind them, happy with the new pace.

Northport is just like the village that came with my electric train set. Idyllic. I didn't believe there was such a place back then and I still don't: white, frame churches, a barbershop with a candy-stripe pole and a harbor-side park with a bandstand. I pick her out immediately. She's standing and talking to a guy who is seated cross-legged on the grass at her feet. This is awkward. I need her undivided attention. I decide to kill some time by standing in line for a sandwich and a soft drink. Jeff is completely occupied with his new friend, so I'm free to plan my approach and initiate it ad lib. I look over her way and am startled to see she is no longer in the same place. Has she gone off with this guy? No, I see him, now. He has his shoe off and is pointing out something about his foot to another guy who looks sympathetic. Damn, she's gone! Has she started riding already?

"Excuse me. Hellooo."

I look up to see one of the tour personnel waiting for me to tell her my choice of sandwich, tuna or salami.

"Tuna and a Coke, please."

I take my sandwich and pop and go to stand on a knoll where I can survey the whole park. People are gathered in small groups all over the lawn. Some are standing, others lying down. Very few are sitting and my own numb rear says why. A few stragglers are still descending the hill toward the marina. We'll be here a while. Then zap! I spot one of her two friends standing over to the left and every part of me revs up. She must be there too. Yes, there she is. She's lying on the grass with her head on the abdomen of the third member of the trio. She has her helmet off. She is laughing and this is causing the other woman to laugh so that her abdomen jumps up and down, which in turn causes my woman to laugh all the more. My woman? Strange, but that's how I'm feeling as I watch her.

I discover that I'm moving toward her. My instincts have taken over, not giving another male a chance to beat me to my goal. In moments I'm standing over her, looking down, a sandwich in one hand a Coke in the other. I have given no thought to what I'll say. The three women look at me with surprise. I have to say something.

"Hi."

I notice that the one who is standing is giving me a dubious frown. I look down. My dream girl is looking up at me. I discern a hint of puzzlement, but there is also a very friendly smile that says she will consider my intrusion with an open mind.

"Hi, yourself," she returns.

A very rapid sequence of thoughts zips by. I have always assumed that if I were able to confront her, she would immediately look into my blue eyes and recognize me as the interesting guy she has seen at Steiner's office. I am faced, at this instant, with the apparent untruth of that assumption. I don't want to say, "Remember me? We both go to the same analyst." Her friends might not know she sees an analyst. The reality here is that I know I have to say something immediately or look like a clown. As I said, all these considerations flash by in a nanosecond. When that happens—all that cognitive concentration—a guy tends to neglect his social composure, which allows the jaw to slide downward into a demented gape.

She is looking up at me with the sympathetic, hopeful expression of a parent willing her dumbstruck kid to remember the words to that song at the third-grade spring concert. Maybe it's the encouragement I see there in her expression that causes me to remember that I'm still wearing my helmet and sun glasses. I take off the glasses and hold the earpiece between my teeth and desperately begin to fumble with the helmet strap. I do this with a sandwich in one hand and a Coke in the other. I think I hear the woman standing next to me give a snort of laughter.

My woman extends both her hands toward me. "Let me hold those for you," she says.

My hand touches hers in the exchange. Everything else is now blotted out. All thoughts of looking stupid cease. What her friends think of me is as unimportant to me as which county we're in.

I get the helmet off. If she still can't recognize me I'll be a guy standing there, helmet in hand, with her holding my sandwich and Coke while I've only managed to say, "Hi."

"Of course," she says. Her smile broadens to include me in a special category. She laughs. "Yes, it was the helmet."

I take my lunch from her and put it into my helmet. She springs easily up and introduces her friends.

"These are my good friends, Marcia and Billie."

My vocal chords come through for me. I say in my best baritone, "Pleased to meet you. I'm David Brahms."

"And," she says, playfulness in her voice, "I am Fahra."

She tells the others, "David and I have known each other for months, but we've never met. Figure that one out." With that she takes my arm and begins leading me away adding, "I'd like to get another drink."

Recovering my social skills, I ask the others if they'd like something also.

"Thanks, a 7-up."

"Make that two, thanks."

Three things are at the front of my mind. The first is the feeling of her hand on my arm, the second is that she has a foreign accent—one I can't identify, and the third is the pleasure of now knowing her name.

While Fahra waits for me on a bench, I run the drinks back to Marcia and Billie. They are sitting on the grass, now, and I know by the way they look up at me that they've been talking about me. They thank me and say something, which, with my mind locked on Fahra, I don't comprehend, but I smile in response and trot back to the bench.

I've been carrying my sandwich and Coke in my helmet. I'm so thirsty my tongue is sticking to the roof of my mouth, not a good condition if one is embarking on the best conversational performance of one's life. I open the can and take a swallow, and then I begin to recite a prepared opening speech in automatic mode, much the way a tipsy Barrymore must have gotten through the first act of Lear without knowing he was even in the theater.

"Isn't it weird how you can become so familiar with a person, seeing them for years even, without knowing his or her name?" I say.

She smiles past this invitation to comment on the obvious and asks, "Brahms. Are you by any chance related?"

"Actually, yes. He's something like a great, great third cousin. The musical gene got lost along the way, however. I can't even carry a tune."

I yell at myself. Not that way stupid! Don't say negative things about yourself. She'll have to say it can't be true, or else appear to agree that I'm defective.

She smiles, playfully. "Maybe he couldn't carry a tune either. Maybe that's why he played the piano instead of singing."

She helped me step around that nicely and she now doubles back to pick up my opening.

"You're right. Among other unnatural aspects about seeing a psychoanalyst is the repeated passing by another patient with only a nod, when you're sharing the same experience. I'm happy that we've remedied that situation.

But I haven't seen you for several weeks."

"I know. I had to change my appointment times. I'm a surgery resident at Northwestern and my schedule changed at the hospital."

Like a formal musical piece, conversation tends to follow convention. A theme is introduced and the variations follow. A talented conversationalist, like a gifted composer, may come up with unexpected twists, but they are still variations. At this point the theme is of our both seeing Steiner. She can ask what I think of him. That would put me on the spot, especially when I know that whatever I say may come to her mind in her free associations during one of her sessions and be reported to him. Or, she can be more personal and ask why I'm in analysis. That might be too intrusive on just meeting me. I am preparing myself to reply to one of these variations, but she has unexpected news.

"What do you think about his retirement?"

"Retirement?"

"Yes, didn't he tell you?"

I'm thrown into a quandary. Can this be true and if so, why didn't he tell me?

"When did you last see him?"

"Wednesday evening."

"That explains it. I saw him Wednesday and he said nothing. He told me yesterday. He said he would retire at the end of August."

And, I think, he'll be on vacation the whole month of August: they all do that. What does that leave, a month? I say this.

"He said he wouldn't be taking a vacation this year. That means he's giving us two months advance notice. From what I've been told by a friend, that's a very short time; six months is usually the minimum notice analysts give their patients."

I feel better thinking that he didn't forget to notify me, but I'm still surprised.

"Why do you think he's retiring?" I ask.

"Well, he is old enough. I have a friend—the one I just mentioned—she's a social worker who hangs out with a professional group that gossips about all the psychotherapy crowd." She adopts a mock conspiratorial tone. "So, what do you want to know?"

"Well, you said he was old enough to retire."

"Mid-sixties. More?" She smiles.

"Will you tell him I asked?"

"No. If you promise not to tell him I told you."

I laugh out loud. She gives me an inquiring look.

"I feel like we're kids telling each other secrets about the parents."

"Yeah, so, weren't they the best secrets?"

"You're a very bad girl. So tell me."

"First of all, although you probably know this, he is highly regarded professionally. He keeps to himself pretty much—only sees a few close friends socially. They, by the way, call him Mordie."

"Mordie? Can you see yourself calling him Mordie?"

She laughs. "I couldn't force my vocal cords."

"You say 'he sees socially.' Isn't he married?"

"He's a widower. A sad story. His wife and their only child, a son, were killed in a boating accident a number of years ago and he never remarried. The son was a student at Northwestern. He had taken his mother out into the lake in his small sailboat, where they were rammed by a drunk in a powerboat."

"Damn!"

"Yes, and according to the story, Dr. Steiner withdrew into himself . . . permanently."

Psychological trauma. I wonder to myself why he didn't avail himself of his own medicine, but then, I think that some things can't ever be "cured." Hearing Steiner's story causes me to feel a little guilty about baiting him about the usefulness of analysis.

"I guess the guy deserves to retire and have some years devoted to enjoyment. I hope he moves to a southern state where he can get outside for exercise. I bet the only exercise he gets now is walking from his chair to the waiting-room door."

"I agree, and that consulting room pallor of his could use a healthy dose of sunshine."

Sensing that we've covered the subject of Steiner's retirement, Fahra changes the subject. "Do you enjoy your residency?"

The word "enjoy" generates a dilemma. "Ah," I say. "There's simple enjoyment as in 'Do you like ice cream?' That question can be answered with an unqualified yes. My residency? Yes, I enjoy my residency, but . . ."

"Not when you're awakened in the middle of the night to attend to something that should have been handled by the previous shift."

"You either have a lively imagination, or you've known other surgery residents. No, that's not enjoyable but I'm grateful that I'm there to get the annoying call."

"You mean grateful to be a surgery resident?"

I decide not to mention my current aggravation.

"Yes, and to be at a good place like Northwestern."

She studies me for a moment with a distant smile.

"That's nice," she says.

I have to point out here that again my mind is being fragmented, taxed to manage the conversation and at the same time to sustain salvos of emotion fired off by my visual impressions of Fahra. I have never experienced the way her eyes positively grip me as we speak. Hers is not a passive gaze, nor even an engaged interest, but rather an active, almost tactile handling of my words, like sensitive fingertips grading and sorting opals.

Her eyes are gray-hazel, as I'd thought, but what I hadn't been able to appreciate before is the dark gray band that encircles her irises. Sharply defined lips, full with ever so slight an upward tilt at the corners. They are perfectly designed for kissing, and she shouldn't be offended if every passing man stops her to do just that, any more than the mother pushing a cute newborn in a carriage can be offended by ladies stopping her so they can take a peek and go, "oo" and "ah."

"And do you enjoy what you do?" I ask.

"Yes, I enjoy being able to work at something interesting, but unlike you, it's not what I hope to be able to do later. I work with computer graphics."

"But it's not art. Is that what you mean?"

"Partly."

I am about to ask her more about her work and where she does it, but the tour leaders call for us to get back to our bikes. We get up and start toward her friends.

"I detect an accent," I say, "But I can't place it." I don't say that it is a wonderfully exotic accent, one that bathes her words in a confection like Turkish delight.

"I'd be very surprised if you did identify it. Even Professor Higgins would have to give up."

For a moment I don't know whom she's talking about and then I do and I laugh.

"Well, I'm no Henry Higgins, so you'll have to help me out."

A call that penetrates stonewalls interrupts all conversations in the park. The Obergruppenführer is demanding that everyone saddle-up. I have to think of something quick to insure our next meeting.

"How about dinner tonight? I'd like to continue our talk."

"That would be nice, David. I'd also like to talk more,

but my friends and I have made plans."

"Tomorrow. You're riding tomorrow aren't you? Maybe we could ride together. No, forget that, I could never keep up with you."

"Actually, I'd like to take a relaxed ride in this beautiful countryside. I do plenty of the hard riding back around Chicago."

I want to ask her more about that, but we are now with her friends and the time for chatting is past. "Glad I met you," is shouted back and forth. Fahra picks up her bike as if it weighs five pounds. Maybe it does; it looks expensive, made of some exotic new compound like moon dust. She swings onto the saddle and twists far around on her seat and waves to me. "Till tomorrow, David," and they are off.

Hearing my name spoken has never meant so much to me. I want to be no one except the person named David with whom she has a date in the morning.

At this moment, it occurs to me that I don't have any way of contacting her, no address or phone number—no last name even. What if it rains tomorrow?

7

The remainder of the day's ride will be a snap. I've found a reserve of that kind of masculine energy that, if felt at the wrong moment, inclines a young man to foolishly charge enemy machine guns crying, "For God and country!" I know that Fahra and her friends will already have left the finish area by the time I get there, so there's no rush. I'm meeting her tomorrow, so my future is secure for as far as I care to think ahead. Jeff is somewhere behind me with Tracy. He has let me know that I will be loading the bikes into the car and returning to the cottage alone. He is going to go off with her in her car. He said he was angling to get her back to the cottage in the evening and order in some pizza, at which time I'm to say I feel like eating something else and leave for a prolonged, restaurant meal, ordering something requiring lengthy preparation like Peking Duck.

The evening spins out as he planned. No Peking Duck for me, but three tedious hours in a crowded bar watching a nighrt ball game. The big surprise of the night is that Tracy is not at the cottage when I get back. Jeff says things went "Great," but I wonder. We'll see in the morning if he rides with her.

I wake up from a very tense dream. In the dream it is night and I hear a herd of horses stampeding in the dark. I'm afraid they're coming toward me, but I can't see them; I only hear the pounding of their hooves. Awake, my heart racing, I lift myself up on an elbow. Through the window I see a pale, gray light. Next I become aware of the sound, the pounding. For a moment I can't identify it, then I discover it's above me—rain hammering the roof. All sleepiness dissolves in an instant and I'm standing at the window staring into the gloomiest sight of my young life. A downpour. This means no bike ride. I go back to the night stand and pick up my watch and carry it to the window. 7:14. The tour group is to assemble at 9:30. I look back outside and try to analyze this rainfall. It's heavy at the moment and the sky is very dark and dense. There is no wind. Unfortunately, I have to concede that this is no passing shower. I hadn't looked at the forecast and I wonder if Jeff had. I make a move toward the doorway of the adjacent room where he's sleeping, and then I throttle back. I tell myself to take it easy. There is nothing I can do at this hour anyway.

I begin to think of what to do if it's still coming down like this at 9:30. Is there a number I can call? I go out to the living room, turn on the lamp and find the papers sent to us when we signed up for the tour. I scan down until I come to a heading, "In case of rain." I read, "If rain prevents riding on two of the three scheduled days of the tour, a rain-check will be issued for full credit for another three-day tour held by Peninsula Bike Tours Inc. No credit will be given if only one day is missed because of rain." I'm not looking for credit. I need to know how I'm going to get in touch with Fahra. There are two phone numbers, one an 800 and the other a local code. I figure the latter is the Obergruppenführers cell phone. I decide I'd better not call before eight, although I'm sure she is already dressed and doing push-ups. When one can think of nothing else to do—make coffee.

I put the coffee on and then return to the bedroom and get dressed. Resigned to the steadiness of the rain, I wander around the cottage looking for something to fill the time. There is nothing to read, no magazine, not even the instruction manual for the Weber grill. Either Jeff's brother cleaned out all the reading material at the end of last summer, or he and his wife are dyslexics.

At 8:30, snoring is still pouring out of Jeff's room. I find his car keys on his night stand and go out through the rain to his car and drive to the top of the hill to make my phone call.

An industrial strength, "Yo," greets me.

It crosses my mind to reply, "Yo, ho, ho," but my urgent need to contact Fahra dictates control.

I identify myself. "I'm calling to find out about the rain." I know as I speak I have floated a very fat pitch right over the center of the plate.

"Yes, it is raining."

I steady myself. "We will not be riding today, I understand that much, but I haven't heard, nor do I have access to, a weather report to know what the forecast is for tomorrow."

"More rain. Eighty percent chance they say, so don't worry, you'll be getting your rain check in the mail."

The impulse is to say that I'm not worried, but I stick to business. "If that's so, I mean about the rain, then my concern is learning how I can contact another person from the group."

There is silence for several beats. "I guess you call them at the number he or she gave you. That's usual, isn't it?"

I know she's pissed at having to give out all those rain checks.

"I seem to have misplaced the number. Would it be too much trouble to look at your roster and give it to me?"

"We don't usually give out information about the tour participants." There is something in the tone that says, "What the hell, why not? We're going broke anyway."

"OK, what's the name?" she asks gruffly.

"Well, you see, I don't know her full name but her first

name is Fahra."

She sees all right, only too clearly. "Sorry dude, if the lady didn't give you her last name, what do you think that means? I have another call, so I have to hang up, but don't worry; you'll get your rain check."

"What do you think that means?" I ask Jeff across the table in a booth at a crowded, breakfast joint called The Early Bird.

He is applying himself to a heap of hash browns topped with two fried eggs. He ponders.

"Well now, let's see. First, there's the possibility that she has no last name. It's like this; she belongs to a gypsy clan that shuns last names in order to avoid easy identification. 'Which one of you stole the chicken?' 'It was Sasha.' 'OK, which one of you is Sasha?' 'Who?' 'Sasha.' 'Sasha? Did you say Sasha?' Jeff demands looking at me.

"Sasha?" I repeat, bewildered.

"Are you asking me?" He feigns incredulity. "There's no Sasha here. You had better ask people in the next village."

"OK, OK. I knew I could count on you for a straight answer. Fuck you, by the way."

"Was that nice? Just keep in mind that I know Tracy's last name. She wanted me to know."

I decide to change the subject. "Maybe the rain will stop. It's only an 80% chance that it will continue tomorrow."

"I'm not going to sit around here waiting to find out. I've got better things to do with what remains of the weekend back in Chicago."

"You're not interested in a lazy day around the cottage with Tracy?"

He looks at me while he works on a big mouthful of hash browns. I believe he is wondering how much to tell me about the previous evening with her. He swallows and says, "Better things back home. I want to leave right after breakfast."

"You can't. You know why? Because, you're going to fall over dead with your last swallow of that cholesterol bomb."

"Brahms, you've made a pitiful failure of your chance with that broad and you can't face it. With all that dough you've spent on that analysis of yours, I'm surprised you can't see that you're displacing your self-loathing onto your best friend. I, who have done everything I could to help you connect with her—have done, and will still do."

With this he gets out of the booth and stands and makes an announcement to the jammed restaurant.

"David, here, doesn't know the last name of the woman he rode with yesterday. He's really desperate. Her first name is Fahra. Can anyone here help him out?"

I slide down in the booth. "Jesus Christ, Jeff," comes out automatically.

Jeff looks hopefully around the room. He smiles and says, "Well, thanks anyway. There was just the chance." In several of the booths people are cracking up.

"Shit," I say with mock envy. "Why didn't I think of doing that?"

The drive back to Chicago is dismal. Jeff is playing Eminem and bobbing his head around to the beat. I hate the music and his carefree attitude. I play the memories of Fahra over in my mind. She is fantastic. I can't understand why she isn't here with a man instead of those muscular friends of hers. Is it possible . . . no, not the way she took my arm yesterday. How can someone so precious have been overlooked? The way she put her hand on my arm definitely meant something serious. She didn't have to do that. Of course she didn't. It was an invitation for me to pursue her. I'm certain it was, but how can I contact her? As I said, the ride back to Chicago is dismal.

As we pass the exit sign for Valparaiso, I reach a point when I've exhausted the memories and Jeff has had enough of the rapper. We begin to talk of the residency and I query him about the dramatis personae of the vascular surgery service, which is the service I'd like to go onto as soon as I get a chance.

"Of the three vascular teams, Boyle's is the best. Carducci and Sanborn are good surgeons, but Boyle is a born leader. He keeps everyone charged up and working in high gear. He was a quarterback at Tulane, you know."

"Do I have a choice about which team I'll be on?"

"You don't, but Harvey Beckstein does. He makes the assignments."

I think of Beckstein, the chief surgery resident. He, more than any of the others, made a point of cutting me when I was on Atkins's shit list. The fall-out from Atkins's animosity has a half-life that might endure for the remainder of my training.

"Then I'd better prepare myself for a less than rah-rah rotation. I have trouble with gung-ho leaders, anyway. One is compelled to take on their goals or be branded a dud. I have this perverse need to be the disappointing team member."

Jeff looks over at me appraisingly. "You know, Brahms, I think you've got that about right, and it's too bad. Life is a lot easier if you can draft a little."

"Draft?"

"Like the way one race car driver 'drafts' behind another car, letting the other car meet the wind, while he rides easy in the vacuum the first car creates."

I look at Jeff. He has sized himself up about right, also, but I don't say it.

Jeff drops me off in front of my apartment building. The sidewalk is wet, but it has stopped raining in Chicago. We say we'll see each other on Tuesday and he pulls away.

I enter my apartment and walk into the kitchen to get a beer from the fridge. My answering machine gives a beep. There are three messages. I hit the button and proceed to open and pour the brew. The first message is a drugstore chain telling me I can get 10% off all cosmetics tomorrow. Next message: the downtown branch of the library wants me to pick up the book I put on reserve. And then the machine, to demonstrate what a wonderful invention it really is, begins reproducing a most beautiful sound.

"David, this is Fahra Esma. How awful that it rained today. I called the tour director this morning and was told that you had called earlier requesting my telephone number. She gave me yours. Anyway, I'm sorry we didn't get to talk more, so I'm suggesting that I meet you in the lobby of Dr. Steiner's building after your session next Thursday. I'm pretty sure you said your appointment was at four-thirty, so I'll be there at a quarter after five. Perhaps we could have a coffee. If there's a problem with that you can leave a message for me at work. Just ask the receptionist for my voice mail." She leaves her office phone number.

The first thing I do is look up Fahra Esma in the phone book. Not there. I rewind and play the message again. There is a surging through my body as if my heart were a happy puppy. She said 5:15 on Thursday. I'll have to make arrangements to delay my return to the hospital. So she called to find out my telephone number. She wanted to get in touch with me as badly as I want to see her. I sense discordance, so I replay the message. "I called the tour director and was told that you had called earlier requesting my telephone number." Right. She didn't say she'd called to ask for my number. It was only after she learned that I had called that she asked for it. Does it matter? I don't think so. She called me didn't she: what more do I want?

Something else bothers me. She hasn't left her home telephone number. Voice mail, a built-in buffer. She's approaching me with caution—no need, like mine, to rush into this relationship. This was going to be no easy conquest. It was like applying for admission to medical school; she was giving me an interview, but that was only the first baby step toward entering the class.

8

My Thursday afternoon session with Dr. Steiner begins with him telling me he will be retiring and our last session will be August thirtieth. I reply, with a note of triumph, that I had already heard the news from Fahra and describe our meeting. He is silent.

I think of his retirement again and tell him I wasn't expecting to end my sessions with him so soon and I've been wondering if he thinks I'll be ready to stop. He, of course, asks if I think I will be.

"Yes . . . I think so."

He doesn't comment so I ask, "Do you think I'll be ready?"

"I think you have made progress."

Damned by faint praise. I decide to leave it right there. I wonder why he is retiring, but don't ask. I'm reluctant to involve my thoughts with anything except that I'm meeting Fahra after today's session.

The forty-five minutes finally comes to an end and I rush through the waiting room, hardly noticing the man who always raises the New Yorker high enough to cover his face, and I dive across the hallway and stab the elevator button. The indicator shows that all the elevators are at the top floor. I stab again and watch the lights. Nothing, no movement. What the hell is happening up there? Maybe I should start walking down. No, now one car has just descended to the next floor. The others do likewise. They all stop there. Are the analysts on the 20th floor all visiting the ones on the 19th floor? I'll walk. I sprint to the stairwell and begin to spiral downward floor after floor. It's dizzying and I almost spiral past the lobby level. I take a moment to compose myself before opening the door into the lobby. I'm trying for a confident debonair smile, not easy for someone who has just made a barely controlled fourteen-floor fall. I don't see her and instantly fear I've been stood up. Then she walks into the lobby through the doorway that leads into a restaurant. She is reading the blurbs on the back of a paperback. I'm thrilled to see her, thrilled that she is here to see me, thrilled that she wants to see me. I walk up to her.

"What's the book?"

She turns it over. *Special Topics in Calamity Physics.* Calamity Physics? What the hell is *that* and what comment do I make?

"Sounds interesting," I say feeling foolish.

"It's wonderful. I think you'd like it. It has nothing to do with physics, of course."

"Right, well where'd you like to get that coffee?"

Fahra drops the book into her purse saying, "How about Cosi down the block?"

"Good choice." I've never been there. I tell myself to be careful about this dissembling.

Cosi is a typical coffee house where you place and pick up your order and then find a seat. At this hour there are plenty of empty tables. She steps forward and orders a skimmed latte and pays for it. I feel that I have failed to act quickly enough, but I would have had to trip her and step over her body to get to the cash register first. She stands next to me as we wait for the drinks.

"It must be difficult fitting your appointment with Doctor Steiner into your busy schedule at the hospital."

Her tone is so gentle and unruffled that it is like oil poured on troubled waters. I relax.

"Because a friend is the one watching my coming and

going it hasn't been a problem. Otherwise, it might have been impossible. How about you, can you get off from work easily?"

"Yes. As long as I meet my assignment deadlines, no one cares about hours. To avoid any complaints about leaving for my appointments, I make sure I meet my deadlines. Don't get the picture of great time-driven pressures. The deadlines usually allow more than adequate time for me to complete my work."

"What are your assignments like?"

She looks up at a display on the wall of the coffee house. It advertises the "drink of the month." In bold brush strokes, a woman is shown kneeling in a garden planting new flowers. A large daisy behind her is holding a cup of "spring blend" coffee and saying, "Coffee Break."

"That's mine," she says.

"No kidding." What a dumb thing to say.

She laughs. "I think I know what you mean. We see these images around us all the time and never stop to think that they have been made by real people, people we might even be having coffee with."

"Right. Was that your idea?" I say gesturing toward the daisy.

"Partly. Usually the copywriter gives me the concept and the copy and I'm supposed to guess what he or she has in mind and produce it. You can imagine how difficult this can be if the other person is very firm about my creating exactly what is in his or her mind. Most of the people I work with aren't so concrete."

"But one guy is, right?"

"Actually it's a woman."

"A real bitch, huh?"

"Absolutely the most incredible bitch, a witch in fact," she says with mock seriousness.

"Is she the one who drove you to see Steiner?"

"Not really. There were other issues, as they say, but I have talked about her a lot."

"Me too." When Fahra looks at me with surprise, I quickly add, "Not your witch, my witch. A male witch. He was the Chief of Surgery and he had it in for me. Made my life miserable. I know what you're thinking, that no one can make your life miserable unless you let them, but this was different. Really." What the hell was I babbling on about?

"David, I'm not arguing."

I can see that she isn't. "Yeah. Right. But you see, I never could convince Dr. Steiner that this guy was really the cause of my problems. Problems can have real causes."

"Of course there are causes other than psychological ones. Sometimes I think analysts haven't even accepted the germ theory of disease?"

We get our lattes and find a table. While standing there she had glanced several times out the window onto the street. I'm worried that it's a symptom of boredom.

"Your job sounds interesting," I continue, "But I got the impression up there in Michigan that you weren't too happy with it."

"I'm sorry if I gave you that impression. Actually, it's fun and challenging—in a frivolous kind of way."

"Frivolous?"

She glances up at the picture of the accommodating daisy. "I have trouble thinking this will help solve many of the world's problems."

That puts a different light on the moment. It negates any thoughts that my coffee companion may be a breezy babe out to live the good, fast life, working-out and cycling to keep her terrific figure while enjoying the income from a glamorous job. Solve the world's problems?

I try to put a serious note in my voice, which is hard,

because the feelings generated by my good fortune to be sitting opposite her are anything but burdened with the world's problems. "And how would you like to make a serious statement and what would it be?"

"Where art is concerned, I'd like to be able to spend my day making a serious statement about what I think and feel."

It occurs to me that my next words can make or break me. I can't process what I'd just heard her say fast enough to really respond truthfully; I just sense I shouldn't make a mistake.

"I can see what you mean, talking daisies fall a little short."

I can tell that my response has passed, so I venture a little farther. "And, you aren't able to concentrate on serious art because?"

"The usual reason: I have financial obligations and my job makes it possible to meet them."

Does she mean that she has a child to support? Again I don't know how to proceed. I can only wait for her to take the lead. A guy asks if he can take one of the chairs from our table. The interruption breaks into the flow of the subject of her obligations and she seems uninterested in taking it up again. I change the subject.

"Fahra, I'm curious as hell about your accent. I thought I was pretty good at identifying one, but I'm stumped."

"Stumped? I don't know that word."

"It means to be baffled. It must be an old Anglo-Saxon word."

"I'm stumped! I like that. English has so many interesting ways of saying things. OK, my accent. As I said before, I'm not surprised that you can't identify it. What's your guess?"

I shrug. "The German quarter of the Navaho Nation?"

She nods deeply. "Not bad."

"You're kidding."

"Well, yes I am, but you got part of it right. My father was Turkish and my mother is Egyptian. I was raised in Bosnia and I attended university in Munich. I say I was raised in Bosnia, but actually for a few critical years, the years when I was learning to speak, my family lived in Peru and the maid who was with me much of the time spoke Spanish."

"Wow. So you're . . . uh . . . Bosnian?"

"I have a Bosnian passport, yes . . . and a green card and I'm applying for citizenship."

There are many questions stirred up by this new information. I find myself making a joke to give myself time.

"And David Brahms was born and raised right here in Illinois to American parents who spoke only English. That's why he hasn't an accent."

She raises her eyebrows.

"I have an accent?"

"A genuine mid-western accent." Then she adds with an impish smile, "A very nice mid-western accent."

"Thank God for that."

Things are very pleasant. I couldn't ask for a better beginning to our relationship. The portents for smooth sailing are good. That is, except for her frequent glances out the front window of the coffee house, an action that could be read as disinterest, if it weren't for her apparent total attention to me the rest of the time.

She glances again and abruptly gets up, asks me to excuse her and heads toward the restrooms. The odd thing is that she takes her coffee cup with her. Another odd thing, she's gone a long time. Waiting for her to return, I notice a big guy wearing a Cubs windbreaker come in and go to the counter where he buys a cookie. He munches on it as he looks around the room. Our eyes meet for a moment, but he seems more interested in another lone customer, a guy with a pony-tail who is reading a book, seated several tables away. I begin thinking of what Fahra has said about her background and what I'll ask her when she returns. The guy in the Cubs jacket finishes his cookie and walks back to the men's john. Just after he goes inside, Fahra comes out of the women's restroom, walks quickly over to me and announces that she must leave. I start to get up, but she puts her hand on my shoulder pressing me back into my seat and says she is in a hurry and that I should stay and finish my coffee. Suddenly, she's outta here.

I'm confused. A moment before she went to the john, she seemed to have time to talk. What the hell just happened here? Was it something I said? I try to go over the conversation to the best of my memory, but my part seems to have been very neutral, nothing that should have caused offense. I'm devastated, bushwhacked.

9

Summer is here and Chicago is great in the summer. Almost every day there is some kind of festival and with the warm weather the rich mixture of people we have here from all over the world is able to get outside and rub elbows.

The one good thing about my research gig is the absence of night-call. Well, I don't escape completely; they have me plugged into the ER night shift twice a month, but compared to my old schedule it's retirement. My problem is playmates. Jeff makes the scene irregularly because he's busy with his new source of women. Having run through the nursing staff he now hangs around a folkdance school. He has actually enrolled in classes. Can you believe what some predators won't do? I've halfheartedly taken a few nurses out for a movie and food. Halfheartedly, because I'm really only interested in seeing Fahra.

So, what about Fahra you might ask? Walking back to the hospital after she'd fled the coffee shop, I was thinking she was giving me the message to stop bothering her. Then I reconsidered. Her leaving the way she did was unusual enough to allow me to hope that the cause wasn't an aversion to me. Maybe she felt ill. That's all I need, a little hope and my feelings for her take over from there. I've left messages on her voice mail and she has answered. She is always pleasant, but always busy. I've asked her to the Blues Festival in Grant Park, the Irish-American Heritage Festival, the Folk and Root Festival and both the 52nd Street and the Old Town Art Fairs. She declines nicely. I'm afraid to ask her to do something several weeks ahead, where it would be unlikely she already had plans, because I don't want to be confronted with a reality that she' simply doesn't want to see me.

I've been calling weekly. I figure a once-a-week phone call can't be construed as harassment. I called this morning and it's now nearing noon and that's when she usually returns my calls. Tonight is the Turkish Festival and I'm counting on that holding a special appeal for her, her father being Turkish and all. The time is at hand, though, when I'll have to accept the final meaning of another "no." I go on entering numbers into the computer. I'm beginning to lose my human identity. I have become an accessory: keyboard, mouse, monitor, Brahms.

The phone rings. I say "hello" several times before picking it up to tame the frogs in my throat and construct something that sounds manful and upbeat.

"Hello" I say into the mouthpiece.

"Hi, David." It's like honey flowing into the earpiece.

"Fahra, I've called to tear you away from the talking daisies and take you out to all the fun we can have tonight at the Turkish Festival."

"I'd like to see you tonight, but maybe not the Turkish Festival."

I can't believe my luck.

"Great. But I thought being part Turkish you'd like to have some Turkish food and maybe you'd run into some Turkish pals."

"I'll pass on the festival, but if you'd like some Turkish food, I can take you to a place where we'll eat much better than we could at the festival."

"It's a deal, when and where can I pick you up . . . er, ah, I don't have a car."

"That's no problem. I should be able to leave work at five. I'll meet you at the El station at Grand. It's equidistant from my office and the hospital. The restaurant is near one of the El stops."

"Great, I'll see you there." This is the first time I've had a date at an El station.

She's wearing light colored linen pants topped with a black tunic. To my eyes, she stands out from the other people the way the movie camera picks out the star, leaving everyone else out of focus. She is carrying a brown paper bag, which she hands to me when I walk up.

"The restaurant is BYOB."

Independence once again, not like she's making a point but only following a natural course. We board a Brown Line train and find a seat together. From a pants pocket she takes what looks like a pillbox and hands it to me.

"For you and your kitchen; it's a timer."

She takes it, opens the lid and sets it for 30 seconds and hands it back. She has a mischievous smile and I soon know why when the tiny gadget lets out an alarm that causes all heads in the car to turn our way.

"How does it do that?" I gasp.

"Same question I asked and I didn't get a satisfactory answer beyond, 'there's a chip in there'."

"Where'd you get it?"

"One of our clients is an online kitchen equipment dealer. We did their catalog and they gave us a number of these to pass out among the staff. I got us both one."

The word "us" sticks in my mental filter. It is the first time she has referred to us as "us."

"Thanks for thinking of me. I'll have a three-minute egg for breakfast tomorrow."

We get off the train at the Western station and walk down Lincoln half a block to the Anatolian Kebab. There is one other couple in the restaurant. A tall willowy waitress with an enigmatic smile floats over to our table. The greeting she gives Fahra says Fahra is a frequent and favored customer. Fahra introduces me and hands the waitress the bottle of wine. I hear her name as Sasha and I'm about to say that I know someone named Sasha, when I remember it was just part of Jeff's horsing around at the breakfast joint up in Michigan. I take a quick look around the room. I make it out to be one waitress and one chef, whom I can see through the open kitchen door. Pleasant place—no over-the-top ethnic embellishment.

I open the menu. "What's good?"

"Really everything is good. Take a chance on something you've never had. You can't go wrong."

I scan the page of entrées. "I've never had a stuffed squash before."

"You'll like it."

The tall waitress returns wearing the same Mona Lisa smile as before. Either she has a joint going in the back room or she is viewing her fellow beings, including me, with amused detachment. Fahra orders for both of us. The waitress pours the wine and takes the bottle away before I can see what it is. It's red. I sip it and recognize a healthy, chewy cabernet.

"You seem to be having more free time than I understood you to have," Fahra says.

Trying not to whine, I tell her about Dickson Conway's treatment of us residents and especially me. Apparently I fail at this, because she discerns my true attitude.

"I think you are much unhappier about this than you let on."

"Ah yes, I guess you're referring to the way I gnash my teeth."

We both laugh and she adds seriously, "Can he do this on a whim, just add time to one's training?"

"I'm not really sure. The problem is, to fight it I would have to make an enemy of Conway. It would involve going way over his head. If I were to win, he'd have to lose in a way that would be embarrassing to him, especially at the beginning of his tenure, and I'll still have him as my chief for a number of years. Also, future superiors would know me as 'that guy who blew the whistle on Conway.' People in authority positions don't seem to like the idea of hiring guys who blow whistles. Odd, don't you think?"

"But you're not alone. Do you think he could sustain this program if you all stood up to him?"

I don't know what to say.

She continues, "Tyrants only become established because individuals don't check them immediately. Not one of the monsters of recent history would have survived long if everyone opposed them right away."

This mouthful could have sounded preachy, but it was said in such a matter-of-fact manner that I hear it as sound observation.

"Yeah, you're right. In the beginning Hitler, Milosevic, Saddam, Amin were just crazies with a few crazy followers, but later they became too powerful for any individual to resist. But, you've got to admit, Fahra, it's human nature to do nothing and hope the problem will go away. Besides, an individual is afraid he or she will end up standing there all alone."

"True. That's a common reaction but, if you don't mind continuing in a serious vein, I'd say that although it may be a part of our genetic make-up to hide from danger and place one's own interests first, the contrary attitude can be developed in a society, an attitude that puts the community's interests ahead of selfish ones. An example is when a person rushes to help someone who is in trouble, while risking his or her own life. At the time of the World War, your whole country worked together and died together to defeat Hitler.

"What I'm saying is that a readiness to stand up to

coercion, abuse and tyranny can be developed in a society."

The beginning of a new relationship with a woman had never been like this. To appreciate my predicament, one has to understand that a second year surgery resident is not really a full member of "society." For about the last ten years my mind has been totally given over to medical training, first getting myself into it, then years of holding on for dear life and now trying to get out of it competent and sane enough to start another life—in medicine. Some of the loudest current events penetrate to where I live, but any ten-year-old who puts in average tube-time could beat me in a current events quiz. It wasn't until a couple of months ago that I found out Eminem wasn't candy. So what do I have to contribute to the discussion here at the table? The kind of info I have will put her to sleep instantly and I'll be lifting her face out of the baba ghanoush the smiling waitress slid onto the table while Fahra was talking. When you don't know the subject, ask a question.

"In your opinion, what is needed in order to change an established attitude?"

"Leadership. Any forceful leader can change the attitude of a group. It's a matter of bringing about a change in a group's identity. What is needed is progressive, intelligent, rational leadership. It's that simple. For some time now, the world has had a leadership problem—especially in this country's recent past. The leaders have been followers. They follow the polls or follow the orders of their campaign donors. Leadership has been forfeited to the bigots and zealots. They are always ready to lead, because their warped obsessions tell them theirs is the only way . . . for themselves and everybody else. Let's hope this has changed here."

Wow. "Interesting. You think it only takes a good leader."

I'm half engaged in a discussion and half trying to make intelligent remarks to a beautiful woman I want to impress. "And, what is required of a good leader?"

"As I said, he or she is intelligent, rational and well educated. Also, they've learned the basic lesson taught in kindergarten: don't hit other kids—use your words."

"You're saying, no wars. Do you really think rational leadership can eliminate war?"

"Certainly. We have all the tools we need, but all of us on earth must want to accomplish it. This is where leadership comes in."

"Hey, I'm convinced."

She shifts to a playful tone. "Good. Now you're the American president, President David Brahms, and I have just charged you with the responsibility of knocking off one of the four horsemen, war. What will be your first step? By the way, you don't have to complete your plan this evening. That's asking a lot, even for a great president like you."

I like the sound of this, because it implies that we will have other summit conferences.

"OK," I say, "I accept the charge."

Sonya (that is her real name) bends her six-one down and serves our dinner—smiling of course.

"Now is the instant for instant gratification," Fahra declares, and I sense that she is ready to let President Brahms concentrate on stuffed squash and take up his world-changing program later. We talk about many subjects while we eat, from films (the few I've managed to see) to Turkish cooking. She is very pleasant to be with, having that rare gift of a quick sense of humor that is not at all hostile. But perhaps her most interesting trait is her openness tp discuss divergent viewpoints stated matter-of-factly and without persuasive pressure.

I say what's on my mind. "You're a woman with strong views."

Fahra thinks about this while taking a sip of her wine. "'Strong views' can be a euphemism for wrong-headed or obdurate views. If you think that, then I'm not being a good dinner companion."

"No, I think you're a great dinner companion, so I couldn't have meant that. I'm just not used to a person being serious. Maybe I've never had anyone talk seriously to me the way you have. It certainly doesn't happen with my buddies. There medicine is the only serious subject allowed; almost everything else is treated as a joke. I've had women talk seriously to me about interpersonal matters, but never about world affairs. You're an exceptional person."

"I'm not an exceptional person at all, David, but I have had experiences that are an exception to yours and those of your friends, experiences that have resulted in my being serious about 'world affairs'."

Bosnia comes to my mind. "Bosnia. Were you there when the fighting was going on?"

She hesitates. I sense that the answer to my question would open a complicated and difficult chapter. Sonya glides up and puts down two checks. Fahra thanks her and then turns to me soberly.

"Yes, David, I was there."

10

It is a very pleasant night. Other couples are out strolling or else going into the restaurants along Lincoln. We walk north to where there are gateway pillars into an area called Lincoln Square. I start there, but Fahra stops and says she wants to walk the other way to a branch of the Chicago Public Library. That's fine with me, but I get a whiff of that same watchfulness I observed in her when she kept glancing out of the coffee house window. Maybe this causes me to make note of the fact that when we get to the library, she only browses for a few moments in the new book display then is ready to leave. Did she invent the library visit on the spur of the moment to avoid walking with me into Lincoln Square? Why?

Back out on the street, we look in store windows and comment on their contents as we stroll north again.

I think about telling Doctor Steiner about this date with Fahra at my next session. Following upon this is the thought that our meetings will soon end.

"Only a few more weeks and we'll see Doctor Steiner no more. Funny, I had been wanting to stop treatment, but now I feel sad knowing it's coming to an end."

She is clearly surprised by the shift in subject. She walks on a few paces then says, "Yes, I feel the same way."

She turns to me and asks seriously, "His manner has changed lately. He seems to be pushing me to accept his ideas. He's impatient. Have you noticed this also?"

"Now that you mention it, impatience seems the right word. I have put it down to his realizing that he has little time left to bring me around to facing up to his version of the truth. Dragging me toward the truth is more like it—before he has to give up and accept me as a lost cause."

Fahra laughs. "I don't think *we* are the problem, David. I think he's coming to the end of a long career and is ambivalent about leaving it. If only he can tie up all the loose ends, it will feel like completed work."

We walk as far as the El station at Western. Fahra enters the building and walks to one side and away from the other people, who are heading for the stairs to the train platform. She turns to me, obviously preparing to say good night.

"I enjoyed the evening very much. I'd like to see you again when I can." She smiles and says playfully, "I'm looking forward to your master plan for a rational world."

"Great, only this night has a lot left to it." I look at my watch. It's only a quarter past eight.

"I'd better be getting home. I really must start early tomorrow. I told you we don't have demanding deadlines, and then one comes along."

"At least let me see you home."

"It's only one more stop and you're going back downtown. You'd be wasting a ticket, and I live near the station and it's a very safe neighborhood."

Ordinarily I'd push right past this kind of protest. Women want a guy to say that no trouble or expense is going to stand in the way of his seeing her home safely. But, I sense that Fahra would not be impressed. She would understand the attitude I'd be conveying, but would still view the action as a pointless bit of conventional chivalry.

So instead I say, "I've enjoyed the evening also, and I won't be happy until I can see you again."

She puts her hand on my shoulder and leans forward and kisses me—half on the mouth and half on the cheek.

"Good night, David."

She turns and I watch her effortlessly mount the steps to the northbound platform.

Sitting in the train car on the way back to my stop at Fullerton, I'm more than a little frustrated, but at the same time I'm pleased. I enjoyed the evening and the good night kiss. A lingering awareness remains, however, that she had been critical of my reaction to Conway's screwing up my training. She thinks I should fight back . . . for myself and for the others who will follow me. By the time I hear the recording say, "Fullerton: the doors open on the right side of the train at Fullerton," I have resolved to accept my duty to challenge the monsters that chance puts in my path and do my best to defeat them. Conway is not a major monster, but he is the one in my path. Descending from the platform I'm already planning my counterattack. I have ruled out going to the hospital administration. For reasons of their own they have clearly signed-on to Conway's assuming the office of Chief of Surgery. Likewise, the medical school has given the nod to Dickie's appointment as full Professor and Chairman of the Department of Surgery. A complaint from me would be unwanted trouble best ignored.

The warm night appeals to me to stay out longer, so instead of going straight home I walk past my street and continue up Halsted. I stop when I come to several outdoor tables arranged on the sidewalk by a tavern and order a brew. I sit and watch the people pass by and slowly drink the beer. I particularly notice couples walking along hand-in-hand. I have a fantasy of walking past with my arm around Fahra's waist. I pay the waiter and resume walking and thinking, and shortly before ten o'clock, I close a large loop back to my apartment building.

I will call the American College of Surgeons' offices in

the morning and find out to whom a letter of complaint about a surgical residency program should be addressed.

Thirsty for another beer, I get one from the refrigerator and sit down at the table I use as a desk in my living room and begin a rough draft of my letter. I want an attention getting opening sentence, but nothing comes to mind. I need a zinger like "Man is born free, but everywhere he is in chains." Nothing. For the hell of it, I write across the top of my clean sheet of paper "Happiness is a world without Dickson Conway." I drift into the doodling mode, waiting for an inspiration. I doodle a stick figure and above it a huge foot descending Monty Python fashion to squash the little guy. "No! Nooo!" he says. I smile at my successful attempt to avoid the work required by the letter. I'm really too tired. I'll write it tomorrow. I go to bed telling myself I've made a start—sort of.

In the morning I stick an orange in my pocket to eat when I get off the train and peel a banana on the way to the El. One should always start off the day with a good breakfast. The disaster called my residency is pushed to the rear of my awareness; center-focus is Fahra and my certainty that I have found the person with whom I want to spend the rest of my days.

I get in line with early morning joggers at the Starbuck's near the hospital, get an espresso with a double shot, and make my irresolute way into the hospital where I find a pack of police cars parked around the entrance. Walking to the elevators, I notice more activity than usual. I get into the elevator with some other people wearing lab coats that are a different color than the ones we use here at the hospital. They all get off at my floor. I step out into the usually deserted hallway to see a crowd. What the hell is going on? There is a heavy concentration of uniformed police among them. I slip into my little cubicle and close the door. I do this without thinking, needing a moment perhaps to consider what I've just seen and where I fit in. I go to hang my backpack as usual on the fire extinguisher that's mounted on the wall. The fire extinguisher is gone. I wonder who took it. I hang the pack on the wall mount instead, and as I turn away I notice something on the floor and bend down to pick it up—a penlight. Half of the barrel is covered with a blue rubberized material. "Welch-Allyn" is printed on the clip. I've seen this particular penlight before, but where? I start to put it on the desk near my computer when it comes to me. I'm pretty sure the penlight belongs to Mike Moran. I remember his saying it had belonged to his father when he was a surgery resident. Mike always carries it. I'm certain it wasn't there on the floor when I left the office last night. As I was leaving, I took my backpack off the fire extinguisher and I would have seen the flashlight. What was Mike doing up here in my room? I drop the penlight in my pocket, planning to find Mike and return it. I'd better find him today, because, since his month-long sentence in research prison has been served, he could leave any day now.

OK, now to find out what the hell is going on outside my room. I open the door and step out to investigate and discover I'm in the path of a large black guy wearing a suit.

"Who are you?" he demands as if he had just encountered me wandering the halls in his own house.

"David Brahms. I work here."

He stares at me a moment considering this and says, "Come with me."

He leads the way to the small office used by the lab technicians and points to a chair saying, "Stay right there," in the tone used to train Labrador pups. I'm the only one in the room at first, until a cop comes and stands inside the doorway away from the hubbub in the hall in order to make a call on his cell phone.

Before he starts dialing I manage to ask, "What's this all about? Why are you guys here?"

"You don't know? Head honcho here died last night. Found in the stairwell. Skull fractured."

"Head honcho? You mean Dr. Conway?"

He nods and begins talking on his phone.

While I'm still in the process of fully coming to grips with the meaning of that brief head-nod, Lieutenant Gemiano comes into the room. With a slight motion of his hand, he shoos the other cop out of the room and sits on the edge of the desk and looks down at me.

"You again, Brahms."

How does a self-possessed person respond to that? Smile and shrug?

"I'm told you worked here with Dr. Conway?"

"That's right."

"You worked alone with him?"

"I have to qualify my first answer. I mostly work here alone. At infrequent times, he would come into the lab to do some things of his own and ask me a few questions about my progress on a project."

"You're saying you don't actually work with him, only for him."

"That's right."

"When was the last time you saw him here?"

"Perhaps a week ago. I'm not sure the exact day."

"What did you talk about?"

"You mean, then? We didn't talk. He thumbed through a stack of records I was taking numbers from and left without saying anything."

"Doesn't sound very friendly. The two of you on bad terms?"

Now what should I say? How deep dare I go into my feelings about my captivity?

"Not at all. I would say he had no feelings about me at all. I'm just a guy entering data into a computer."

"And your feelings about him?"

If you sat opposite Julius Caesar or Alexander the Great or Attila the Hun and were asked a question on any subject, I don't believe you would have been free to weigh your answer. That's how I experience Mario Gemiano.

"I didn't like him. He has me doing a job that I think is a waste of my time."

Understand it is inconceivable to me at this moment that Conway's death was not accidental.

"When was the last time you were here on this floor?"

"I left yesterday at twenty to five."

"Four-forty. That the time you usually leave?"

"Usually five-thirty or six."

His cell phone rings and while getting it out, he asks in a distracted way, "Why'd you leave early yesterday?"

He says, "yes" into the phone twice and breaks the connection and puts the phone away.

"I left early because I was meeting a friend."

He stares at me as if he were tracing the neuronal connections in my brain.

"You didn't come back later?"

"No."

"What did you do last night?"

I'm beginning to realize there is something wrong here. The questions are leading in strange and unexpected directions. Assuming, as I am, that Conway had an accident, I expect the questions to relate to the physical features of the lab, such as, "Are banana peels usually left lying on the stairs?" Instead, Gemiano is asking about what I did outside the hospital.

"I went to dinner with my friend."

"What's your friend's name?"

Now, I'm beginning to weigh my answers. "I'd rather

not say."

"Because?"

"It was a first date. I wouldn't want her decision to go out with me to result in her being involved in anything here at the hospital."

He smiles a little. "Hey, I can understand that, but all the same, it might be necessary for me to know her name as we go along."

I don't like the idea of "as we go along."

"How long were you with her?" He continues.

"Not late, eight, eight-thirty."

"Then, what did you do?"

"Took the El home, went for a walk before I went into my apartment."

"You live alone, right? It's a new apartment, right?"

"Yes."

"Am I hearing that you were with no one from eight last night until this morning?"

"No one I know. There were people around when I was walking last night."

"But no one you could call upon as a witness?"

Witness? Witness? He's talking about an alibi. Could it be that Conway's death wasn't an accident?

"I have been assuming that Doctor Conway died in an accident. Am I wrong?"

Lt. Gemiano stands up, then delivers the kind of noncommittal "at this time" statement one is familiar with on the evening news. However, his momentary delay before he did so, shouts the truth.

11

As he leaves the lab techs' office, Gemiano tells me that Conway's lab is off limits until further notice, so I take the elevator down and walk to the Surgery Department office. Mike Moran coming along the hallway toward me. I stop him.

"What do you make of all this, Mike?"

He seems preoccupied and uncharacteristically abrupt.

"I don't know what the big deal is. Guy falls down and hits his head. Why make a big deal of it?"

I remember the penlight and dig it out of my pocket and hold it out. "This is yours I believe."

Mike hesitates before taking it from me as if he's not sure I'm not playing a trick on him. He clips it on the pocket of his scrub suit and charges off down the hall without saying anything else—no "Thank you" no "Where did you find it?" I continue on to the office where several other residents have congregated. Their information is no more than mine. Ralph Springer, coming out of his office and seeing us, walks over. He looks grim.

One of the other residents asks, "Anything you can tell us?"

Springer looks down at the floor. His expression as well as his hesitation says he is considering how much to say.

"Don't be spreading this around, because it is only an impression I have." His eyes sweep the inquisitive group and I can tell he knows that whatever he says won't be confidential very long.

"I'm hearing between the lines that the police think Dr. Conway's death was not an accident."

"Not an accident: you mean he had a stroke?" one of the guys asks.

"No, not that. If I'm correct, they think he was killed."

"Killed? You mean murdered?"

Springer nods.

"Outta sight," someone utters.

"Apparently the police have found several indications that point to that," Springer adds.

"Unfucking believable! Who would want to kill Dickie Boy?" one of the guys asks, but his sarcastic tone cancels the question. Nervous laughter follows this and he restates, "OK then, who didn't want to kill him?"

Ralph Springer says, as he walks away, "Anyway, this will mean that we're going to have the police underfoot for a while." He notes our questioning expressions and adds as he continues toward the elevators, "I'm not holding anything back, just telling you the vibes I'm picking up."

I follow him to the elevator and ask, "Doctor Springer, the detective in charge told me the lab is going to be closed to me until they're finished. Do you want me to work somewhere else in the meantime?"

"Sure, Polk called in—caught a bug. You could help out on his ward until he's well."

"Right."

It's good to be doing actual medical work again. Pat Polk's ward is part of the trauma unit and his patients at the moment are mostly burn cases. The worst is a 40% skin surface third degree case, a guy who set fire to himself while doing a little home plumbing job. Not many years ago this would have been a death sentence, but now he has a good chance of recovery. I'm able to finish up on the ward in time to make my appointment with Dr. Steiner at 4:30.

This afternoon it's the bejeweled matron who bursts through the door into the waiting room from Steiner's inner office and marches past me without a glance. I say "Hi" to Steiner as I pass him and settle on the couch. I wait for the squeak of his chair to tell me to begin.

"It happened again. Without an assist from any unconscious conflict resolution, another obstacle has been removed from my path: Dickson Conway was murdered last night in his lab."

This time I catch Steiner unprepared. He is genuinely surprised.

"I heard from another patient that he had died, but murder? Are you sure?"

"That's the way it looks. The police are swarming over the lab, so I worked today on one of the wards. I'm thinking that it's very unlikely that anyone taking Conway's place would want to continue this dumb project that I've been drudging away at and if I'm lucky, they'll cancel Conway's whole research mania."

Steiner apparently hasn't been listening to my wishful thinking.

"But, what makes them think he was murdered?"

"Search me. Springer only said the police had found something that indicated it wasn't an accident. It boggles the mind to think that someone could be murdered right there in the hospital, and for it to happen on the research floor is unbelievable." Mike's penlight comes to mind. "There's something that bothers me. I found Mike Moran's penlight on the floor of my room. You know, I've mentioned him before."

"Yes, your friend from your college fraternity."

"Right. You see, I'm sure the penlight wasn't there when I left the hospital yesterday. I hang my backpack on a fire extinguisher near where I found the light and I'm sure I would have seen it. When I gave it back to Mike this morning, he acted oddly. I don't think he liked it that I knew he had been up there on the floor last night."

I say nothing more and Steiner reminds himself that he is my analyst and asks, "How do you feel about Dr. Conway's death?"

"Great. Free and clear. Nothing can stop me."

"Invincible, in other words?"

"Not a word I use much, but yes."

"Nothing can hurt you?"

"I sense you've got something in mind."

"I have in mind the 'big hurt', of course, the one you have been fearing for so long."

I know immediately he's talking about my childhood fear of my father. And at the same time, completely unbidden, a question presents itself: how will I feel when my father dies? I suddenly recognize Atkins's and Conway's deaths to be psychological previews of my father's death and the feeling of freedom I'm experiencing now to be a preamble to the freedom I'll feel then. This is suddenly sobering and disturbing.

This is a very good place to do some explaining. The incident that sent me into therapy was, as I've described, my passing out in the emergency room when I saw the boy's finger hanging from his hand by a shred of skin. This, of course, was the focus of my early work with Steiner and it wasn't long before I recalled—relived—a scene in an operating room when I was thirteen. My father was the Chief of Surgery at a small hospital in my hometown, Woodstock, Illinois. He had always assumed and planned that I would follow him into medicine, my opinion regarding my own career being irrelevant to his plans for my life. One day he announced that it was now time that I had my introduction to the operating room and the next day I would "scrub in" with him.

Nervously, I entered the surgery locker room the next morning and donned a green scrub suit while getting some good-natured kidding from a couple of other surgeons who were preparing for another case. There was another surgeon there, also, a man whom I knew from parties at our house. He was going to assist my old man. This man, however, didn't kid me, remaining uncharacteristically quiet. I stood anxiously beside the two of them at the sink and went through the hand-scrubbing ritual for the first time. I was very nervous, but also excited to be venturing into the big-time adult world. We walked into the operating room where a gowned and masked nurse held up a surgical gown for me to slip into. I followed my father's example in every move, afraid I'd mess up and do some dumb kid thing like scratch my ear. Then came the gloves—snap, snap.

I was not really going to participate in the operation. I was only there to watch. I took up the spot my father indicated near the patient's head. I began to relax: I was being called upon to do nothing more complicated than to stand there. The patient, a guy about thirty, was draped with sheets while the nurse-anesthetist put him to sleep. I became embarrassed when I saw that the drapes were arranged to expose his penis. Huge embarrassment followed when a nurse began swabbing his shaved genital area with antiseptic. It was then that I noticed that there was something wrong with his penis, it was misshaped, bulging on the one side. My father asked for a scalpel and looked over at me.

"This man has carcinoma of the penis. He didn't want to admit to himself that the lump he felt was anything serious, so he allowed it to grow to a point that, now, we can only do a complete amputation."

The other surgeon pulled the man's penis up with a

pair of forceps, my father made an initial incision, blood flowed, and that was the last thing I knew until I awoke some time later on a cot in the surgeons' lounge with a big goose egg on the back of my head.

My father was pissed. He reamed me up one side and down the other for embarrassing him. He had violated hospital rules to make it possible for me to have this unusual experience, and I had screwed it up. He had grave doubts about my whole future, certainly as a surgeon, but also as a man.

So this is how I came to understand my passing out in the ER when I saw that boy's dangling finger. Steiner hadn't been satisfied with leaving it there, of course, but also related it to my decision to become a surgeon, a need to master the unconscious fear I had of my father, a man who cut off boys' dicks. This fear, according to Steiner, existed long before I entered that operating room at thirteen. That experience had only revived and crystallized my fear. After that, my faltering ego had one of two choices, run like hell from any activity that would symbolically represent a conflict with my father, or try to master my fear by becoming the thing I feared—become the man with the knife.

The way Steiner saw it, my father, as many fathers are, had been threatened by competition from a son and without being aware of the reason, had been demeaning and even physically brutal at times, maintaining consciously that his harsh treatment was only aimed at "making a man" of me, the result he really least desired.

I keep saying "according to Steiner," but while I don't have the clear conviction he has, I think he's got it right.

Steiner, in bringing me back to this underlying story, has put a damper on my high spirits, bringing me down from "invincible" to mellow. The thought crosses my mind that if Ralph Springer is correct and Conway was murdered,

I hope the person who dispatched him gets away with it.

Steiner has finished invoking and reviewing the operating room incident. I don't want to contemplate it more, so I talk till the end of the session about Fahra and what an unusual person she is. Steiner says nothing.

Walking the long seven blocks back to the hospital, I have time to think more about the idea of Conway being murdered. If I set aside the usual causes for the murder of someone who moves in Conway's circle: robbery (the 12th floor of the research pavilion is an unlikely place for a robbery), a lovers' quarrel (that happens in a motel or when one's wife discovers a motel receipt, not in a research lab), unpaid gambling debt (a parking lot in Las Vegas, the Mafia being uncomfortable in academia). What does that leave? Could a rival author, afraid Conway would beat him into print with a paper on the cost-effectiveness of various combinations of ward personnel, be the perp?

What I'm really afraid of is that it was one of us residents, one of the seniors most likely whose plans were screwed up by the extra month tacked on to the end of their training. Mike Moran heads the list. The Johns Hopkins fellowship was withdrawn and given to another person when he'd been unable to begin there on July first. That would make anyone want to kill. I think of Mike's unusual behavior in the hall outside the surgery office this morning when I gave him his penlight. There's no doubt that he was up on the research floor last night.

Hating Conway. Why am I so quick to begin thinking of the seniors' motives, when no one has a greater motive than myself? I notice that I've begun to walk faster. I think of Fahra. I want to talk to her.

I take out my cell phone and call her office number hoping she hasn't left work yet. I tell her voice mail that I need to talk to her. She calls me back in a few minutes and at first says she can't see me today. I tell her about Conway's murder and she picks up the anxiety in my voice and says she could talk to me for a few minutes if I can meet her in half an hour in the gallery on the first floor of the building where she works. Seems like an odd place to meet, but I agree.

I send a text message to Jeff at the hospital. "jf cn u cvr 1 hr dvd"

A minute later, ":-)". Smiley face.

I enter the gallery where I'm to meet Fahra and make a quick appraisal. The walls are covered with antique botanical prints—that's all. I wonder how they can make a go of it in downtown Chicago where the rent must be breathtaking. I see a dark-haired, dark-eyed young woman sitting at a desk near the rear of the room. She notices the scrub suit I'm wearing and recognition appears on her face. She's expecting me.

"Hi, I'm Alifa Baghdadi. You must be David," she says coming around from behind the desk. "Fahra is coming soon. Would you like a cup of tea?" She begins walking through an archway into a small side-room. Here three armchairs are placed around a coffee table. One wall is covered by floor-to-ceiling bookshelves, and on the other walls hang beautifully framed, colorful prints of tulips, irises and some flowers I can't name.

She has gone over to a compact alcove where a carafe of water sits on a hot plate. She is awaiting an answer from me.

"Oh yes, I'd love a cup of tea."

She busies herself making the tea and says over her shoulder, "This is the deal closing room. In an oriental carpet store I'd be giving you mint tea; here it's Darjeeling. How can you decide not to buy after you've accepted my hospitality?"

I like her.

"Are you a friend of Fahra's?"

"Yes. Small world, our mothers knew each other as children. Cairo."

"Really." I remember that Fahra told me her mother was Egyptian. "You have an interesting gallery."

"Oh, it's not mine." She places a silver tray with cups, tea, sugar and slices of lemon on the table. "I could never afford it. It's a hobby for the lady who owns it. She loves old prints and sees it as a form of public service to bring these prints to people's attention so that they can enjoy them in their homes."

I picture the lady in my mind, a gray-haired matron wearing expensive clothes and museum-grade pearls, whose chauffeur parks at the curb while she toddles into the gallery to check on her good work before continuing on to a luncheon at the club.

"Ah yes," I say, "I have a mental picture of the old dear."

"If you're picturing a hard-driving federal prosecutor, then you're right. Bet you weren't."

"You're right."

Fahra comes into the gallery and sees us sitting in the side-room. Alifa leaves, exchanging a kiss as they pass each other.

Fahra is wearing a tan jumper over a white T-shirt. She sits opposite me, her eyes focus deep into mine, trying to understand and read my thoughts.

"I can't believe what you told me—murdered right where you work?"

"On that floor at least. I don't know the gory details of where or how . . . or exactly when. The thing is, there can't be too many suspects. For instance, it's unlikely Conway interrupted a thief trying to rip-off a computer. What thief would risk carrying the thing down twelve floors in one of our elevators? I'm worried that one of the other residents—actually one in particular—whom Conway shafted, wanting to talk to him alone, went up to the lab and lost it when Conway blew him off. I believe the cops are hearing about the trouble we residents have had and will concentrate on us."

"On you, for instance," Fahra says.

I utter a grim laugh. "For instance."

She studies me seriously for a moment. "Do you think it would be wise to contact an attorney?"

The idea startles me. I have never thought of consulting an attorney for anything. Fahra sees this.

"Those in power have the upper hand. They are used to having things their way and can easily justify their actions to themselves, disregarding your rights, especially if you are not thoroughly aware of what rights you have."

This is all new to me. I have never been concerned about the police taking advantage of me. The truth is, I think of myself as a member of the establishment, not a potential victim of it. We do, indeed, have different backgrounds.

"Isn't it a little early to be talking to a lawyer? I mean, I haven't been accused of anything."

"Some of a person's worst mistakes are made in the beginning by saying more than he or she should."

"Yeah, I guess so." I don't really think this applies to me, but I agree in principle."

We talk a bit about how this might affect my training schedule. I have it in mind to segue into plans for being together this evening, and I start in that direction, but she tells me she has agreed to do some work for a friend and can't. There is something wrong here. I think she likes me. She acts like it. But then there's this odd, cool restraint, even though my instincts tell me she's a warm, giving person. She leaves the gallery out a side door into a hallway with access to the elevators. We say goodbye at this side door and I drift back into the gallery where I see Alifa looking at me with sad understanding.

I heave a resigned sigh and ask, "How much are these pictures, anyway?"

"They vary. Some are more rare than others. The one you're looking at is one of the earliest botanical prints, 1613 by Basilius Besler. It's twenty-five hundred."

"Really, I expected it would be more. But don't wrap it up just yet. Nice meeting you, Alifa."

"And, I enjoyed meeting you, David." As I turn to go, she says quietly, "It would be a shame if you misjudge her."

I'm surprised and don't know if I heard her correctly. If so, I want to ask her what she meant, but the telephone rings and she answers it. Standing there watching her, it occurs to me that she may not want to say more, so I leave.

12

The sidewalk outside the gallery is now in shade, but I feel the still-hot concrete through my shoes. I walk the half block to the corner and stand lost in thought and wait for the little, green walking figure, instead of sprinting through a break in traffic—my usual technique. Alifa's words are on my mind, "It would be a shame if you misjudge her." She is Fahra's friend, so it figures her judgment about her is positive. Then it must be that she is afraid I have, or will come to have, a negative opinion of Fahra. And her fear, in turn, must have been aroused by what she witnessed at the gallery between Fahra and me and Fahra's abrupt departure.

The light changes and I start across Wells Street. I notice a big guy all in black leaning against the building at the corner. I notice him, because he seems to be watching me. But now that I look his way, he shifts his gaze a few degrees to my right. I say seems to be watching me, because I can't see his eyes since he's wearing blue-mirrored, wrap-around sunglasses. Although his head is turned a bit to one side, I can feel his eyes and the feeling isn't any friendlier than the "fuck you" attitude I read on his mouth. I walk past him and keep heading east on Huron.

There's something familiar about him. I think I've seen him recently, but I'm clueless. Maybe around the hospital. After walking about twenty-five yards, I throw a glance back over my shoulder. He is no longer leaning against the building, but is now standing at the corner watching me. He immediately looks into a store window when he sees me turn around. Is he also wondering where he's seen me before?

Back at the hospital, I find that the police have vacated the lab and I'm free to return. No thanks. I'll continue working on the trauma unit until Polk gets back. After that, I'll request a meeting with Ralph Springer at which I'll ask to be placed on one of the vascular teams. On the ward I ask people what they've heard about the investigation—zero.

The speculation about the cause of Conway's death changes with the evening news. Sitting at the bar in my neighborhood tavern, John's Place, I hear the earlier rumors confirmed: Dr. Dickson Conway was murdered. A blow on the head with a small fire extinguisher did the job. It's really too weird to believe. I find myself wondering which small extinguisher was used. There is—was—one in the room where I've been working. It had been standing on the desk next to the computer when I first arrived there to work. I had the thought when I saw it there that someone feared the computer would suddenly burst into flames. I had fastened it back into its mount on the wall near the doorway and had been using it for a coat rack. The memory of that fire extinguisher not being in its rack this morning is interrupted by John, the owner and patron saint of this sanctuary, placing a glass of Guinness on the bar in front of me. For a moment I experience this as clairvoyant, but then I always order a Guinness.

John's Place is a sanctuary, a bastion against the the mean-spirited, the superstitious, the irrational and the narrow-minded of the world. Other bars also create a kind of "our club" atmosphere, but not the sort of club I want to belong to. John is the reason for our esprit de corps. Mid-forties, gray haired, tall and quietly affable, he is unobtrusively the arbiter of our membership. The "others" are artfully examined for the depth of their foolishness, and if judged to be irredeemable, are smoothly encouraged to take their business elsewhere. Fortunately, business is good enough to permit that luxury. If the "others" of our country ever take over, John's will be the last stronghold of rational humanism. We will barricade the doors and fight to the last man and woman.

"Do you know the dude who was killed?" he asks wiping the counter and tossing the towel over his shoulder with a well-practiced move.

"Indeed I do, he's the same gentleman I was telling you about who screwed up my training—not the first gentleman but the second gentleman."

He looks puzzled for a moment. "Gentleman? Ah yes, *de mortuis nihil nisi bonum*, speak kindly of the dead. That 'gentleman' bit puzzled me at first; I knew him by that other name you'd called him." He studies me a moment. "You must be pleased, yet your tensed shoulders tell me you're uneasy."

"Yes, the perfect word. I would be at ease if only the police knew who "offed" the . . . er gentleman."

"Why's that?"

"Of all the people I know, I'm the one with the strongest motive to have done the deed. The police will thik so too."

"I see. Do you have a lawyer?"

"You're the second person today to raise that question."

"And did you follow through?"

"No. It seems like overreacting, and besides I don't know a lawyer—a good one—one I could trust—and afford."

"We have some good ones who come in here. Say the

word and I'll introduce you."

"Yeah OK, but I want to wait a while."

"Better to be prepared."

"That's what the other person said too."

The next morning's rounds are about half way through, when a nurse pulls me aside and tells me there is a call for me, a Lieutenant Gemiano. I pick up the phone with plenty of the "unease" John identified. Gemiano is probably interested in what I know about the lab's fire extinguishers.

Faking composure, I say brightly, "Good morning, Lieutenant. This is David Brahms."

"Brahms, I want you to come to Police Headquarters as soon as you can break away from there without putting anyone's life at risk."

I'm knocked completely off balance.

"You mean come there now?"

"That's the idea. One of our cars is in that drive-through at the hospital entrance. He'll bring you over here."

I hear him hang up. Police Headquarters? Now I wish I had a lawyer I could call him to meet me there. But I don't and I judge that it wouldn't be a good move to keep Gemiano waiting. At this point, I'm still thinking in terms of being cooperative—of having him like me.

I tell the staff doctor leading the morning rounds that the detective in charge of the investigation wants to ask me more about the lab. I don't say where this talk is to take place. The plain-clothes man in the car downstairs displays no interest in me. All the way down Michigan Avenue he busies himself with the instruction manual for his new cell phone, glancing up from time to time at the traffic.

He pulls up at 3510 South Michigan still concentrating on the manual and glances over at me as if surprised to see that I'm still there and says, "Fifth floor."

I ask the receptionist on the fifth floor for Gemiano's

office and I'm passed down the hall from secretary to secretary as if they were sorting mail, until I end up knocking on a door that is opened by the same black guy who yesterday morning told me to "Stay right there." He steps aside and there sits Gemiano behind a desk.

"Sit down, Brahms. This is Detective Barrows," Gemiano says nodding toward the other guy. His tone is friendly enough.

I'm nervous anyway and am trying my best not to show it. I know myself well enough to recognize that the reason for my mounting anxiety is because the truth is I'm happy that Conway is dead. Knowing the source of the anxiety does no good. My mouth is dry.

"How long did you tell me you've been working in . Conway's lab?"

"Since the first of June."

"People tell me these haven't been happy days for you. Conway sort of shanghaied you. That about right?"

That was about right, but I don't like the direction Gemiano is heading.

"He wanted me to spend more time doing research."

"More time than you wanted to spend, right? You've already told me it was a waste of your time."

I kicked myself for saying too much at our earlier meeting. "I guess you could say that."

"What is going to happen now that he's dead? Will you go back to clinical stuff on the wards?"

"I don't really know." Who had this guy been talking to?

"In other words, Dr. Conway's death is very convenient for you?"

I say nothing.

"When was the last time you used the fire extinguisher that's in the room where you work?"

So it was that fire extinguisher!

"I've never used it, Lieutenant."

"Oh, but we found your fingerprints on it."

"My fingerprints?"

"We're going to take a set of your prints this morning to be sure, but the same prints we found on the extinguisher are on your computer keys and all around your desk."

"Oh, now I remember. I picked it up and hung it in its wall-mount when I first started working in that room."

"That so."

All the time this exchange has been going on with Gemiano, Barrows has been leaning back in his chair and looking on with quiet amusement as if watching Cyrano duel with a court fop. His eyes seem to brighten in anticipation of Gemiano's next thrust.

"I want to go back to the night of April nineteenth, Brahms. To help you place the date, it happens to be the night that Dr. Atkins was run over and killed."

There's no doubt about it, this is an interrogation, and I wonder if I should, as I'd seen people do in films, say that I won't answer any more questions until my lawyer is present. But in spite of the warnings received from Fahra and John, I'm still thinking that if I cooperate, Gemiano will see that I'm a good guy.

"I told you before, I was home that night. But Dr. Atkins's death was an accident, isn't that right?"

"Hit and run. You say you were at home . . . but as I recall there was no one with you."

"I was alone unpacking." Then I add, "I remember that day clearly, because that's the day I moved like I told you before. My friend Jeff helped me move the larger things and then left."

"When did he leave?"

Late afternoon."

"Larger things. Like how large?"

That question surprises me. Why should Gemiano

care how large my furniture is? Is there a law against moving sofas?

"A sofa, a bed, desk."

"How'd you move em? You have a truck?"

"I borrowed a friend's van."

"A van. What kind?"

"Ah," I laugh, realizing that I don't know the make. "You know, standard van, or rather a mini-van, actually. We had to leave the rear door open when we moved the sofa."

"What's your friend's name?"

"Friend?"

"The guy that let you have his van?"

I don't like this, dragging a friend into something like this when the guy had only been doing me a favor. But I have no choice.

"Peter Graham."

"Is he at the hospital with you?"

"Yes."

Gemiano throws a glance toward Barrows, who gets up and leaves the room.

Gemiano opens a file folder on the desk in front of him. There look to be half a dozen single sheets of paper in it. He studies the top sheet for a long moment before closing it.

"You haven't had a smooth experience in your training have you, Doc?"

I start to say something confirmatory, but catch myself and ask, "What do you mean by that?" I have, at last, given up the idea that this guy is an uncle.

"I mean, it looks to me as if these guys, Atkins and Conway, had it in for you." He pauses to give me a chance to agree, but I only look blankly at him. He goes on as if I had agreed. "Atkins says here that you were, 'immature.' Why do you think that was?"

"No idea. I don't think anyone had it in for me."

He can't know that Conway read the file to me . . . or can he? He has recognized that I'm no longer going to be easily manipulated and so he changes his tactics.

"I told you when we talked before there might come a time when I would need to know the name of the woman you claimed you had a date with the night Conway was killed. That time is now . . . name and address."

I think about it for a few seconds. If I don't answer and say at this point that I want a lawyer present, he would assume I have something to hide and I will, without a doubt, end up having to reveal her name anyway.

"Her name is Fahra Esma. I don't know her address." This is true.

"OK, her phone number."

"I don't know that either." True again. Yeah, I know her work number, but Gemiano didn't ask that.

"You don't know her phone number? How'd you get the date?"

"She called me." True again.

"And you didn't ask her for her number?

"Sure I did, but . . ."

"But what?"

'She seemed not to hear me."

His look becomes derisive. "Do you think she's giving you a message?"

"She might call again," I say.

"Yeah, right. So, that's it. Fahra Esma?"

"That's it."

He is looking at me as if it weren't a desk between us but a poker table instead. He is pondering whether to raise the bet or just meet it. He assumes a relaxed attitude and says, "That's all for today, BerahmsStay handy . . . know what I mean?"

13

Gemiano doesn't provide a ride back to the hospital, so I start walking to the Bronzeville El station. I think about what just happened and the fact that Gemiano is considering me to be a suspect in both the murder of Conway and Atkins. I picture the fire extinguisher hanging on the wall. Waiting at the station for the next train north, I call Peter Graham to warn him that he might hear from the police about my borrowing his van. He already knows. Barrows has been quick to contact him, telling him his car is going to be picked up for inspection by the police lab. I don't hear overtones of pleasure in Peter's voice.

"I was planning on driving home to Indianapolis this weekend. What's going on ?"

"Sorry, Peter. I don't know what they're looking for. Maybe they only want it for a few hours."

"That's not what it sounded like. 'Impound', doesn't sound like a few hours . . . or even days."

"Oh shit. Impound, eh?"

What can I say? I'm sure he had already reminded himself that this is what happens when you do someone a favor. I can't even think of any remedy for his spoiled trip home. I certainly can't pay for a plane ticket to Indianapolis.

"Well, tell me if there's something I can do, and, again, I'm sorry." I hang up.

Now I have to call Fahra to tell her that Gemiano has her name, and judging by his rapid action with Peter's van, she can expect to have him on her doorstep, soon. Once again, I'm shunted to her office voice mail. I'm not sure how much I should say on the voice mail. I ask her to call me at the hospital and have me paged. I wonder how she's going to take my giving her name to Gemiano. Something tells me that she's not intimidated by police questioning, or is that only wishful thinking?

Before returning to the trauma ward I decide to see if Jeff is free to commiserate with me. I take out my phone and text a message, "jff F2T dvd?"

"Y"

"Cmng."

"OK"

He's free for a minute, but it's not commiseration he's up for when he hears my story.

"Graham said he was going home this weekend? That bastard! He agreed to cover for me Saturday night so I could go to my folkdance class. But, hey, he can't go now because the cops have his wheels, right?" He seems pleased.

I'm riled by his insensitivity to my troubles, so I fire off, "But wait, if you were any kind of a friend, you'd loan him your car so he can go home and see his old folks one more time before it's too late. That's certainly more important than your having one more dance lesson, as you call it."

"Do I hear jealousy? You can't get that Arab chick to give you her phone number, let alone a dance lesson."

"She's Bosnian," I retort stupidly and leave.

I go back to my ward where a nurse tells me that she had just checked on a man who'd suffered a chest injury in an auto accident yesterday, and discovered that his breathing has become labored. Several ribs on the right side of his chest had been broken in the crash. In a case like this, anticipating the possibility of a pleural effusion developing (the accumulation of fluid in the space between the lung and the chest wall and diaphragm) I'd written orders for his respiration to be checked every hour for the first twenty-four hours.

I know the moment I walk into the room the guy is in considerable distress. I percuss the right side of his chest, tapping a finger I hold against his chest with a finger from my other hand. Over a normally inflated lung, the sensation you have is of tapping a ripe watermelon, but over an accumulation of fluid it feels as if you were tapping a leg of lamb. It's clear that an accumulation of fluid fills the lower third of his chest cavity, the secretion of oozing blood and tissue fluid caused by the injury.

I ask the nurse to bring me the sterile tray of instruments I'll need for a thoracentesis and I clean an area of his lower chest with antiseptic solution. I then inject local anesthetic into the place in the skin where I will insert a long needle into the pleural space. Although this is generally a safe procedure, something still feels very wrong about pushing a long needle into a person's chest. The same goes for that initial incision into the skin when performing any surgery. I insert the long needle and attach a syringe and draw back on the plunger. Pink, clear fluid quickly fills it. Not much bleeding, that's good. I draw off 500cc of the fluid. Immediately, the guy feels better and is breathing normally. I stick an adhesive bandage over the hole. All done. It's possible I'll have to perform this procedure again, but hopefully not.

As I wash up, I become aware that this total immersion in my work had taken my mind off Lt. Gemiano for a time. Now I'm back to being his major suspect in two murders. I wipe my hands, shaking my head. It's too much. The sum of all that has happened to me, beginning with the gulag of Northpark General followed by the exile in Conway's "research" lab and now this new horror, has worn away my capacity to hold things in perspective. I feel alienated from the whole program here at the hospital. This sort of thing is not happening to anyone else here. I'm alone.

It crosses my mind that I should be telling this to Dr. Steiner. Once again I hear myself whining and I don't like it. What can he do anyway . . . invite me to analyze my feelings? Screw my feelings. What I need is some kind of action. Even if Fahra does call back, I don't want to have her sympathy. I need to do something. An idea comes to me and I dig the Chicago phone book off the shelf in the ward nursing station. I find the number of John's Place.

A woman answers and over the clatter of bar noise, I ask for John.

A moment later, he asks, "What can I do for you, David?"

"You can give me the name of one of those good lawyers you were telling me about."

"Good move. His name is Marty Frumin. He's sitting here at the bar right now, and I was telling him about your situation—hypothetical, of course, no names. You can supply those yourself."

This is surreal, but what the hell. "Thanks John, put him on."

The voice is of a guy who sounds middle-aged.

"I think John stages things like this, what do you think?" he says, a smile in his voice.

"His ways are beyond our knowing, friend," I reply. "The name to go with the story, by the way, is David Brahms. I'm a surgery resident at Northwestern."

"So John said, a surgery resident, but he said nothing about Northwestern. I'd be happy to talk to you about this, Dr. Brahms."

"David."

"David. What's your schedule like?"

"It's difficult to get away during the day, but I have some evenings free this week . . . this evening, for instance."

"My office address is in the phone book, Martin Frumin. I'll see you at eight."

"I'll be there."

I put down the phone. Did that really happen like that? If he's in his office at eight, it did.

A few minutes later Fahra returns my call. I tell her that Gemiano now knows her name.

"But not your phone number. That's only because I didn't know it."

"He'll find out what my number is with no problem, but that's fine. I have nothing to tell him. I didn't realize that you didn't know my home number."

She tells me and I add it to my cell phone.

"Also," I tell her. "I followed your advice and have an appointment with a lawyer this evening."

"Good. Where did you get his name?"

"From someone I trust to know good from bad. I'll make my own judgment after I see him. "

"Let me know how it went with him."

Her interest feels very good. "I'll do that."

Six o'clock, time for the change of shift and my ward work is done. I stop by the nurse's station to say that I'm leaving. It's important at this point to get off the ward before a new patient comes up from the ER or Admitting. Once that patient arrives on the ward, he or she becomes mine to work up. That could involve another two hours, maybe more.

The lawyer's office on Fullerton is on the second floor of a corner building only three blocks from John's Place. Occupying the first floor is a store calling itself The Lincoln Park Wine Broker. The building's vintage architectural details make me think of the 19th Century. There is a large south-facing bay window up there in what must be

Frumin's office. I would bet someone stood there at that window in October of 1871 and watched the hot glow of downtown burning during the Great Fire. The street number with an added "B" is painted on a glass door to one side of the wine broker's front display window. I'm looking at a flight of wooden stairs when I open the door. This set-up brings to mind ambulance chasers. It's certainly not the high-powered lawyer world the movies have taught me to expect. Certainly not a place where Michael Douglas would practice. Maybe Paul Newman after years on the sauce. I'm slightly reassured by a sign that tells me elevator service is available at the side street entrance. The stairs end at a small landing and a solid door with the name, Martin Frumin, Attorney. I open it and step into a room with a single desk and three chairs facing it along the wall. A hallway leads off one side of this room toward the back of the building. To my left is the open doorway to an inner office. A large man, whom I remember having seen before at John's Place, now fills that doorway.

"Hi, I'm Marty Frumin."

"David Brahms."

He shakes my hand and ushers me into a large office, where I identify the bay window I'd seen from the street. The room is furnished comfortably and appropriately for someone engaged in the practice of law, wood and leather and many red and tan bound law books. There is no intention here to manipulate a client toward thinking that the man behind the desk is anything other than an experienced middle-aged man who is confident that he can advise a client about what is possible and decent where the law is concerned. The single name on the door and the single desk for a secretary says he isn't pushing hard. His relaxed confidence says it is of his own choice. Coloring this first impression is the fact that John recommended him.

"John gave me a description of an interesting situation," he begins. "He likes to do that. I think he is really a law professor masquerading as a tavern keeper. A professor posing hypothetical questions was my favorite part of law school, so I welcome it."

"I'm afraid I don't have the objectivity about this to see it as interesting," I return, "Or even to understand it. In fact, I feel uncertain of just why I'm here. I don't know what you can do to help me. I guess I'm ah . . . getting scared, and my friends have been asking if I've engaged a lawyer."

"I don't know what I can do either. Why don't you tell me your story and we'll see."

I begin with Atkins's death, but Frumin makes me go back to the beginning, the very beginning, applying for the residency, who it was who interviewed me and so on. He is very thorough. He ends up focusing on the events immediately preceding my banishment to Northpark General Hospital.

"So the only unusual thing that happened prior to Atkins "loaning" you out, was that fainting spell in the ER?"

I nod.

He retreats into his own thoughts and this allows me to observe and take stock. He is large, as I said, maybe six two, two forty. I decide he was definitely an athlete, but I can't figure which brand. He is bald and his scalp is deeply tanned. Tennis without a hat? If so, he's not overly cautious. He has a naturally friendly look, large features that form a smile quickly. All the same I can't picture a maître d having the nerve to turn him away.

Marty emerges with, "I don't buy it. Fainting at a new and unpleasant sight might make Atkins think you weren't ready for combat duty, but I can't believe it would cause him to try to hurt you by screwing-up your training. There must be another reason."

His tone is so certain and dismissive of an easy explanation, like my fainting, the one which I had accepted because I knew of no other, that I'm ready to hear his next idea.

"My hunch is that the answer to that question, why first Atkins and then Conway had it in for you would tell us something of vital importance about those men, and knowing that is central to our work of clearing you with the police."

I don't really follow this. "You know, Marty, there is something that bothers me. Even if we were to find out their reason for messing with me, how does that really help me? I mean, I would still have the same motive for killing them and it's because I have a motive that Lt. Gemiano is breathing down my neck, not because they had a reason to bedevil me."

"That's not the point, David. Look, somebody killed them and it wasn't you. My judgment says you're not a killer and more significantly," he grins, "John says you're not. Since we can't prove you didn't kill either man—you have no alibi—our best way to make Gemiano go away is to give him the name of another person with a motive, means and opportunity as strong or stronger than yours." He looks hopefully to see if I got it.

I nod. "I'm listening."

"I think we'll have to learn as much as we can about both of them. That's all we have to work with now."

He's talking as if there's no doubt about his being on my side. At least that much is reassuring. It feels very good. Money comes to mind. How can I afford the luxury of having so expensive an ally? I start to push that question aside and plunge into talking with him about how we're going to go about learning about Atkins and Conway, but I realize that after I have already accepted his help the issue of his fee will be more difficult to bring up.

"We need to discuss your fee, Mr. Frumin."

"Marty. Yes, of course. As you know, professional advice—legal, medical—is expensive. Years of concentrated study and all that. I used to have a doctor friend whom I could call up to put me straight on medical questions—not medical-legal issues, but miscellaneous medical questions as they arose in my work. My friend died. I was thinking that a young guy like you would be able to give me the latest information."

He's lost me. It seems like the subject changed and I wasn't paying attention.

"What I'm suggesting," he continues, reading the bewildered look on my face, "is that we swap expertise. I'll help you with this problem of yours without other recompense, if you'll agree to be my general medical advisor . . . for a reasonable period of time."

What he'd said sounded OK. I try to imagine how Jeff Richards would respond were he in my chair. Immediately I hear Jeff asking for a definition of "a reasonable period of time" and suggesting that I was buying "a pig in a poke," since I don't know how good Marty Frumin's advice will be. But that's Jeff and not me. Even if Jeff were right here whispering these things in my ear, I'd still say what I'm about to say.

"It's a deal."

"Good. Of course, you're entering into this agreement on what is called 'good faith,' since you don't know how helpful I'll be."

"The thought did occur to me."

"Excellent. Now, we need to divide up the task of researching your former Chiefs. Why don't you go into their medical backgrounds—training and so on, and I'll check into their financial and legal records?"

Marty Frumin starts writing out a list of facts he needs for his research that I should be able to supply from the public records of the Surgery Department. We part with a handshake. I was right, earlier. This is the action I needed to take. I ache to be able to relate all that has happened to Fahra.

I walk to John's Place and on the way I call Fahra's number but get the machine. I leave a message that the meeting with Marty Frumin went well and I'll call later. I wonder if Gemiano has contacted her and I begin to consider what trouble he might cause her. Is her alien status really in order, or has she failed to dot some i's and cross some t's? In other words, has my bringing her to the attention of Gemiano caused her a big problem?

I take a seat and order a Guinness from Susan, one of the bartenders, and wait until John is free and thank him for putting me in contact with Marty Frumin.

It isn't long after this when Jack Plamondon comes in, spots me and climbs onto the stool next to me. He does this in a hesitant way, as if he had decided to avoid me, but then realizes that I've seen him. It was Jack I had replaced on the ward, making it possible for him to take a rotation at Children's Memorial Hospital. The hospital is only a couple of blocks from the bar. The way he's looking at me isn't the way you'd look at a friend whom you hadn't seen for a while. His is more like the expression you'd have if you'd heard this friend was wanted in all fifty states for kidnapping.

"How's it going, Jack," I say brightly as if I haven't noticed anything out of the ordinary.

I can see that he's having a problem finding the right thing to say to me.

"What's on your mind?" I prompt.

"Well it's ah . . . Well, we heard you'd been arrested. You know, for killing Dr. Conway."

"What? You heard what?"

"Yeah, one of the guys just returned from being downtown at Northwestern and that's what's going around the hospital this evening down there."

I stare at him as if he were talking in tongues. Finally, I say, intelligently, "What the fuck!"

His face shifts to a, "Let's get this straight," expression. "You haven't been arrested, then?"

"Does it look like it?"

"Well, I mean, you haven't . . . you aren't . . . "

"Are you asking me if I'm a fugitive?"

"Yeah . . . well are you?"

"This is the first I've heard of it. To my knowledge, there is no warrant out for my arrest.'"

"Is that so? I'm sorry."

"That there's no warrant for my arrest?"

He laughs. "You know what I mean. Shit, what's this all about, Dave?"

I ease back, too. "Beats me. I was asked to go to Police Headquarters this morning, where the lieutenant in charge of the investigation asked me some questions, but there was no hint of an arrest. And there is no reason there should be. Damn rumors! How in hell did that rumor get started?"

"Probably it's because everyone else would have wanted to kill Conway if they'd been in your shoes."

"Whatever, I don't like it."

"Yeah, I don't blame you."

Although he had just come into the place, he says he has some errands to run and leaves. Now what was that all about?

I walk the five blocks home. The apartment caretaker, Michaels or Nichols, I can't remember which, is in the lobby mopping the tile floor, a task that is long overdue— but at nine-thirty at night?

"Oh, Dr. Brahms," he says when he sees me. "I wanted

to catch you before you went up to your apartment." He puts the head of the mop in the bucket and pushes the bucket over to the wall, leaning the mop against it.

"The police were here . . . with a search warrant. They made me open your apartment. They had this paper."

"Search? To search my apartment?"

"Yeah. Understand, I stayed right there at the door and watched them. I wasn't gonna let them walk off with something valuable like. And I locked the door when they left."

This beats everything. What could they possibly hope to find in my apartment?

14

The caretaker walks up the two flights with me. I can tell he is feeling guilty that he'd opened my apartment for the police. I'm not sure he was legally required to do so. He hangs around the doorway after I unlock the door, watching my reaction to what I'm about to see.

"Good God!" pops out of me. I stand looking at the shambles for a long moment and then turn, thank Michaels—I remember his name—and back him out of the doorway and close the door.

No attempt has been made to hide the fact that a search was made. Everything taken down from shelves or out of drawers is right where the item was dropped after being examined. My apartment has a living room, a kitchen, an alcove with a dinette table, a bedroom and a bathroom. I go to stand in the bedroom doorway and hesitantly look in as if I were about to view the scene of an axe murder. Apart from the absence of blood, this is exactly what I'm looking at.

All of my clothes are piled on the bed and the mattress is askew where they have lifted it to check beneath it. They even took the pictures off the walls.

I've read descriptions of people's reactions to having their homes broken into. Violated is a favorite verb. I feel raped—by an entire cell block. I pick up my few shirts and refold them, handling them like wounded pets and put them back in the dresser. I re-hang the pictures, two colored etchings of alpine scenes I got at a garage sale. I'm fuming, but it's beneath the surface like the molten magma below the earth's thin crust. The crust in my case consists of disbelief—shock.

I begin to feel the anger and I also sense that I'm afraid
of it. I need to talk to someone. I take out the card Marty
Frumin gave me. He had added his home number and I
call that. The machine answers, so I tell it what has
happened here.

I still need to talk to someone so I start to dial Jeff's
number before remembering he is on call at the hospital. I
dial the hospital's number. The operator is surly. She's
reluctant to believe that I'm a doctor named Brahms.
Finally, I'm connected to Jeff's ward, but the nurse says
she hasn't seen him for a while and suggests he might be in
the resident's lounge. She gets the operator again and asks
to have my call transferred. After waiting a long time, I
hear the dial tone. Disconnected. Dismissed.

I go to the kitchen to get a beer and believe that even
the food in the refrigerator has been moved around. I count
the remaining beers and try to remember how many I've
drunk since I bought the six-pack. I decide none are
missing. I'm disappointed. I'd like to be able to yell,
"Thieves!"

I take the beer and go to my easy chair, put the cushion
back in place and sit down. I take a few swigs of the brew
and begin to calm down. Maybe it's like sucking my thumb.
Whatever.

What could they have been looking for? They were
very thorough; books have been taken off shelves and
riffled. I spot a couple of bookmarks on the floor. So, they
hoped to find something like a piece of paper. Or maybe
they were just damn thorough and I shouldn't try to guess
at what it was they wanted to find.

What should I do about this? Raise hell? And how does
one do that? Yell at Gemiano? He would expect that and
merely say it was a routine part of a murder investigation.
Should I call him and inquire quietly what it was he thought
I had in my apartment that would link me to Conway's

murder? I finally conclude that the question of what I should do is just the kind of thing for which I need Marty Frumin's help.

I spend the next hour putting the apartment back in order. The phone rings. It's Marty. He says he checks his office machine before going to bed and got my message. He's calm, says that he'll check in the morning to see if a proper warrant was issued. Since the caretaker let the cops in, it was not an illegal entry. He suggests that since they could have found nothing, the search may result in getting them off my back. On that optimistic note, we say good night.

It's as I turn off the living room lamp, the light coming in the window from the street reflects off the top of the small table I use as a desk. I freeze. Something *is* different. I turn the light on again. It comes to me what's different and my heart shrivels. There is nothing on the table now. What had been there when I'd left this morning was a letter, the letter prompted by Fahra's attitude that one should take action. I was writing to the American College of Surgeons making a formal complaint about Conway's screwing up my training. At the top of the sheet I had written, "Happiness is a life without Dickie Conway." Below this I'd doodled the giant foot descending on his head.

I think of calling Marty back, but decide to wait till morning. At least one of us can have a good night's sleep lulled by the sweet fiction that Gemiano found nothing in my apartment of value.

I fall asleep, because I'm very tired, but I awake several times from anxiety dreams that I can't remember. Up till now I've experienced each of the setbacks in my training as individual events. Telling the story to Frumin has had the effect of bringing them together into an epic. I'm starting to feel like one of those characters in Greek dramas cursed and pursued by the gods. Those poor mortals have usually committed some unpardonable boo-boo, like having hubris. Hey guys, check me out. No hubris!

I can tell Marty is not pleased by my news when I call in the morning. He handles it calmly enough, telling me to sit right down and, to the best of my memory, reproduce the letter the police have taken. He says Gemiano will have to give him a list of items taken from the apartment, but will not have to give him a copy of the letter until and if I'm charged. He tries to reassure me that it is the flimsiest kind of circumstantial evidence and nothing a prosecutor would try to build a case on.

I've told a lot of lawyer jokes in the past, but at this moment, I'm very happy Marty is there for me.

When I enter the hospital the next day, it's pretty clear that the rumor of my arrest has spread and been accepted. Those who don't know me well stand back and stare, while my friends come up and ask for details. I keep repeating that it's a groundless rumor. I say nothing about the search of my apartment, until I see Jeff.

"Now, this is just between us, right?" I begin.

He crosses his heart. I reach over, take his hand, and move it to the left side of his chest and make the cross, again.

"Hey, so I haven't finished my cardiovascular rotation, yet," he counters.

I tell him about the search and the letter and the doodle of the stamping foot.

"Don't worry," he says confidently. "I know what your drawings are like. No one will be able to tell what it's supposed to be. Besides, Conway was not trampled to death. If he had been, then you'd be in deep shit."

"Now, why didn't I think of that?"

"Something else though," he says.

"Yeah?"

"I saw Peter Graham in the lounge last night and he told me about the cops taking his van away." He pauses and looks me in the eye seriously. "Did you notice if there was a dent in the left front fender of the van when you borrowed it?"

"Dent? No, I didn't see a dent. Did you see one when we were using it?"

"No, I didn't either. Well anyway, there *is* a dent. Peter says he only noticed it when he got the van washed, a week after you returned it."

"It was beyond dirty when I used it; it was muddy."

"The thing is that there's this rounded dent—no scratches—and Peter doesn't know when it happened. He said he hadn't run into anything himself and no one else borrowed it. He didn't mention it to you, because it could have happened in some parking lot after you used it and he felt sure you would have told him if you'd done it. Oh, and the dent's in the left fender. The side of the car that the witness said hit Atkins."

The significance of this stuns me. What we have here is concrete evidence that the van, which was in my possession the night Atkins was run down, had hit some object with enough force to cause a dent in the left front fender, and the man who owns the van can't swear that it hadn't happened while I had it that night.

"But," I point out emphatically, "If I had hit Atkins, the dirt would have been rubbed off and Graham would have been certain to have seen it."

Jeff is nodding. "Right—maybe, and that's what I said to Peter. He reminded me, however, that the streets were covered with dirty slush that night and what dirt might have been rubbed off in a collision with Atkins would have been re-deposited in no time."

I consider this soberly. "Old Peter has been doing a lot of thinking. I thought you said he was sure I would have told him if I'd had an accident."

"Right. He was sure of it . . . if you had hit another car or a post or . . . "

"But, not a person. He didn't think I would tell him if I'd hit Atkins."

"Well, would you have? In that case Graham would have expected you to smear lots of mud over the dent and hope he wouldn't notice it."

"That's just great," I sigh.

I call Marty's office. He's not there, so I tell the story of the dented fender to his secretary, Ethyl Mann. Why? Because she actively solicits my trust and presents a soft shoulder. The only thing better than having an understanding lawyer is having one with an understanding secretary.

It's not enough though. I want to talk to Fahra so I call her office and leave a message on her voice mail. There is something about doing this that reminds me of the earlier time when I was sure she was avoiding me. Could that be happening again since I pulled her into my problem with Gemiano? I can't stand this limbo, so I decide to pay another visit to the gallery where Fahra's friend, Alifa, works.

At lunch hour, I sprint from the hospital to the gallery. I make two observations as I open the gallery's door, the first is that there are no customers, the second is that Alifa made a sudden move to hide something below the level of the desk top where she's sitting. She recognizes me and relaxes and brings a sandwich back up on top of the desk.

"They don't give you a real lunch break, huh?"

She smiles. "No, there's no one to cover, and it's just as well, because I can save money by packing my own."

"What is it today?"

She looks at the sandwich. "What did I make this morning? I was sleepy. Humus, I believe. Yes, humus and cucumbers."

Alifa gets up and carries her sandwich to the little side room with its rich Persian rugs and comfortable chairs.

She's wearing a caftan-like dress of some diaphanous material that flows exotically. Her body has a soft look. She's not fat, but I don't think you could find a hard muscle anywhere, probe as you might.

"Let's sit here. You'll have some tea won't you?"

She pours a cup for me.

"I doubt that you are here as a customer."

"One day I'll surprise you, but today you're right." I drink some tea, then put the cup down. "The reason I came here today is to ask you to tell me about Fahra."

The cheerfulness leaves her face. Seriousness takes its place. "What is it you want to know?"

"The last time I was here you said that you hoped I wouldn't misjudge her. Obviously you guessed I'm . . ."

"Puzzled?"

She's correct, but it's more than puzzlement I feel. I'm hurt . . . make that deeply hurt.

"Yes. I'm confused," I say.

"You care about Fahra very much don't you."

"Right again." I hazard the question, "Do you think she knows that?"

Alifa nods and says with warmth, "Yes, of course she does."

"But I feel that she's avoiding me."

"This puts me in a difficult position. I have sympathy for your feelings, but Fahra has very good reasons for her behavior and I would not be her friend if I ignored her decision to handle this in her own way."

"You said you hoped I wasn't misjudging her and yet you are going to do nothing to prevent me from drawing the only conclusion I can; she—for whatever reason—is prepared for me to move on and forget her."

Her look says that she wishes very much that I hadn't come and presented her with this dilemma.

"OK, she may not even want me to tell you this much, but I will tell you some things about her that should help you understand her better."

She glances up to take in the gallery as if to assure herself that she is free to forget her duties for the time she needs.

"Fahra has known much pain in her life. She is careful to avoid causing more . . . for herself . . . and others."

She pauses, but she knows she has begun a tale that will require much more telling.

"As I believe she told you, she and her family were in Sarajevo during the war, Fahra, her younger sister and her parents. Her parents were professors at the university, her father an archeologist, her mother taught history. Their religious background was Islamic, but they were not religious. In his courses, he, Professor Esma, naturally treated the Christian and Moslem students alike, so the family was unprepared and startled when a group of Serbs came into the university and took Fahra's father and several other professors captive. The family did all it could through Serbian friends to clarify the situation and obtain his release, but it never happened. It was only after the truce, that Fahra and her mother learned that he and about fifty other men had been executed the same day they were captured."

"Jesus," I murmur.

"Before the truce, Fahra, her sister and her mother managed to escape to Germany, one of the only countries that would accept Bosnian refugees. One of Fahra's aunts and two uncles weren't as fortunate. After the truce, when they learned the truth about Professor Esma's death and the death of her aunt and uncles, they felt they could no longer live in Bosnia. Luckily they managed to remain in Germany. This was largely through the efforts of one of Fahra's German professors. I don't know if she told you, it was there in Munich that she attended the university and got a degree in fine arts."

I am listening to Alifa with divided attention. Anything

I can learn about Fahra fascinates me, but I am also listening for the explanation of why she is avoiding me. Nothing I have heard so far answers that question. Alifa hesitates. She has a look of someone who realizes she has painted herself into a corner. Maybe she's afraid if she says anything more she will have to violate her resolve to honor Fahra's wishes.

"Yes?" I nudge.

She exhales deeply. Her expression now says, "What the hell, if Fahra is angry with me, so be it."

"OK, in Munich Fahra and her mother became friendly with a Turkish family who had a son named Ahmad. To Fahra he was only a friend, but he began to develop very strong feelings for her. She told him that she didn't share his feelings, but it didn't deter him. His parents counseled him to accept this reality, but to no effect.

"He was crazy about her—I mean really crazy. The situation became critical when he began following her and causing scenes when she was with her friends. Ahmad threatened one of the young men in Fahra's art class and this man made a complaint to the police. A magistrate ordered Ahmad to stay away from both the young man and Fahra. At first it seemed to have solved the problem. He moved out of his family's house and for a while no one saw him. But then one night after a concert, Fahra's friend took a shortcut home through a dark park and was attacked from behind and hit on the head. His skull was fractured and he almost died. His wallet was taken, so it could have been a robbery, but Fahra was sure Ahmad had done it."

It's a horrible story. I imagine how this new violence must have been overwhelming to Fahra, coming as it did after the terrible, violent fate of her family. And what is more, although illogical, she probably blamed herself for her friend's near fatal injury.

Alifa continues, "What Fahra did was to apply for a visa to come to the United States to attend graduate school.

When it was evident to Ahmad that she'd disappeared, he surfaced and began questioning people concerning Fahra's whereabouts. Eventually, through some channel he learned she had gone to New York and the Parsons School of Design. By the time he learned this and followed her to this country, she'd completed the course at Parsons and had moved here to Chicago. Fahra knew it would be too much to hope that her move to the U.S. would be the end of her problem with Ahmad, but at least she'd accomplished shifting the danger zone away from her family and friends.

We sit silently studying each other.

"And that's why she won't see me?"

"She is torn. She is tough like a Spartan. She will sacrifice her own happiness as long as she prevents harm from coming to those she . . . "

Here she stops, probably thinking she has said too much already.

"Does this Ahmad know about me?"

"Fahra is beginning to think so."

Many questions leap forward to be answered all at once, like the hands that shoot up together when a teacher announces an exam.

"Does he talk to Fahra?"

"He leaves messages."

"What kind of messages?"

"Notes where she'll find them. She had to get an unlisted number, because he was calling all the time. And, of course, he follows her."

"Why doesn't she go to the police with this evidence of his stalking her?"

"You forget, she did that once and it did no good. It ended in the attack on her friend."

"But this is Chicago."

Alifa laughs. "You mean the police here are more effective than the German police?"

I laugh too.

"He must not have a job if he's able to follow her around."

"Not an hourly job, but he is actually able to cope fairly well. Fahrah says that for generations his family has made its living trading and bartering. If they see a flock of chickens they can buy cheap, they buy them and find someone to sell them to at a profit. Then they look for cheap corn to sell the buyer to feed his chickens. Ahmad is continuing the tradition. He will find you anything you need—even drugs it's rumored. Also he has a small Turkish band that plays for parties, weddings and some restaurants. He plays a traditional stringed instrument, the *saz*."

"If he's able to manage his band, he probably isn't crazy in all areas of his life."

Alifa nods. "Just about Fahra . . . and any other man in her life."

"I'll bet he's not a legal immigrant."

"You're right."

"Why doesn't Fahra report him? That would quickly solve the problem."

"It would solve one problem, but she is also concerned about the safety of her family if he were to return to Germany."

"What does he look like?" As soon as I ask the question an image comes to mind of the big guy who had stood across the street from this gallery, watching me.

Alifa's description is of the same person.

"Yes, I noticed him the other day when I left here. And yes, now I remember where I've seen him before. He came into the coffee house that first day I had coffee with Fahra. She must have seen him coming toward the door, so she quickly went back to the women's restroom. When she came out, she immediately left the restaurant—and me."

"She told me about that. She knew it must have hurt your feelings, but she couldn't take a chance of being seen with you."

I understand more now about Fahra's behavior, but if she feels at all about me as I do about her, she would confide in me. The most important thing is for us to be together. We can deal with life's problems if we're together. Clumsily, I try to say this to Alifa.

She nods. "Yes, I understand that you might think that, but it is not that simple." She smiles as if at herself. "I'm sure what I've just told you explains her keeping a distance between you, but there is something else which I'm sure causes her to hesitate."

Again I can identify in her expression that struggle one has after having partially revealed confidential information about another person and not being sure what to say next. I wait, but my attitude says I want to know everything.

"Fahra has never said this to me in so many words, but I believe she would hesitate to quickly get deeply involved with someone whom she finds attractive until she is sure that he respects her very serious dedication to social issues."

"What do you mean by social issues?"

"Organizations. Those working for peace . . . against violence, for disarmament, anti-capital punishment, anti-poverty, human and animal welfare. She is very active in all these areas. Almost all of her time away from her job is spent this way."

"And cycling," I add.

"Even that plays a part. She says she must have exercise to remain healthy and have the stamina for her activism."

I think about what Alifa has just said. She has described a person very different than myself. I'm in sync with the causes Alifa mentioned, but I've never done anything about any of them except vote, and occasionally put my hand in my pocket for odd change to drop into a canister. I'm also surprised to hear about Fahra in this way. I'd thought of her as the epitome of femininity—sweet and lovable. So, there's more than sweet and lovable. It hasn't changed my feelings about her one bit; in fact, she has just become more interesting..

"I suppose this strong need to work for peace comes from her experience of violence . . . her father's murder."

"Of course," Alifa murmurs.

So be it, I think to myself. I begin to wonder why Alifa has told me this. Is she saying that Fahra and I are not suited, that I'm not the right man for her?

"Are you saying we won't be compatible? That I should forget her and move on with my life?"

This surprises her.

"No!" she responds. "I only want to help you understand the situation." She stares straight ahead for a few moments and then shakes her head. "I think you're right. I think I was telling you exactly that, but now that you've said it . . . No, I don't want you to forget about her, but I'm afraid something very bad is going to happen."

"Don't be. I can take care of myself." I realize as I say this that it has the ring of an automatic cliché phrase. I maintain the expression and pose that goes with the line, but I'm thinking that the statement, "I can take care of myself," is pure bullshit. I've never been involved in a real fight and I'm good at avoiding situations where fights might occur.

"You are only one of the people I am afraid for," Alifa adds.

"You mean Fahra."

I hadn't thought of Fahra being in danger. After all, this Ahmad didn't attack her. But then, what might jealousy drive him to do? Then, I think of Alifa.

"Is there someone else you're afraid Ahmad might harm apart from Fahra and me?"

Her silence becomes meaningful.

"You mean yourself? Because you're her friend?"

She sits looking at me and her eyes tell me, "You are

here talking to me aren't you?"

"You think he knows that I'm here?"

She shrugs. I remember that it was just across the street that I had seen him standing, keeping watch.

"Yes, I see," I murmur. "I'm sorry."

Suddenly she laughs. "Don't worry . . . we can take care of ourselves."

At first I hear the remark as sarcastic and derisive, then I see that her smile is friendly. She's kidding me, but at the same time she is saying, "We're now in this together . . . for better or for worse."

15

I get to the ward station in the morning and sit at a computer and begin reviewing what the night shift has recorded about my patients. I see where the IV tech has been called to work on a non-functioning IV on a new burn case. The resident on duty decided to insert a central line. This had to be done, because fluid management is critical in this case and will be required for an extended period of time. He inserted a plastic tube in a vein in the patient's arm and ran it along into the large vein, the superior vena cava, which empties into the heart, insuring that there will readily be a way of giving the patient needed fluids. I finish looking at the reports, finding the status quo with my other eight patients and I'm logging-out, when I get a call from Ralph Springer saying he wants to see me in the office of the Chief of Surgery. He is once again Acting Chief.

The secretary is not at her desk, but the chief's door is open and Springer seeing me come to the doorway, waves me in. Ralph Springer is an elegant guy. He exudes natural confidence and perfect manners. "Brahmin" is the word that comes to mind. Not haughty mind you, in fact, he's very friendly. He's just . . . lofty. As I understand it, he was Ivy League all the way, down to kindergarten. Also he's very resilient. I've never seen him look discouraged. He seems to take the uncertainty that has become the norm here in the department in his stride, marching forward like an eighteenth century infantryman, ignoring the fact that two of his comrades have just fallen at his side.

"Have a seat, David." He smiles encouragement at me. "Shall we try once again to get you back on the normal course in the program?"

"Ah yes, normal course," I say in a manner to imply that I've vaguely heard of such a thing.

He tells me he wants me to join a vascular surgery unit. I'm to write summary notes on all my patients on the trauma unit today, and report to Dr. Carducci tomorrow. I thank him, but I'm cautious about letting myself believe in a "normal course."

"Oh, by the way Brahms, what is all this interest that the police have in you?"

How much do I tell him? I play it safe.

"I imagine it's all part of a routine investigation. I was working in the place where Dr. Conway was killed. They want to keep going over my recollection of what was happening in the lab. I didn't—don't—know anything more to tell them."

"Then they are through questioning you?"

"I would think so."

"Good."

Probably meaning I was coming very close to achieving the status of persona non grata.

On my lunch hour, I begin my research assignment given me by Marty Frumin on the professional histories of Drs. Atkins and Conway. On the Northwestern University web site I find Conway under the medical school link and the faculty bios. There, mention is made of his former position with the NIH. Following this, the piece mentions that he trained at Ford Hospital in Detroit after graduating from medical school at Hanhemann in Philadelphia. There is no mention of where he was an undergraduate. The web site had already deleted the bio of Mason Atkins, but on another site I find a partial bio on Atkins related to his being a speaker, last year, at a Pan-American Surgical Congress. Here I discover that he got his medical degree from NYU where he also was an undergraduate.

Truthfully, I was hoping to find that they both went to

the same medical school or were college roommates. According to Jeff the two were known to have been friends. I'm looking for the link that would account for a strong enough relationship to cause Conway to take over Atkins's program and to thwart my progress. I carry this fantasy of Atkins penning a note to dear ole Dicky, "If anything happens to me, ole buddy, grant me this last favor: see to it that David Brahms becomes so discouraged that he throws in the towel and quits medicine."

I smile at this extravagant bit of egocentrism, but this self-awareness doesn't shake my certainty. There has to be some strong link between them. I could look both of them up in *Who's Who in Medicine*, but I doubt if the bio there would go beyond what I already know. There has to be more complete information in the university's personnel files. Whom do I know who could help me? Jeff has dated someone in every department of the hospital. The problem is that he has a tendency to leave a trail of "don't darken my doorway again" kind of sentiment. I decide to go around to his ward and see what's possible.

Jeff is sitting behind the mahogany-wrapped counter of the nursing station making notes on a computer. The nurses are very busy with something on the far side of the station, so I lean over the counter and ask Jeff if he has intimate contacts in the Personnel Department.

"No, I never took out anyone from there, but it's a great idea, Dave. Thanks."

"It wasn't meant as a suggestion. I need access to their files on Atkins and Conway and while I know you work fast, I can't wait for you to undermine a pretty clerk's morals enough for her to give you access to the files."

"I have another idea. If it's just biographical information you want and not performance reviews and that sort of thing, as an Editor of the Surgery Department newsletter, I can call them and say we're doing a piece on both of the former Chiefs and want all they have on their background."

"Terrific."

Jeff reaches for the hospital telephone directory and looks up the number of Personnel and dials. He speaks to the Director's personal secretary, who hears his request and says she'll get the info to him before the day is out.

Jeff hangs up and, pleased with himself, smiles at me. He takes the notebook he always carries from his jacket and flips a few pages and makes a notation.

Since it seems to be related to the phone call he's just made, I ask, "What are you writing down?"

"You owe me one more. I added another check beside your name."

"What? How many checks have I got already?"

"Enough. Enough, so that when I call in the debt at the right time, you'll have to devote years to getting me elected President of the American College of Surgeons."

As it turns out, when we look together at the material sent up that evening from Personnel, there is nothing there to warrant a check beside my name. The only relevant fact is that Conway had gotten his undergraduate degree from the U of Connecticut. So, they weren't college roommates as I had hoped. No high school is mentioned in the information, but that's probably not unusual.

"Jeff, there has to be someplace where these two came to be close friends."

"Grade school? High school? They married sisters?" Jeff offers.

"Hey, right. I've been thinking solely of professional and school connections; there could be many more opportunities for them to have met and bonded."

"Right. People don't build the kind of shared prejudices we're postulating unless they work together, or belong to the same club . . . or family. As far as the record shows, they haven't worked together, so it would have to be in some sort of social relationship where we'll find a connection."

I have an idea.

"An obituary usually lists surviving relatives."

"Good idea. I've got to run. Let me know if I can help."

"Maybe you can call in a favor or two from your list." I produce a snide grin and motion toward the jacket pocket that holds his notebook.

"Sure, but it means the checks get transferred to your column."

On my computer at my apartment I access the *Tribune's* obit archives, which I have to agree to pay for. Here I strike gold. Conway's survivors include his wife, Lenore, his daughter, Meredith, Michael and a granddaughter, Megan. Only one relative is listed in Mason Atkins's obit, a sister—Mrs. Lenore Conway. Could Jeff's wild suggestion that they might have married sisters be at least half true? Hell, it's got to be true. It would be too much of a coincidence if there were two persons named Lenore Conway. Conway married Atkins's sister!

I immediately call Jeff at his apartment, get his machine (folk dance night) and tell the machine about the good luck. The reason there was continuity in the program to torment me is now evident. What isn't clear is why? I had never heard of either of these guys until I entered the surgery program, so how could they have it in for me? It could work either way; Atkins could have been the prime mover and passed it along to his brother-in-law, or Conway was the one with a grudge against me and asked Atkins to act for him. Later he took up the project himself once he became chief. Either way it made no sense. Could either of my parents have done anything to inflame them? My father is a local boy. He trained at the University of Chicago and only practiced in Woodstock, Illinois. There is nothing in their histories to suggest that either Atkins or Conway had been in either place.

I make myself a can of Campbell's tomato soup and pour myself some wine out of the vacuum-stoppered half bottle on the kitchen counter.

Although I have no more idea than I had before of what their reason could be, this digging for connections in their backgrounds has resulted in my solid belief that both men's treating me the way they did, was not an unfortunate random coincidence, but a conjoint, deliberate undertaking. If only I had some solid proof.

I wonder when it was that Dicky Conway met Lenore Atkins? High school? College? How far back does their friendship extend? Again, I'm not sure how knowing that will help me to understand the attitudes of the two men toward me, and what's more important, how knowing that can convince Gemiano that I'm not a murderer. But this is the assignment Marty Frumin gave me.

I'm tempted to call Fahra to tell her what I'd discovered. I stop myself, because it occurs to me that Fahra is hearing a lot about my troubles, not the mental image I want to implant. I think of calling Marty, but remind myself that the news I have can easily wait until his office hours. He claimed he was happy with the arrangement for his fee, but how much weight will that bear?

I walk to John's Place and climb onto a stool at the bar. I notice that the artwork has been changed. It happens about once a month. John donates his walls as a showcase for little known Chicago artists. A curator from the Museum of Contemporary Art, one of my fellow club members, does the picking. There has seldom been a work that I wouldn't want on my own walls. Surprising, how many talented people there are walking about.

The cardboard placard on the bar tells me that, "Guinness is Good for You." I know this to be true.

John doesn't inflict sport TV on all his clientele, but he has one screen pointed toward an alcove off to my left. I can't hear what they're saying, but in a reflection that bounces off a front window and back to the mirror behind the bar I can see that it's that jolly group of ex-jocks punching each other on the shoulder and making predictions about the upcoming game. Everyone must have noted that their predictions are always balanced so that team "x" gets two votes and team "y" receives the same. Gotta keep the consumers in both cities happy. Hey, it's all show-biz. But then so much is.

Looking at the mirror, I see Peter Graham enter the bar. I remember that he is doing a rotation at Children's Memorial now. I see him notice me, pause a moment, and then decide to come and take the stool next to mine.

"I got my van back today," he announces with the same tone my father had when he said, "I see you've finally mowed the lawn."

"Gee, I'm sorry for the inconvenience. Of course, I had no idea that this would happen."

"The bastards didn't bring it back, they merely informed me that I could pick it up at the auto pound. I spent half the day dicking around before I got it. The seats were still all pulled apart."

"Pulled apart?"

"I mean they were pulled out of place, where they had looked under them and didn't bother to put them back."

I was clearly associated in his mind with all this.

"You don't think I wanted that to happen do you?"

This forces a wedge between what he'd like to feel and what he logically knows to be true.

"Of course not. It's just one of those things that happens."

I knew the extension of that thought was, "When you loan your car to a god damn friend."

"Did the police say anything to you . . . about finding anything in the van?"

"Not a thing. Jeff told you about the dent, right? I took

another good look at it. It's about four inches in diameter and an inch deep."

"Like a baseball had hit it?"

"More like a soft ball."

I'd already told him that I hadn't hit anything and there sure as hell was no softball being played in the city of Chicago on the day I borrowed the van. What disturbs me is the fact that the police aren't thinking softball, they're thinking Atkins's head.

At this moment, John comes into the bar dressed to the nines. He says he's going to a play at the Steppenwolf Theater and then on to a party given by one of the theater's big donors. Before he leaves, he pours each of us a heavy shot of Highland Park scotch, gratis.

16

Peter sips his drink and says, as if confessing, "I wanted to be an actor." He glances at me to see the effect of his sudden confession. He sees he has tweaked my interest and not my contempt, so he adds, "I was in the theater arts program at Indiana University."

"Is that so? Why did you make the switch to medicine?"

He sips his scotch before answering. As he begins to speak, I can identify a long-held wish to talk about this past period of his life.

"My family never had any money. My father injured his back on a construction job and never again held down a regular job. I was only eight or nine when it happened. We lived on his workmen's comp and a little my mom earned doing proofreading at home for a small publishing house. As a kid, I knew things were tight, but my parents didn't burden me with the details of 'just getting by' so I never considered the realities of making a living when I considered a career choice. I wanted to be an actor. I saw myself as another Christopher Plummer."

To my eye, Peter's appearance was more aligned to be another John Goodman.

"I was fortunate to get a scholarship to Indiana, and there was never a question about a major—theater arts was it. Some things happened during my sophomore year that changed my outlook. For one thing, I had to have a root canal and a crown on one of my teeth. The university dental school fielded that, but I asked and discovered that in the real world it would have cost me a bundle. At the same time the rear end went on the old VW Jetta I was driving. I couldn't afford to have it repaired, so I gave the car to my mom, who gave it to some charity for the small tax deduction. I started walking, and as far as I could see into the future I saw no chance of replacing my wheels. Then, a guy who had been well known for his acting ability in university productions before graduation, came back to see some of his old friends on the faculty. He'd spent several years in New York trying to get work and had no luck except for some very incidental walk-on stuff. He worked as a night watchman, a job my Dad did now and then for short spells. A bell went off in my old noggin. What are the real odds Peter old man that you'll do better than this former campus star? I reviewed the careers that could both be interesting and guarantee a decent living. Here I am."

I had always viewed Peter as a contented person, so I ventured the question. "Any regrets?"

"None. But I also think I could have been very happy being a working actor. As it is, I'll settle for a yearly subscription to the Steppenwolf—when I can afford it."

I was certain that a good portion of the money he had been able to save so far in the residency had gone into those "wheels" I had borrowed. The van must represent freedom from poverty to Peter, and yet he had loaned it to me. I can understand how the police confiscating it and the fact that it was dented meant much more than I had appreciated.

The uneasy tension between us, when he first sat down beside me, has vanished, so we say good night on the sidewalk outside having established an easy friendship once again.

Peter begins walking the short distance to Children's Memorial Hospital and I head in the opposite direction. After three blocks, I look both ways before crossing Fullerton to my apartment. There is no traffic in the near eastbound lane and a lone car is coming in the far lane. Following that car by a comfortable distance is a line of traffic. I decide to cross part way, wait for the single car to pass and then jog across before the next cars arrive. I am thinking of the conversation with Peter and my surprise at his secret thespian ambition.

I'm half way across the first lane, when suddenly I'm aware of movement to my left and catch the reflection of streetlights off a windshield hurtling toward me. A reflex throws me forward, even though it's directly into the path of the car in the next lane. I skid face down onto the pavement to the sound of screeching tires coming at me. Then I'm lying on the pavement staring at a front wheel about a foot from my head. I hear a car door slam and someone yell.

"That son-of-a-bitch! Fucking fool!"

I start to roll over in order to get up, but there isn't room between my back and the bumper of the car that hangs over me. I inch sideways.

"He tried to hit you! You know that, man?" The same guy yells at me.

Now, traffic has stopped in both directions and I hear the short whoop from a patrol car that has pulled out of line and comes to stop a few yards away. Two cops jump out, that anxious look on their faces wondering if this is just an accident or that situation, always expected, that will cost them their lives.

One of them looks down at me where I'm still sitting on the street and says, "You all right?" He kneels next to me. "You think you can get up?"

"Yeah, I think so."

He grabs my arm and helps me up. I become aware of a smarting pain in both knees and look down to see both of my knees through ripped pant legs. My right hand smarts. The heel portion is abraded and oozes blood.

"Yeah, I think I'm basically OK." The black guy who

was driving the car I just crawled out from under begins, "That car tried to hit him. Really did. It go right at him, but he dove in front of my car and the other guy had to swerve away. I got good brakes. Another car would'a run over this man."

I take a good look at his car for the first time, a Porsche. Thank God he forked over the fortune to buy it. I take him in also, thirties, tall, athletic, wearing a warm-up suit.

I put out my hand, then realize I'm handing him a bloody mitt and take it back and hold out my other hand. He gives me a fist bump.

"And thank God you've got great reflexes," I say from the heart.

The police have him move his car to the curb and get the rest of the traffic moving, then one of the officers takes our statements. I have no facts to offer, but the Porsche driver does.

"You could say I was ready to stop. I saw this van without lights start to move away from the curb as this man here walked out into the street. It accelerated and aimed right at him and if my car hadn't been coming, it would'a come right into this lane an' hit him. I'm sure of it."

The cop looks at me. "What about that?"

"Beats me," I lie.

"What can you tell me about the car?" the cop looks back at the other guy.

"I didn't have time to do a lot of studying, understand, but it was a dark color, like I said, a small van, maybe an SUV."

I limp on into my apartment. I take two kitchen chairs and wedge each under the front and back door knobs. I go into the bathroom and start to draw a tub of water and then I imagine how the water is going to feel on my scraped knees and turn off the tap. I take off my jeans and roll them up and throw them into the laundry hamper. I'll worry later about whether they can be mended. I spend the next fifteen minutes gently cleaning my abrasions and applying gauze pads and Neosporin. I'm not experiencing much pain but I throw down 800 mg. of ibuprofen for good measure. A half tumbler of Clan MacGregor, the house scotch, in hand, I sink into my one easy chair and begin to think seriously about what just happened.

The guy with the Porsche was sure the car was out to run me down. OK, say he's right. Who besides Ahmad would want to kill me? He must have been behind the wheel. This crazy Turk is out to kill me. What can I do? What would happen if I went to the police? A dark SUV is not the kind of description that's going to get the cops excited. I suspect that even if I knew where he lived and went there immediately, he would either not be there and have a good alibi, or would have parked the car away from his apartment and be there sitting cross-legged on a cushion smoking his bong. I think of several scenarios along this line and conclude that all I can accomplish by making a complaint to the police about Ahmad is that they will have a place to start their investigation once he's killed me.

Maybe I should carry a gun. I don't like having had that thought. I believe that all guns should be gathered up and melted down for their steel to replace the old El bridges. Besides, how would having a gun have helped me, tonight? Even the Sundance Kid couldn't have gotten off a round as he was diving for the pavement. I'm feeling very vulnerable. Ahmad is like a heat-seeking missile; there is no getting away from him.

The phone rings on the table beside me. It's Jeff.

"Hi killer, it's Mr. Serendipity, your society sleuth."

I have a strong urge to tell him my tale, but I discern that he has one of his own. "What's up Mr. Serendipity?"

"I went to the cafeteria for coffee and pie this afternoon

and Ralph Springer was sitting there alone, so I sat with him. It came up that he was going to New Hampshire next weekend to visit his son at his school, St. Paul's School. The talk moved along and it came out that Ralph went there too, and so did his whole fucking family back to the Mayflower. So, here's the serendipity part; Ralph says that Mason Atkins and Dickson Conway went to St. Paul's—for a while. 'No kidding.' says I. 'Tell me more'.

"I can't remember the exact path of the conversation after that, but here's the gist of what I learned. These guys, Springer, Atkins and Conway, come from 'old' families in the East. That always slays me, as if anyone's family is older than anyone else's. I mean all our families are traceable back to Homo erectus. Right? Anyway, everyone in the residency has heard that Springer was Harvard all the way. One of his ancestors lent John Harvard a hammer to build the school. Turns out that the Atkinses loaned him a saw and the Conways loaned him a shovel. The only ones in both families who didn't go to Harvard were the few rebellious problem children who went to Yale. OK, you're wondering, why did Mason and Dickey go to NYU and Connecticut respectively? The answer is that they were kicked out of prep school, kicked out of St. Paul's for some horrendous reason that scotched their chance of going on to play hockey for the dear ole Crimson. You understand this was tricky, getting this information. I didn't want to appear to be a voyeur and cause Ralph to clam up like a gentleman of the old school should do. You would have been proud of me. You owe this tidbit, by the way, to my mastery of the art of subtle seduction."

This last sounded like the Mafia offering to do one a favor. By using his information he was saying that I would never again be able to criticize his deceitful manipulation of women.

He went on. "Springer said no one ever heard just what it was that Atkins and Conway did to bring down the roof.

It wasn't for lack on interest. Both of them were seniors and stars of the hockey team, and hockey is a big fucking deal at St. Paul's School. It's like they invented it or something. Springer was a freshman and didn't know them personally, but when they were expelled right in the middle of the hockey season, the whole school talked of nothing else. Apparently the word got around quickly to the Ivy League's admissions officers."

"Quite a story," I said. "I gotta give Atkins and Conway credit for bouncing back the way they did."

"I don't want to hear that credit bullshit. You know very well how they advanced their careers—the same way as a lot of other hot shots do, and you know it very well: they were pricks."

When Jeff hangs up, I have an idea. I'll take a look at the St. Paul's School web site and see if they are listed among the alumni. I go to my computer and wait forever for the dial-up connection. I get the web page and see that there is a link called "e-lumnet," which I click on only to find that they want a password to let me look at the alumni directory. So much for that.

And this is the report I am making to Mordecai Steiner at our next session.

"I told the cops that I had no idea who would want to run me down, but it was a lie. It was Ahmad. No question."

"And why didn't you tell that to the police?"

"Because, even if they located him, don't you know he'd have an alibi. He was going to kill me. It's a sure thing he'd have worked out an alibi ahead of time."

"What do you intend to do?"

Steiner was talking in the present about problem solving. Damned if it didn't have me off balance.

"I suppose that if I happened to find a sympathetic ear among the police and explained about this guy's history . . .

No, forget that. They wouldn't do anything. They're too busy to afford to watch Ahmad or protect me."

"Then you intend to do nothing?"

I hear my father saying critically, "So. Once again you're not going to stand up for yourself." Did I really hear criticism or was this more of what the shrinks call the "transference."

"Funny thing, I've always totally rejected violent solutions to problems, but the only effective way I can think of to stop Ahmad is to kill him before he kills me. The guy is really a dangerous psychotic, but from what Alifa has told me about his functioning, it would be next to impossible to get a judge to rule that he required long-term hospitalization. Long term, like forever. So, what else is left?"

The meaning of this off-the-cuff analysis hits me and I'm stunned. I've just logically concluded that I'm going to be killed unless I kill someone first.

"I wonder if you can let yourself see the thread that runs through so much of the fears that you have experienced over this past year," Steiner says. He is using his tone of psychoanalytic reasonableness. The tone that announces that he sees something clearly that I haven't a clue about— but should—if I weren't so defensive.

When I don't answer, he continues. "I ask you this at this point, because I think there is enough material for you to be able to see what you have been doing. Each item when taken singly is not conclusive, but if you will allow yourself to see the overall pattern it should convince you of the coloring you have been adding to the facts."

He pauses, but since he can see I'm only going to listen, he has to continue to develop his argument.

"So, what are the facts? Dr. Atkins sent you for a rotation at Northpark General Hospital. Residents have, in the past, gone to outside facilities for some of their training. True, as you told me your friend had discovered, never to that hospital and it is true that he didn't consult you, but you have no proof that if you hadn't been sent one of your fellow residents wouldn't have been chosen. In other words, there are no facts to support the motive of personal animosity that you attributed to him. Furthermore, even if those who know you wouldn't agree with his opinion that you needed more basic clinical work before continuing surgical training, he has a right to his opinion.

He pauses again. I'm sure he's expecting a strong reaction from me, but I disappoint him.

"OK, the next fact is that Dr. Conway wanted someone to do tabulating work in order to produce a paper for publication. One legitimately can say this was a selfish thing, but again you see it as personal. Don't you think that you were the easy choice, since, at that time, you were not actively part of any of the surgery services? To use another person, he would have had to come into conflict with the faculty member who headed that service. The next fact is that you have seen this Ahmad in locations to suggest that he has followed you. Limited to what you have told me—and I am not referring to anything told me by anyone else—you have no support for the idea that he intends you harm. You do not know that he was driving the car that almost hit you and you have only the opinion of the other driver, whose perception was likely influenced by the intense danger of the moment, that the car actually swerved to hit you." He pauses to get a breath before concluding his argument.

"As I said before, your feeling that you are the object of someone else's anger cannot be supported when we look at the individual cases. What can be appreciated when viewed as a series, a series of events that you must agree are unrelated, is the personal interpretation you are giving them."

"So you think I'm making it all up?"

"I think you hated your father and always expected

him to retaliate. Where Doctors Atkins and Conway were concerned you expected them to retaliate for daring to think that you could be a surgeon who would challenge them. Where Ahmad is concerned you are afraid he will retaliate for your wish to possess his woman just as you were afraid your father would retaliate for your wish to have your mother all for yourself."

His words are calm, but there is certainty there, as there would be in the words of the experienced voice coach who advises the young student, "I think you should consider becoming a dentist."

I have two almost simultaneous reactions: anger, and the feeling that he really dislikes me and has just attacked me. At the same time, I can recognize that these same reactions of mine exactly repeat the pattern he has just outlined. What the hell, my analogy about the voice coach is of the big father saying to the child, "You'll never be the man I am."

What can I say—he's right.

I tell him about finding out Atkins and Conway were classmates.

He says nothing.

The session is at an end and I get up and leave without a word. As I exit the waiting room going into the outer hallway, I bump into a patient I haven't seen before, but I'm so lost in my thoughts I don't acknowledge the collision. I ride the elevator down, swirling in a combination of insight about myself mixed with confusion. I walk along Adams to the El stop and climb the stairs to the platform admitting to myself that even the notion that Ahmad is after me is based solely on Fahra's unproven belief that it was he who attacked her friend in Munich. It could have been anybody. My train comes in, almost empty. I enter and take a seat next to the window. I hardly slept last night and I feel like I might doze off right here. The train doors close and I happen to look out of the window.

Leaning against the wall of the station platform is a tall, heavyset guy wearing a Cubs jacket. It's Ahmad. He smiles at me and raises one hand and draws his finger across his throat. With his other hand, he waves bye-bye, and I don't think it's just because my train is pulling out.

17

The train leaves the station and I'm looking at the familiar building fronts along Wabash. What I thought I'd just seen—Ahmad smiling at me and making a motion that he'd cut my throat—reminds me of dream scenes from movies. Could that explain what I'd just seen, a dream? Did I doze-off? I'm wide awake now, however, and around me are the familiar sights and sounds of everyday: other passengers, the rumbling of the car, the advertisement over the window telling me my future will be secure with a correspondence degree from Hudson College. If it was a hallucination then I'm around the bend, projecting my feelings into the real world as Steiner keeps insisting. My hold on sanity is very shaky at this moment. I sense that someone is looking at me—the guy across the aisle. Is he staring at me because he perceives that I'm running off the rails? I look over at him. He's black, about my age, wearing those puffed-out pants, backwards cap, MP3 player headphones around his neck.

He says, "That dude back there don't like you, man."

Reality locks firmly back into place again. This guy saw Ahmad, too—saw him threaten me. I'm not crazy. I feel like giving the guy a five.

"Guy's a pain in the ass," I say, with a dismissive shrug.

He smiles and with the flick of his wrist has his headset in place and is in his own dream world.

An alarm bell rings in my head. Since it wasn't a dream, this proves Ahmad is threatening to kill me and, without doubt, drove that car last night.

I'm on a Red Line train. I decide to get off at Fullerton and transfer to the Brown Line that will take me to Fahra's stop. She'd said her apartment was only one stop beyond the one where we'd parted after dinner at the kebab place— one stop past Western. I take out my phone and scroll to her number. No answer. The machine comes on and I say that I want to see her and that I'll call again soon.

I make the transfer between trains at Belmont and immediately consult the map of the Brown Line route. Rockwell is the stop past Western. On the map it looks very near to Western. Two high school girls are jabbering away across the aisle as if they had been lifted from their seats in the classroom and deposited here without interruption, completely unaware of a city of three million people around them, until I speak.

"Excuse me."

They both give me that wary, big-city teenage girl appraisal to determine if I am a rapist, a desperate addict gathering money for a fix, an exhibitionist, a smart ass, or a dumb tourist. I have to be careful how I phrase a simple request for information.

"If either of you is familiar with this train route, can you tell me how far it is between the stop at Western and the next stop at Rockwell?"

They look at each other to determine if the other has recognized a hidden obscene meaning in my words. Do they dare allow me to penetrate the boundaries of safety? Once I'm deemed safe, then there's the question of how to answer me and diss me at the same time.

The bolder of the two uses the technique of answering barely audibly and obliquely while shooting her friend a knowing smile. "Not far. Maybe three blocks."

"Thanks, that's helpful," I say with my best, clean-cut smile of moral rectitude and promptly look away.

Satisfied that they've handled this play passably, they take up where they left off.

It's likely that Ahmad might think that I'm going to Fahra's. Since, having a car and with favorable traffic, he can make it to the Rockwell station before I can, I decide to get off at Western and walk. If Ahmad plans to cut me off, I figure he will park where he can keep an eye on the Rockwell station exit.

I descend the stairway at Western and think of a way to kill some time. Fahra mentioned that Ahmad never goes to the kebab restaurant, so I walk there and order a Turkish coffee from Sonya.

Again, as on the night Fahra and I were here, there is only one other table taken. A couple is holding hands across it and whispering words they've infused with magic. I see this and look away, giving them the private room they imagine they have.

Sonya, again smiling enigmatically, puts the coffee in front of me then floats away. Aromas of coffee and cardamom envelope me. I stir in some sugar and take a sip. The strong, black syrup seems to travel straight from my mouth to the base of my brain, where it gives it a kick. Suddenly, a parallel universe is illuminated. It is a different one than the one in which Dr. Steiner perceives me, the one in which I have created a detour from my life's path by imagining that I've been thwarted by two wicked step-fathers. The world that the oriental caffeine has just switched on is one in which the Chicago Police Department really believes that the abuse I've had to endure was real enough to make me commit murder. Gemiano is satisfied that I had a strong enough motive. Starkly sobering is the realization that with the dent in the fender he has completed the triad of motive, means and opportunity. Why hasn't he arrested me? My fingerprints were on the fire extinguisher. I was in possession of the vehicle that could well have killed Mason Atkins. Seeing him walking alone on a dark, deserted street provided the opportunity. Premeditation? Gemiano had my doodled sketch of Dicky Conway being squashed by Bigfoot.

This is an amazing sensation, this hyper-alert mentation I'm experiencing. I am inside Gemiano's brain. I feel like I can reach over and pull his social security number off the shelf of his memory. I answer my own question. He hasn't arrested me yet, because he has no hard evidence that couldn't be easily challenged by a competent attorney. If I were a poor, black guy who'd likely be represented by a disinterested public defender, Gemiano would be getting a warrant right now. But, as sure as he is of my guilt, he knows he can't put me away and keep the door locked—yet. He needs something more.

I take out my phone and punch the re-dial button. This time Fahra's home. I tell her where I am and that I want to come to her apartment. There must have been special urgency in my voice, because without hesitation she tells me the address.

I walk there checking all the parked cars I pass. Typical Chicago two-flats, upper and lower, make up Fahra's block. Her address is mid-block and features a tall pine tree in the front yard. Her doorbell is above her neighbor's, so I figure hers is the upper. A light goes on in the entrance foyer and behind the lace curtains of the door glass I see her hurry down the stairs.

She's smiling. "Hi, come in. I'm glad you're here."

She leads the way up the stairs and steps aside to let me enter the apartment. What strikes me first is the color: colorful rugs, wall hangings, paintings and the multi-color display of a floor to ceiling bookcase.

"What a pleasant room," comes out spontaneously.

"Thank you. It's comfortable."

Beyond the main room, I can see a sun porch filled with plants and through its windows the pine tree. Glancing to my left, I see a desk lamp lights a computer keyboard in what was intended as a bedroom, but which Fahra has made into her study. I think of my place. It has suddenly become measly and barren.

"Have you eaten?" Fahra asks.

"No." I hadn't given food a thought.

"I was about to make myself an omelet. Does that interest you?"

"Very much."

"*Aux fines herb.*"

"My favorite kind of herb."

A quick look tells her I'm joking and she smiles. "In that case you must be an expert with the chopping knife. She hands me a chef's knife and gestures toward a cutting board on which are assorted twigs of grasses. I recognize parsley and chives.

It's a very pleasant feeling I'm having standing beside her at the counter. Telling her about Ahmad's threat and my dive away from death last night are hanging there in my awareness, but I don't want to alter the present mood. Eating the delicious omelet by candlelight with a glass of cold Frascati is another mood I decline to diminish. Sitting with her on the couch and realizing that she is entirely open to my first caresses and their possible extension is certainly not to be disturbed with thoughts of Ahmad. In fact, all traces of Ahmad have dissolved long before our bare bodies touch and I sink— thrust into sweet oblivion.

I climax into a fourth dimension. I have an overriding consciousness that I have reached a zenith, a fulfillment of all that life has to give. I have stretched out and touched the top. Lying back and looking up at the room's ceiling, which is still open to the stars, I sense that I have floated down a little from that ultimate height, but in its place is the rich knowledge that, with Fahra, I now possess the key to reach out again and again to what will remain the highest mark of my life's reach.

I look back at the seamless way in which it all happened. Completely unexpected. I know it isn't because Fahra is "easy" in the usual meaning of that word, but that for her our making love seemed to have an inevitable quality.

Fahra rolls onto her side and kisses me very tenderly.

"Confused?" she asks, her voice intimate.

"Ah, no."

"You ought to be," she continues. "First I seem to shun you. I don't let you know how you can contact me except by my office voice mail, and then I barely let you finish your omelet before I have you in bed."

"Now that you put it that way."

She laughs. "I'm a little confused . . . by my sudden, well, like a dam breaking." She lays her cheek against my chest and hugs me tightly and I have my arms around her.

"In for a penny in for a pound," I hear her mumble to herself.

"What's that?" I ask.

"It popped into my mind, a saying I read in an English novel. Letting go. Investing everything."

She props herself up on an elbow and looks me in the eye. She is smiling the contented smile of a very happy person.

"Oh David, I thought I would never feel like this. I had made up my mind that I wouldn't let it happen, but of course I didn't really know what this feeling was." She laughs happily. "Let me start again. I knew that to be truly happy one must make a full commitment to something—usually another person. But that sort of commitment opens one up to terrible pain if that person is ever lost. Most people, young people, have not experienced that kind of pain by the time they find themselves desiring to make that kind of total emotional investment and so they blithely make it. I, on the other hand, have felt so much pain at losing people dear to me that I had made up my mind that I wouldn't—couldn't—go through it again. I knew there were many interests and activities that could fill my life without my having to run the risk of loss, and I resigned myself to limit myself to these. I was ready to sacrifice full happiness in order to avoid pain.

"I felt myself strongly attracted to you, David, right from the beginning. I was aware of it the first time I saw you in Dr. Steiner's waiting room and from the wonderful moment at the lunch stop on that bike tour: I was falling in love. It was easy at first to keep my distance, because my fear of commitment was reinforced by my fear that you would be in danger if Ahmad learned about you. After Alifa told me that you knew the story and had come to know about you, that rationale for distancing myself fell away and I was left with . . . how shall I put it . . . feelings of love versus a wish to avoid pain. It's pretty clear which won out."

Fahra has been telling me this in a light-hearted manner, as if she were relating a joke on herself.

"So you see, it is not so sudden really. I have been in love with you for quite some time now. It's just that tonight the dam broke. But . . . "

She pauses as if not knowing how to continue.

"But what?" I prompt.

"Well, I don't really know what you want our relationship to be."

"That's simple. I want us to get married. That must be clear."

"Well, yes, that is what I thought, but I may not be what you imagine me to be. While I love you and would want to be the wife you'd want, there is another side to my life that I am very committed to."

"If you mean your investment in social causes, Alifa told me about that. I'm all for your having interests that are important to you."

Fahra studies my face soberly and then says, "I can't expect you to understand that my commitment is more than an interest. Surgery is more than an interest for you, am I right?"

"Surgery? Sure surgery's a good part of my life."

"My dedication to doing all I can about the problems I see in our world is just as much a part of me, David. Just as surgery is your life's work, this is my life's work. Later on, after I'm a citizen, I might decide to run for public office. I just want to be sure that you know who I am."

I can't say that I completely understand the meaning of the dedication she's speaking of.

"What about art? I thought art was important to you."

"Yes, it is, but this other is just as important—perhaps more important."

I'm tangentially aware that she has been trying to tell me that she has no intention of being the good dutiful wife that I may have assumed I'd have someday, but my emotions, lying here feeling her bare flesh against mine, have no room for considerations of any real incompatibility. There can be no serious disharmony anymore than there can be a conflict between my right hand and my left. I can't see that I am taking a chance at all, but I am able to realize that she is taking the chance that opening up to me will not result in the same pain she has known in the past. She has asked me for no promises. She is accepting the responsibility for her choice and I intuitively know that if I were to betray her trust, I would hear no recriminations. No ceremony or document could make me feel more married than I do right now.

I spend the night, intending to leave very early in order to be on the ward in time. I leave after coffee and toast with the sure knowledge that my life has moved up to a new and never imagined plateau.

I have no thought of Ahmad until I hear the door open on a car I have walked past and hear him scream, "You die you son bitch." I look back and there he is coming toward me. One block away, on Montrose, there is morning traffic moving and I instinctively start running toward a place where there will be other people. I can run fast and Ahmad is not gaining on me as I round the corner and cross the less traveled westbound lane and dance my way between cars heading east toward downtown. I am about to start waving to someone to stop and pick me up, when I see the roof sign on a Yellow Cab. I wave and luck is with me; he has no passenger. He pulls up, stopping traffic.

Ahmad was held up by a knot of westbound cars and has lost enough time for me to slide into the cab and tell the driver, "Downtown. Northwestern Hospital," without the guy becoming alarmed that he has picked up a fugitive.

I'm shaken. Part of this is because of the violence that I barely avoided, but just as much is due to the abrupt shattering of the bliss I'd been feeling and the new fear that Ahmad's discovery of my having spent the night with Fahra would mean that she is likely now also in danger.

My hand is shaking as I scroll to her number on my phone. I tell her about Ahmad, both the attempted hit-and-run and what had just now happened. She is stunned. I tell her that she must be careful, because I figure she's in danger now. I get her to agree to take a cab to work today and say I'll call her later. I take an anxious glance through the rear window of the cab. Looking over my shoulder has become a part of my life.

18

Today contains a "first" and a "last." This is my first day on the vascular surgery unit and this afternoon I have my last appointment with Dr. Steiner. Wanting quickly to bring me up to speed and make me feel one of the team, Dr. Carducci has assigned me to assist him tomorrow on a iliofemoral artery bypass. That means that during any break in routine ward work today I have to bone-up on the anatomy of the pelvis and upper leg as well as the surgical technique we'll be using. My mind isn't up to it. Try as I do to concentrate on what I read, my other problems take priority.

I stand an extra moment outside Steiner's door, looking at his name. I'm feeling a sense of loss. There will probably never be a time in the future when I can really speak my mind freely to another person without first considering the social situation.

As I enter his inner office, he motions toward a chair across from his.

"Why don't you sit down Dr. Brahms."

I understand this will not be the usual session. I realize that anything I might have reported about Fahra and me or about Ahmad is not today's business. Today is about leaving. What we say is very routine, but behind my words is unspoken feeling. Soon there is nothing left to say except, "Goodbye." Less than a quarter of an hour since I walked into his office, I am standing at the elevator pressing the down button.

What I understand, as I step out of the elevator is that I no longer have a daddy to run to. The problems of

Gemiano and Ahmad are mine to solve on my own.

I I have to find a way to neutralize Ahmad. I can't have him lurking on the fringe of my life able to dart in and ambush Fahra and me. Better judgment tells me that confronting him aggressively is not the solution. First, I'm not a match. Second, even if I were to be the victor, Ahmad has friends. Both parties to a dispute come away happier after negotiation and compromise. That means I have to meet him. The problem is how to arrange for this meeting— and to survive long enough for there to be a negotiation.

I go out on the sidewalk and check in all directions. I see an average inventory of shoppers, office workers and at the corner the guy who toots the sax in a random way while going through cool moves as if he were John Coltrane. A tourist tosses a coin into the open instrument case at the guy's feet, taking care to stay a good distance away. I cross the street only when I'm sure there is no car that could pounce on me. On my way to the El station, a guy comes out of a doorway to shove a free shopping flyer in my face. I get my heartbeat down to a countable rate and decide to take the advice I gave Fahra this morning and take a cab. I'm slow getting my money out to pay the driver when he pulls up in front of my building. I want time to scan the block. Two buildings to the east a guy, caretaker I guess, is sowing grass seed on a bare patch of ground between the street and the sidewalk two buildings down, but that's it.

Putting the barricades in place once I'm inside my apartment, I call Fahra and she answers. I tell her of my plan to meet with Ahmad and convince him that she and I are, now, a permanent item and while I'm sympathetic with his disappointment, I'm not going away and he should get a life of his own.

Her response amounts to, "You can't really mean that." I understand. But she doesn't fully appreciate my plan, which is to track him to his apartment and present myself unannounced. As it is, he is emboldened by being in the role of the hunter. Opening his door and finding me standing there will catch him off balance and in that moment I will establish a one-to-one conversation between equals. I will break through to that part of him that is rational, that part that is able to work together with others on jobs and harmonize with others in a band. Fahra isn't aware of the kind of instant camaraderie that is possible between two men. A crazy plan? You bet.

We talk a while about her work and I tell her about the procedure I will assist on tomorrow. Before we hang up, I ask her to be very careful until we're sure Ahmad has become disinterested in us. She, of course, has already figured that out, but leaves me able to believe—if I need to—that she will follow my advice.

I make a peanut butter and jelly sandwich, the featured entrée' at Chez Brahms this evening, and open my anatomy atlas and look at the diagrams while I eat.

One thing I will not argue with Dr. Steiner about is the existence of unconscious thinking. We've all experienced becoming aware of a thought that could only be the culmination of a line of thinking that had been progressing without our awareness. I experience this now. I suddenly have the thought, "Ahmad must be playing his *saz* this evening. That's why he wasn't following me."

In spite of my better judgment, which agrees with Fahra's reaction to my suggested meeting with Ahmad, this new idea of *where* I might find him in order to follow him to his apartment has taken over. I'm like a guy suddenly obeying an impulse to plunk down his life's savings on a turn of the roulette wheel. I get my phone book out of the drawer to see if Alifa is listed. There are half a dozen Baghdadis and one is A. Baghdadi. She answers and is clearly surprised when I identify myself. I say that I hope I didn't call at a bad time, but I need some information and hope she can help me.

"I'll be happy to if I can."

"I want to find out where Ahmad works and where his band plays . . . tonight, for instance."

I know she's wondering why I'm not asking Fahra, but she doesn't ask and I don't explain. Her hesitation before answering tells me she is also uncertain about what Fahra's reaction will be.

"I can make some phone calls and possibly learn something."

"Would you do that for me?"

"OK, what's your number?"

I go back to looking at pictures of anatomy, although my brain is not really keeping me company. The phone rings and I'm on it before the end of the first ring.

"Yes?" I say urgently.

"The pregnancy test was negative; you can relax, son."

It's Jeff. I realize there had been an imploring desperation in my tone.

"It's you," I say.

"You weren't expecting anyone else, surely."

"As a matter of fact I was, and don't call me Shirley."

"Ah, that's my Groucho. Since you're expecting another call, I'll make this quick. Dr. Serendipity had a brilliant idea. You told me about the roadblock you ran into because that St. Paul's School site was password protected. It occurred to me that Ralph Springer might use a general password for logging onto unimportant sites like a lot of people do. Like sites other than one's bank account. I got one of the women I know who works in the Surgery Department office to see if she could find out what he uses in the university computer. Again, you're indebted to my mastery of the science of seduction. His password is 'bowwow.' There's some deep hidden meaning there, because I think that's part of a Yale cheer and I know Springer went to Harvard. Anyway, I went to the St. Paul's site and tried it and—Open Sesame. I looked around a little and did ascertain that Atkins and Conway didn't graduate with their class, but they were listed the previous year as juniors. That's all. You're very welcome and I'll get off the line." The line goes dead and I hang up. Bowwow? I want to check out the site now that I have entry, but I have to leave the line free for Alifa's call.

I get myself a beer and sit looking at the phone until it rings.

"The third call did it," she announces. "He's playing tonight at Grand Bazaar. It's a Turkish restaurant with live entertainment. It's on Peterson, 2900. May I ask why you want to know?"

"I'm going to try to talk some sense into him."

There is a long silence.

"Does Fahra know?"

"Yes and no. Thanks a lot for your help. I'll stop around at the gallery soon. So long."

"Be careful, David."

I've made up my mind. Tonight is the time to do it. Better not delay and be sorry later—or not even be alive to be sorry later.

Would it be a smart idea to get Jeff to come along with me? I like the idea of backup, but I reckon that Ahmad will be more likely to see me as friendly and allow himself to talk to me if he's not confronted by two of us. It's eight-thirty. A band would play until ten o'clock, at least. I'll wait another half hour here and then go. I take another shot at the anatomy and find I can concentrate now.

By taking the El to Berwyn and then a #84 bus, I'm able to scope the south side of Peterson until I spot the Grand Bazaar. It's part of a block-long strip of miscellaneous stores. I'd heard of it as a pretty good place for an entertaining night out, good food, lively atmosphere and not expensive. The storefronts nearest to the restaurant are all dark. I walk past the Grand Bazaar's entrance as two couples emerge. Music comes out with them. So, I'm early enough. The question is how early? I, of course, can't go inside. If Ahmad catches sight of me, my plan is dead. My question is answered by a notice stuck on the door, "Live music from 8 p.m. until 10 p.m." I have some time to kill. Light plays onto the sidewalk from the front window of a store at the next corner. I walk there and discover that it's a Korean grocery. I *am* becoming hungry. The peanut butter and jelly sandwich has peaked. Is there such a thing as a Korean candy bar?

This is very much a ma and pa operation, except there is no pa in sight. Four middle-aged women are in the rear having a social hour. One sees me and smiles but goes on with the conversation. No hurry here, browse as long as you wish, so I pick up and read the label—when I can—on nearly every item I don't recognize. Finally, I take a cellophane bag of little cakes called *diafu*. The list of contents looks to be in Japanese, not Korean. The lady comes to the register and I ask what the cakes are made of. We have hit the language barrier.

I leave the store and walk back toward the Grand Bazaar, taking a bite of the diafu. Hmm. Chewy. Definitely an acquired taste. Hunger beats out strangeness.

I kill more time walking along the line of cars parked on Peterson to see if any of them stir a recollection of the car that came at me night before last. No luck. The plan I have is this: I will wait until shortly before ten and then flag down a cab. I've got a story ready for the driver. My former brother-in-law has not been making his support payments and the court can't find out where he's living— no employment record, no social security deductions. I found out he's playing with a band at this restaurant. I'm going to follow him home and get his address for my sister. It seems to me that the story's got a good chance of evoking cooperation—maybe.

I open the Grand Bazaar's door a crack and put my ear to it. It's 9:50 and this is about the fifth time I've done this.

To any observer I must look like a hesitant swain about to present himself at his loved one's door, only to open it a crack and then lose nerve and walk away again. This time, I hear loud applause. Either they played their last number of the evening or they're about to. Time to flag down the next cab. 9:57 and no cab. Not being a regular consumer of taxi rides, I haven't allowed for the fewer cabs that cruise at this hour. I check the door again—no music. I hustle across Peterson willing there to be a taxi's lit roof-sign in sight.

Ahmad comes out of the restaurant with two other men. All three are carrying instrument cases. His seems like a banjo case with a very long neck. I sink down below the roof of the car I'm standing behind and watch. Their conversation goes on for a while on the sidewalk and then there's some sort of exchange taking place. Ahmad is counting out some bills into the hand of one of the guys. They part, Ahmad going west and the other two east.

Occupied with watching them and keeping out of sight, I nearly miss the cab until it is abreast, but the sudden raising of my hand catches his attention and he brakes. Luckily, cab drivers grow to be as sensitive to subtle signals as a Christie's auctioneer. Before I get into the cab, I scan the opposite sidewalk for Ahmad and see him just as he's turning the corner to walk down the next side street.

I appraise the driver. Does he look like he will swallow my story? He's fiftyish, white, ill kempt and looks bored. I'm pessimistic. He looks like he'd love to leave the wife and four kids and duck out of any support payments. It's too late to construct another yarn to explain my wanting him to tail another car.

"I need your help, friend," I begin. "My sister is divorced from a guy who used to beat her up and now she's raising the four kids herself, because he's skipping out of the child support." I sense that I'm much too wordy, but I plunge ahead. "The court can't find him, but I found out he's working at the restaurant across the street and I need to follow him to see where he's living."

The driver looking even more bored and skeptical, turns toward me.

"You want to hire me for some surveillance stuff?"

"Ah, yes, you could put it that way."

"That's a different price scale than a cab ride. Understand?" He has some kind of heavy eastern European accent.

"How much?"

"Triple the meter."

"OK, let's go. He just walked down that side street."

We make the turn and see a parked car about fifty yards down the block turn on its lights. My driver slows to a stop. The back-up lights on the other car go on, and then it pulls away from the curb and drives on down the street. It passes under a streetlight and I feel sure it's the same car that almost killed me.

"That's him," I announce, the excitement of the hunt entering my voice.

My driver manages the tail like a pro. I look at the framed taxi license certificate on the back of the front seat, where his photo is sneering at his passengers. Mikhail Sletnev. Fucking KGB driver without a doubt. When Ahmad parks and goes into a Bosnian grocery/café and we park and watch, I become afraid that there is a chance the meter might challenge the treasury deficit. Luckily Ahmad comes out of the store in less than five minutes carrying a brown paper bag that could contain a bottle of Slivovitz.

We follow Ahmad east on Devon. My driver runs a red light at Clark, then turns north on a street I'm not familiar with and the name of which I miss. At the first intersection, I read Newgard.

My driver, exercising a sixth sense, doesn't follow Ahmad into the next block, but waits at the intersection until he sees Ahmad's stop lights go on about mid-block ahead. My driver, then, turns to the right on Albion and immediately pulls over to the curb.

"He's parking. Do you want me to wait?"

"No. This is good." The meter reads $14.50. I take two twenties and a ten out of my wallet leaving me with six bucks. I hand him the bills and get out and run across the street and peek around the apartment building on the corner. Half way down the block, Ahmad is walking toward me. I see him turn onto the walk leading up to an apartment building. He disappears from view and I trot down the sidewalk to a position where I can see if any lights are turned on in one of the windows. I wait several minutes, but the windows that are dark remain dark. I mount the steps to the entrance. There is the typical mail box/ intercom combination with slots for about a dozen names. I look at it with a sinking realization that I don't know Ahmad's last name.

My eye quickly skims over the name labels. They look like they've been there a long time. One is different from the rest. Next to number 304 the name is written on what appears to be brown paper from a grocery bag. There is a large "A" and the rest is microscript, but it could say Ahmad Basir. I press the call button next to one of the second floor apartments. No answer. I press another and a voice says, "Yes?" I answer, "It's me," slurring it all together. The door buzzes and I go in. The stairway is straight ahead across a small lobby. I start up, planning to quickly and quietly mount to the third floor before the person who just buzzed me in comes to investigate. Before I get to the second floor I hear a door slam loudly higher up. I pass the second floor and climb to the landing half way to the third floor. I'm out of sight of anyone who might come from that second floor apartment to take a look down the stairwell, when "It's me" fails to show up.

I rest and consider what I'm going to say to Ahmad when I knock and he opens his door. I experience a flicker of critical judgment that's asking me just what the hell I think I'm doing here. I don't allow it to advance beyond a flicker and force myself back to the question of what I will say to him when he opens the door. First of all I've got to look relaxed and friendly. "Hi, I'm David Brahms. May I come in?" Yeah, that's good. It appeals to one's hospitality and the Turks are reputed to be dripping with hospitality. After that . . . improvise. I peek around at the second floor landing. No one. I climb up to the third floor. Straight ahead of me, across the hallway is a closed door with a red exit light over it—the back stairs. The first door down the hall to the right is 304. I see that the door is ajar a couple of inches.

I try to assume a relaxed attitude. I get a smile on my face. I knock. The door is so light that my knocking pushes it open a bit more. I can see a dim light in the room. I push the door open more, while saying, "Ahmad." The light is coming into the front room from a hallway to the right. I push the door wider and am jolted to see him slouched on a couch facing me, looking at me from under half-closed lids. Real cool expression. I expect him to say something like, "What the fuck you want, dude?" He doesn't say it. He doesn't say anything.

19

I now smell the burned gunpowder and I study him more carefully. This man is dead. I know it. I walk cautiously over to him to place my fingertips over his carotid artery. Two sensations register at once: no pulse and he's very warm. Of course he's warm, I remind myself, I just saw him walk into the building. I see the hole in his black nylon jacket. It's in the center of his chest, the fabric puckered around it. I see blood through the hole.

This just happened! I twirl around afraid the killer is behind me. No one. On the wood floor, lying in the track of light coming from the hall is a gun, a heavy automatic. I lean over to look at it with no intention of doing something stupid like picking it up.

"What is this? Who are you?"

An old guy is standing in the open doorway to the apartment, looking at me with terror on his face. He turns and runs back down the corridor yelling, "Emma don't come! Go back!"

I'm scared out of my mind and dash out of the apartment and sail down the stairs, passing a startled woman who falls against the wall shouting at me, "Hey you, what you think!" I fly out the front door . . . into the arms of two Chicago cops.

In an instant I'm face down on the lawn with a knee in my back that's trying to break my spine.

"Where's the gun?" one cop is yelling in my ear.

"Upstairs," I answer. Now that was stupid.

"What's your name?" he demands. I hear the other guy talking on a phone or walkie-talkie saying they got the shooter.

It's time to forget I can speak. Handcuffs are being locked onto my wrists.

"Your name, asshole!" I feel a hand trying to get my wallet out of my pocket.

"No. Leave it alone," the other cop says. "We leave everything like it is. I'm going into the building to check it out. Crowley will be here in a minute and he can have the responsibility for fucking up the evidence if it happens. Stay with the punk."

Twenty minutes later and I'm still lying on the front lawn face down. A load of cops has come and some have gone. I don't try to look up, but I hear them comment about me as they pass. "He the guy?" "Drug deal you think?" or they kid the cops that grabbed me. "Fastest you pizza pies ever moved." I learn that the old guy called the cops when he'd heard what he recognized to be a gunshot.

At last my two captors, Brunetti and Baldo, such are their names, are told by a detective to take me to the precinct and book me. I ride sitting bolt upright, my hands shackled behind me. When we arrive at the station I'm processed as if I were doing nothing more exciting than applying for a job. I know I'm allowed two calls. One has got to be to Marty Frumin. The other has got to be to Ben Hawthorn, the Chief Resident on Carducci's service. I'm scheduled to scrub with Carducci in the morning for the graft procedure and it's imperative that I let him know I probably won't make it.

I announce to the guy who is asking me questions and typing a form that I know I'm allowed to make phone calls. I don't specify the number, hoping I'll be able to call Fahra and Jeff before they realize it.

He says, "No shit? We got a fucking lawyer here."

I can tell this guy didn't try out for the part of "good cop."

As far as the form is concerned, I cooperate enough for

him to fill in name, address, phone and social security numbers. They fingerprint me.

Lieutenant Crowley makes his appearance as I'm finishing a coffee that one of the "good cops" brought. I'm taken into a room that I recognize from the many hours spent at the movies as an interrogation room, complete with small table holding a tape recorder. He tells me to take a seat, and I tell him that I'm not answering any questions until my lawyer is present. (Also learned from the flicks.) He looks at his watch. I'm sure, just as in my world, this has to do with the question of when his shift ends. Either he will want to pass me on to the next detective or he will want me for himself. He gets up without a word and returns shortly with a phone that he plugs into a jack in the wall and a telephone book. He sits down and makes a very minimal gesture that says, "Go for it."

I look up Marty's home number, but as I expected, it isn't listed.

"I'll need my cell phone. My attorney's home number is in it."

Crowley, exhibiting admirable patience, has my cell phone brought and hands it to me. I turn it on and scroll to Marty's number.

A young woman answers. Daughter? I identify myself and ask for Marty. She asks me to wait a moment.

"Hi, David, what's up?" he says when he picks up.

"Not anything you might expect, unfortunately. I'm at the 25th Precinct Police Station. I'm being held because I was at the scene of a shooting. A guy was shot."

"Shot? You mean killed?" He pauses for three beats. "Naturally I've got many questions but they can wait until I get there. Until then don't tell them anything, but don't be belligerent about your rights either."

"I understand." I hang up.

"I get another call, right?"

"I've never looked it up but I don't pay the phone bill."

He motions toward the phone he brought.

I know the physicians' number at the hospital. I dial it and ask if the operator knows where Ben Hawthorn is. She tells me that he is signed in, but after trying his ward says he's not there and asks if I want him paged. Yes. I look over at Crowley, who seems totally absorbed in a small journal he has taken from his coat pocket. Finally Ben answers the page.

"Ben, this is David Brahms. I've accidentally got myself enmeshed in an investigation of a shooting. I'm being held for questioning as a witness but what's relevant is that I may not be released in time to scrub in the morning."

"A shooting?"

"Yeah."

"Jesus. I'm beginning to see you as that little guy who goes around with the rain cloud following him. It's not a good thing to miss this case. Carducci picked you especially to assist him."

"There's no place on earth I'd rather be, but this detective sitting across from me may have other ideas. And Ben, I'd very much prefer it if the exact reason for my absence isn't known. If you think you can manage that." I can see that he may think I've asked him to lie. "I'm not wanting you to lie to Carducci. I thought it might be possible to avoid an explanation altogether."

"That will be tough, but I know what you'd like and I'll do it if it plays out that way."

"Thanks. I'll get back to the hospital just as soon as they release me."

Crowley unplugs the phone and carries it out with him. I sit alone in the dingy room feeling like I belong here. How did all this happen? I saw Ahmad walk into the apartment. I took maybe five minutes tops to get into the building. I saw no one, heard no one. I did hear a door slam. I think of the sound and how it didn't sound exactly like a door, too abrupt, sharp. Yes, it must have been the shot I heard. But

I went straight—no, I waited on the landing between the second and third floor for a couple of minutes. The person who shot Ahmad must have immediately come out of his room and gone down the back stairs. There's probably a back door as well.

The door opens. It's Crowley and another guy dressed in T-shirt and jeans. This guy is carrying a small suitcase.

"The technician is going to take some samples for a test," Crowley announces. He adds in a sarcastic tone, "Your lawyer has nothing to say about this."

"He's right handed," he says to the technician.

I start to say that I won't let anything happen until Marty gets here, but I remember him saying not to get hostile about my rights, so I let the guy position my right hand palm down on the table, asking him to go easy since my hand is still tender from my slide on the pavement. He presses several sticky metal discs on the back of my hand, which he then removes and places in little slots in a tray.

"I suppose this is a paraffin test for gun powder residue to see if I've fired a gun," I say to the technician.

"That's right, only no one does a paraffin any more— too inconclusive. This disc picks up microscopic metal particles used in the manufacture of gunpowder. They become part of the residue left on the skin of a person who fires a gun. The discs are put in a scanning electron microscope, where the particles can be identified. Sure thing."

He gets up and leaves the room with his equipment, as an officer from the front desk comes to the open doorway and says, "The lawyer's here."

Crowley nods, gets up and goes out and returns with Marty Frumin. Marty is wearing a tie and jacket. I wonder if he has donned his professional garb for the occasion as a notice to the cops that legal rules must be obeyed.

Instead, it is Crowley who recites the rules. "Counselor, you may advise your client about whether he has to answer a question that I ask, but you may not coach him on his answers, and you may not confer with him about his part in the incident we are investigating. If we hold him you will be able to have a private conference with him, not before. Is that understood?"

This final question is to establish who's in control here.

"Perfectly. I will require a transcript of any recording that you make."

I recognize arm wrestling.

"Mr. Brahms."

"Doctor Brahms," Marty interjects.

Crowley shoots him a tired look and continues, "Tell me in your own words what happened this evening."

I would like to leave Fahra's name out of this, but I can't otherwise explain my following Ahmad. I tell the story of Fahra and Ahmad and finish with a photographically detailed account of this evening. Both of them are listening carefully, but with different motives, one listening for evidence of guilt, the other planning a defense.

At the conclusion, Crowley stretches and says that he is satisfied that there is enough evidence of presumed guilt to hold me on suspicion of murder. He says that it's OK with him if Marty and I talk for a few minutes and he leaves us.

"I probably should have told you about Ahmad, but it really had nothing to do with the other problem of Atkins and Conway."

I expect a lecture about telling one's attorney everything, but he only nods and says, "It looks like you were at the wrong place at the very wrong time. I wonder who killed him."

I'm assuming some kind of old-world vengeance, that or drugs. All those cops who showed up at Ahmad's certainly assumed it was just another drug-related hit. Whoever it was, it has nothing to do with me and I find I don't really care. To me the murderer is a faceless and indifferent actor, a bit-player, who appears, does the deed and vanishes, not important enough to take a bow at the final curtain. It's only at this moment that it comes to me that the triangular problem of Fahra, Ahmad and me is resolved. Maybe in the only way it ever could have been resolved permanently. The next thought leaves me breathless: what if Fahra did it? She knew I was planning to confront him and she must have been afraid of the result. Would she be capable of murder? Perhaps, if she saw it as the only way to protect someone she loves. The fact that I'm asking myself this question would be evidence that I don't really know her if I only considered it squarely. And it's true, of course. I don't know her.

Marty is continuing to talk. "They will hold you at least until they get back the results on your fingerprints and the residue test. Then comes the question of whether or not the lieutenant and his superiors believe your story. Either way, I'll be here tomorrow to demand that you're released on bail.

Marty leaves and they put me in a cell by myself. I lie on the cot expecting not to sleep at all, anxious as I am with the possibility that Fahra pulled the trigger. I drift off however, into tangled dreams that I awake from more drained than if I'd been awake all night. Before he left I'd asked Marty to call both Fahra and Jeff Richards. The situation wasn't hopeless enough yet to call Dr. Luther Brahms.

After a breakfast of a banana and surprisingly decent coffee, I have only a short time to wait before I'm taken from the cell to Crowley's office. Marty is there and he looks pleased, or at least not angered.

"We're letting you go on the strength of your attorney's word that you will remain in the city and will surrender to him and/or us if we want you back."

He shoves a clear plastic bag containing my wallet,

watch, beeper, cell phone and change across the table and also a form for me to sign saying I'd received them.

"You're free to go."

I can't believe it's going to be this easy. I keep expecting to hear someone yell, "Stop!" like in the movies when the hero is almost out the door and the police discover their mistake. It doesn't happen and I find myself getting into Marty's car.

"I gotta respect Crowley," Marty says as he starts the engine. "They could have kept you a while longer, even rejecting bail. They don't have another suspect, and a bird in hand as they say. Crowley confirmed what I thought, your prints weren't on anything in the room and the gunpowder residue test was negative."

I could have told them that.

"But neither fact is conclusive in this case, because they found a sock that tested positive."

"A sock?"

"Yeah, it's a trick to foil the test. Pulling a long sock like a dress sock up one's arm can keep the expended powder fragments from adhering to one's hand and arm. Just peel the sock off and drop it and away you go."

Marty drives out of the police parking lot as I sit numbly taking all this in.

"The lack of fingerprints doesn't mean much either, of course, since the sock is like a glove," Marty adds in a matter-of-fact vein. "By the way, where do you want me to drop you?"

We are headed south in the direction of both his office and my apartment. I tell him my address.

He continues, "I'm concerned about what can happen with this murder. Crowley is being a real *mensch*, as I said. He's giving us the benefit of the doubt—for the time being. That will change if they don't come up with another suspect. But what I'm also concerned with is what this will mean to Lieutenant Gemiano when he hears about it in the morning departmental cross-briefing. "What's Ahmad's murder got to do with him?"

"It might not be difficult for him to see it as part of a pattern." He shoots me a look.

"What do you mean, a pattern?"

"It seems that the people who give you a hard time somehow end up dead."

20

It's only ten a.m. when I get out of Marty's car in front of my apartment building. I should get my buns right down to the hospital, but I don't want to show up until I know what Ben Hawthorn said to others about my absence, and he's likely to still be in the OR. I don't need to compound a bad situation by putting my foot in my mouth.

I take a shower, shave and get into clean clothes. I feel a little giddy from hunger, lack of sleep and all of that adrenaline I've pumped in the last twelve hours. I open the refrigerator and snag a couple of slices of Munster cheese. I grind some espresso and load my stove-top espresso pot. Standing there waiting for it to brew I notice the swimming fish on my computer's screensaver and I remember Jeff telling me he had gotten onto the St. Paul's School site using the password "bowwow." While I wait for the coffee, I can take a look for myself.

I don't have DSL and my server doesn't take its title seriously, so I wait. Finally, I'm logged on and get to the school's site and type in the password in the alumni affairs link. Like a charm, I, an imposter, now walk within the hallowed walls of dear old St. Paul's. As Jeff said, I can see that Atkins and Conway didn't graduate with the class of 1957. I check the previous year's juniors and there they are. Of course there will be no explanation on this site of why they didn't graduate. After Atkins's name on the list, I notice Russell Ayers. I wonder if he's the same Russell Ayers who's on that political talk show, the obnoxious, far right creep I always want to punch out. And here's Dunstan

Beeman. Can he be the movie critic for the *Tribune?* He must be; how many Dunstan Beemans can there be?

I'm impressed already. Counting Atkins and Conway, the first four alumni I come across are probably in *Who's Who.* I'm curious and start to go through the whole class list, but my coffee pot starts hissing and spitting announcing that the coffee's ready. I take down a cup from the shelf. The crack that has been there for some time has entirely spiraled around the whole circumference. I picture the bottom dropping out half way to my lips, so I toss the cup in the garbage can and take another one off the shelf. That reduces my inventory to two cups. I pour the coffee and stir in sugar and take the first wonderful sip. The front door buzzer sounds. Who the hell can this be?

"Yes, can I help you?" I say into the intercom.

"Police. We've got a message for you."

A feisty feeling wells up. It crosses my mind to ask how I can be sure it's the police, but I don't want to get into a pissing contest with them.

"Just a moment," I say and walk over to the front window and look for a blue and white patrol car. It's there, all right. I press the button to open the front door and open my apartment door and wait.

One over-weight man in blue labors up the two flights.

"Lieutenant Gemiano wants to talk to you. You're to come with us."

"That's my only choice?" I ask. Feisty plus a little giddy.

He is confused for a moment but then reads my sarcasm.

"Believe me fella, I can think of better things to do than haul your ass around."

A point. "Be right with you, but I need to make a phone call."

"Do it."

I call Marty's office and find he's not there, so I tell Ethel Mann that I'm being hauled downtown again.

"I'll try to reach Marty but remember you won't talk without your attorney."

"Right."

I gather up the things I'll need to take to the hospital—beeper, Blackberry, stethoscope, penlight—and shove them into my backpack. I retrieve the cup from the garbage and fill it with coffee. I'll throw it away at Police Headquarters.

"You may take me to my appointment," I say in my imitation of the lord-of-the-manor. Maybe it's hypoglycemia.

The cop gives me a look that says he may have a nut case on his hands. "Yeah, right."

The large clock on the wall behind the row of three secretaries' desks in this hallway/waiting room says 12:48. My watch makes it 12:36 and I know mine is right—U.S. Naval Observatory time set two days ago. I ponder whether this whole department runs twelve minutes fast, or if the clock is kinetic art. I've been sitting here one hour and twenty-six minutes by any timepiece. I'm really experiencing hypoglycemia now. I've asked if I can go and get something to eat and I've been told no.

The waiting time has worn away any feistiness. I've sobered to the meaning of this Draconian summons. Gemiano sees the pattern that Marty mentioned. I begin thinking of an alibi for Ahmad's killing. I crisscross the events logically and see that the only fact to support my innocence is that I've never owned a gun. Totally meaningless. In this public arsenal called Chicago, the acquisition of an automatic like the one left on Ahmad's floor would be the work of a few morning hours. The cab driver will say I told him to trail Ahmad to his apartment, giving him a cock-and-bull story about my sister and then left me there only a few minutes before Ahmad's neighbor saw me bending over the gun. It is beyond belief that another person had the time needed to insert him—or herself—into the scene to kill Ahmad and get away unseen. The "herself" consideration refers, of course, to Fahra as the killer. This makes convincing Gemiano that the killer was someone other than me tricky. It could cause him to think of Fahra if he hasn't already done so.

At last, the ploy of making the suspect sit and stew— the cops' version of "icing" the place kicker—comes to an end and I'm taken to Gemiano's office.

He motions to a seat and says, "I see that Crowley didn't think it was necessary to feed and house you. And they say that we waste the tax payers' money, making no attempt at all to avoid needless expense."

These are his first words. He is wearing a wry smile and I correct my earlier impression that he reminded me of the Emperor Tiberius. How could I have thought that, when he's a ringer for Al Pacino? He exudes smugness. I suspect he thinks he's dealing with a wimp, who is bound by his identity to a particular social and professional class, which can't countenance one of its members making a run for it. Because of this he is at leisure to put together his case against me without fearing I'll abscond.

Gemiano drops the facetious manner and hammers me with questions about Ahmad, Fahra and the details about my movements last night. In spite of Ethel Mann's admonition, I find myself answering. He then sits back and clasps his hands behind his neck, rolling his head from side to side as if to relax tense muscles. He straightens up in the chair and speaks to me in a flat, even tone.

"Like Crowley, if I weren't mindful of the daily cost of incarceration, Brahms, I could charge you with triple murder right now. However, there are a few more details I want to check out, and while I do I'll let you support yourself."

I, of course, don't think for a second that his failing to charge me this very moment is because he wants to save the taxpayers small change. He'd love to charge me and be done with it. He's afraid he can't make it stick in court. There is no hard evidence that I pulled the trigger on Ahmad, and a good attorney—I think Marty fits those specs—could convince a jury it was possible that someone else did it and got down the back stairs before I knocked on Ahmad's door. And damn it, that's what happened!

I'm on the point of challenging him to go ahead and arrest me, but I hold off—fortunately. Finally I'm paying attention to Ethel Mann saying, "Don't say anything without your lawyer."

He warns me as I leave his office to be where he can reach me day or night. Yeah, yeah, sure, sure, I think. I'm feeling cocky again, past giddy, past hunger. Gemiano has no case and I'm certain he can't build one, because there is nothing for him to discover to add to the circumstantial evidence against me. He can find no evidence. I've done nothing.

I begin the walk once again from Police Headquarters to the El station. The farther I walk the more agitated I become over Gemiano's attitude. However, it's not agitation over his smugness alone. The more I think about it, his smugness has begun to take on a different meaning for me, pointing to a different outcome than the perpetual stalemate into which I prefer to imagine we're locked. What is causing my agitation is that it's sinking in that he really means what he said; the case is sewn up, only a few details to check out.

I get off the El at the Grand Street Station and walk toward Michigan Avenue. I come to a dead stop on the sidewalk outside Nordstrom's. A guy hurrying along behind me—probably looking at the Harley Davidson in Nordstrom's window—crashes into me.

"For Christ's sake!" he says.

I mouth some kind of apology but I'm not aware of what I say. One thought has totally captured my attention . . . and it has chilled me. Gemiano has a few loose ends to attend to, such as: did Ahmad have any enemies, had anyone threatened him, did Ahmad do any dealing in drugs? If this inquiry is not fruitful, then Gemiano will be ready to charge me with murder. He will be ready to turn the case—slam-dunk or not—over to the Prosecutor's Office. Many a person has been convicted on circumstantial evidence alone. He only dragged me to headquarters to repeat that I wasn't to leave the city and to reassure himself that I was docile.

I walk on slowly absorbing the cold realities of what being charged with murder will mean to me. If I'm convicted, of course, my life is over, either for real in this state, which still stupidly has a death penalty, or else my life as it might have been will be over with a life sentence. But even if Marty is able to convince a jury that there is not enough proof of my guilt, months will be taken from my training, probably resulting in my being dropped from the Northwestern program. And if the real killer is never found, I will forevermore be viewed as the possible murderer. Even if the killer is discovered and convicted, my social circle will permanently see me as having been involved in something very unsavory. "That's Dr. Brahms. Did you know that he was once put on trial for a triple murder?"

The thought that Gemiano might start the legal wheels turning that will grind me down chilled me moments ago. Now I'm getting mad. I have the makings of a great life within my grasp and I'm not going to fumble it away. Gemiano is lumping Ahmad, Atkins and Conway together based on the idea that I benefited by each of their deaths. If the killer of any one of them could be discovered, then the triad would be broken in Gemiano's mind and with that, his certainty about me. This, of course, was Marty's plan. I can do nothing about finding Ahmad's killer, and if,

God forbid, I learn that Fahra did it, there's no way I'll reveal that to Gemiano. But Atkins's and Conway's world is my own. If I am going to help myself avoid my life's certain ruin, I must discover the person who knocked off either of them. Mike Moran was on the research floor the night Conway was killed. He had no reason, as far as I know, to be there. Mike is a good friend. He has gone out of his way on several occasions to help me over the years and I simply can't tell Gemiano about the penlight until I talk to Mike. But, can I afford to wait? Isn't it imperative that Gemiano have this information before he goes ahead and issues an arrest warrant? Apart from my own future, I now have Fahra to think of.

I enter the hospital with the dread of facing Dr. Carducci and being asked to account for my absence this morning. I pass by his secretary, Hilda, and she looks up with a pleasant smile and a normal greeting. I don't know what to make of this. She should at least have the neutral expression of one speaking to a person who has fallen from grace. I continue on to the ward and ask one of the nurses if she has seen Ben Hawthorn.

"I saw him a minute ago, checking on the patient in room 554."

Ben is removing a pair of rubber gloves and is dropping them into the receptacle for contaminated waste when I come to the doorway.

"Ah, David," he says, "I take it all back. You're not the little guy under the dark cloud after all. You're golden."

"What's that supposed to mean?"

"The surgery was canceled last night. Carducci aggravated an old back injury and had to cancel. He asked me to reschedule it, AND to tell you he was sorry."

Once, while an undergraduate, I walked across campus to the building where I was to have a history exam that I was not prepared to take only to find that the place had burned down during the night. I'm having the same feeling

I did then.

"Fantastic," I say.

"Yes, I thought you'd be pleased. Now what about this murder business?"

I give Ben a modified, somewhat skewed version of how I happened along just after this guy was shot.

"And they kept you overnight? I would have thought they would take a statement and let you go."

"Yeah, except that for a while they thought I could be a suspect."

"Ah. That must have been scary."

"That whole world of police stations and interrogation is something most of us manage to miss out on. Like you said, it's scary."

"And there are other things I prefer to remain naïve about, such as starving or being tortured."

21

I'll be spending the rest of the morning in the general surgery post-op clinic, removing sutures, changing dressings and renewing prescriptions, but my main business today is to find Mike Moran. I can't afford to let another day pass. I call to have him paged but I'm told that he's not listed as being present in the hospital. I ask to have him paged anyway knowing that he has no regular duty now and may not have signed in. Next I call the record room, where I'm told he's not there and hasn't been for several days. I'm asked to tell him when I talk to him that his white coat is hanging on the coat rack.

When I get no response to the page, I seek out Ben Hawthorne to see if he has any idea about Mike's whereabouts.

"I'm not positive, David, but I think he left the hospital a few days ago to go out East to start a fellowship."

I don't like this and decide to do what I should have done earlier: ask Ralph Springer.

From our ward station, I call Springer's office. His secretary, Mrs. Tobin, tells me he won't be in until the afternoon. I ask her if she knows where I can find Moran.

"I don't know, Doctor Brahms. I saw him shaking hands with Doctor Springer . . . several days ago I think he was saying goodbye but I'm not sure."

"Thanks, Mrs. Tobin. I'll call back in the afternoon."

Damn! I need to talk to Mike right now.

I continue to automatically do ward work while thinking of my next moves. The fact that Mike's flashlight was in my office looms larger in my thinking. At the time

Conway was killed, having no reason to consider Mike to be the killer, I'd put the evidence of the flashlight aside. After all, Gemiano's attitude of suspicion toward me was only tentative at first. I had felt no real danger, and hadn't calculated how being arrested would impact me. I certainly didn't want to inform on a friend. And, perhaps I wasn't concerned with the person who killed Conway, because I was so happy he was out of my life. The situation is much different now. These facts are staring me in the face: Mike was in my lab the night Conway was killed and he dropped his penlight on the floor right below the rack where the fire extinguisher—the murder weapon—had been hanging. Mike must have hated Conway. Mike has an explosive temper. He behaved very oddly when I returned the flashlight. Still, I can't take this any further until I talk to Mike.

While learning where Mike is and confronting him is my highest priority, I can't afford to ignore the assignment Marty Frumin gave me to learn all I can about Atkins and Conway. An idea had crossed my mind when I saw Dunstan Beeman's name on the list of Atkins and Conway's classmates. I could go and talk to Beeman. I'd had the thought, but no serious intention of acting on it. Now, with my mounting panic, it doesn't seem to be such a wild idea. The question is, will he talk to me?

I call the *Chicago Tribune*, go through the automated options until I get Beeman's voice mail and leave my cell phone number saying I'm a surgery resident at Northwestern and that I want to talk to him about a subject of vital importance to him and possibly a story for the paper. An hour passes without a return call.

Just as I'm about to call Springer's office again I get a call from Mrs. Tobin. She tells me that Doctor Springer called in to say he'd been held up at a meeting and wouldn't be back in his office today. But when she told him I had called wanting to know how to get in touch with Mike

Moran, he told her where on his desk he had placed a note with Mike's telephone number. She reads it to me, a number with a 410 area code. I thank her and immediately dial the number. The phone rings half-a-dozen times before a guy answers.

"Harbor Lodge." The voice oozes irritation.

"Is Doctor Michael Moran there, please?"

Silence for fifteen seconds. I think I've been disconnected and then, "No answer," he says grudgingly.

"No answer? Is this a hotel?"

"It ain't no hunting lodge."

His reply takes me aback so that I don't think to ask where the place is before he hangs up. I press the redial and let the phone ring until it's clear that he doesn't intend to answer again. I'll call later. Maybe I'll get someone else.

I track down Jeff at four o'clock and ask him to cover for me for an hour. I now know this favor will go down in his little notebook, but what the hell: borrow now, pay later.

The offices of the *Trib* are only a few blocks away. I change out of my scrub suit and judge that in my own clothes I look like someone who could legitimately be delivering a package to Dunstan Beeman. I need a package, so I go to the surgical supply room and spot a box containing six filters for the air purification unit used in the OR. The box is about two foot square and six inches thick. It could be a reel of film, if you don't look too closely. "Filters" is printed on one side, but I can hold that side next to my body. My plan could work . . . or I could be on my way to making a complete ass of myself.

As I enter the building, I'm called over to the *Tribune*'s security desk and asked my business.

"Delivery for Dunstan Beeman," I say in my best near the end of the day, one damned last delivery to make before I can meet my friends at the bar tone of voice.

"Is he expecting you?"

"Friend, no one in this world is expecting me and that's just fine. He *is* expecting this film, however."

"Do you know the room number?"

"Sure."

"What did you say your name was?"

"Transamerica Carriers."

He starts writing this down and I add, "I'm Jason, the CEO."

He laughs and motions for me to pass.

Great. I go to the elevator and step into an up car. Now to find out where I can find good ol' Dunstan, whose taste in films sucks, by the way.

A young woman gets on at the first stop. I take a paper from my pocket, which happens to be the receipt for flowers I sent my mother last Mothers' Day and study it with a puzzled look.

"Dunstan Beeman. My route slip doesn't have his office number, do you happen to know it?"

It's incredible what a box under one's arm can do for one's credibility.

"Beeman? I don't know the office number, but he's on the tenth floor—to your right about three or four doors when you get off the elevator—name's on the door."

"Thanks." I put the paper back in my pocket and go back to looking at the elevator wall.

She's right, fourth door to the right. The door is open and I see a woman, most likely Beeman's secretary, making those quick, "get everything in place", movements heralding departure. I move on down the hall before she sees me and asks my business. I stop at a fountain and drink a lot of water, until I see her leave, closing the door behind her. She doesn't try the knob. Either she's left the door unlocked, or else it locks automatically as it's closed. I walk back down the hall and try the knob. It opens and I step inside and close it. The way I figure it, Dunstan Beeman is in the inner office. If he weren't, wouldn't the secretary have locked the door?

I take a couple of deep breaths and knock.

"Come in,", penetrates the door.

I open the door and there he is, older and fatter than his picture in the *Tribune*. He sees the package I'm carrying and he dismisses any thoughts about me other than "he who bears the package."

"What is it?" he asks casually.

A critical moment. There was no defensive challenge. I feel positive vibes.

"Oh this?" I say off hand. "These are filters for an operating room air purifier. I'm a surgery resident at Northwestern, David Brahms."

He tilts his head a bit, curious. He is seeing me for the first time as a person and not just as an animated delivery vehicle.

"I want to talk to you . . . I need to talk to you about two of your old classmates at St. Paul's School, Mason Atkins and Dickson Conway."

That gets his attention.

"Really? How do you know they were my classmates?"

"I happened to be looking at the alumni website. I think you can help me, if you will."

He motions toward a chair. "Have a seat . . . ah, Dr. Brahms."

I made it over the first hurdle; I'm in the door. I relax a bit and take in the room. It has good windows facing east with a view of Lake Michigan. My eye is drawn to a poster for *Citizen Kane*, probably an original. There is a cluster of four or five photographs on the wall behind Beeman. My gaze sweeps over them on its way back to the man sitting opposite me, and as it does, I recognize the familiar, smiling face of Roger Ebert in one of the pictures. He and Beeman are wearing Hawaiian shirts and leis.

"I appreciate your talking with me, Mr. Beeman. I'm in a difficult situation and I need some information."

He says nothing and I wonder if I should suggest the possibility that there could be some gain for him, a story perhaps. I go ahead.

"I left a message on your voice mail saying that the problem for which I need help could become a story for the Tribune."

"My secretary culls my voice mail. There is no way I can deal with all the messages I get."

Either it's true that he never got my message or this is his easy way of explaining the ones he's chosen to ignore.

Whatever. I plunge ahead. "As I'm sure you know, both of them—Atkins and Conway—died violent deaths recently. Murdered, the police think. It so happens that I was not well treated by either of them and their deaths did me a lot of good. The police seem to have no other suspect or suspects and I'm a person with a very good motive. I didn't kill them, by the way."

I can see that his interest is pretty high.

"Last night a guy who had been stalking a woman I care a lot about was killed. I mean, really stalking in the psychotic sense. It was probably a drug-related hit, but the police lieutenant in charge of investigating Atkin's and Conway's deaths sees this guy's murder as one more example of the removal of someone who was standing in my way. This detective has let me know that he's about to charge me with these murders."

I pause to evaluate his reaction and I'm still doing all right.

"The shooting of this guy last night can't have any relationship to the deaths of Atkins and Conway, nor is there any way that I can investigate his death on my own, but if the murders of my two former chiefs are related, I might be able to discover some link to the person who killed them before it's too late and I'm arrested."

I pause, again, take a deep breath and complete the proposition. "I know that both of them, Atkins and Conway, were expelled from St. Paul's School while you were there. I'm hoping you can tell me why."

Beeman is staring at me as if mesmerized. He shakes himself back into the present.

"Wow." He smiles and moves his head in a "can you beat that?" way. "Wow, that's quite a story. How was it that they didn't 'treat you well'? I think that's the way you put it."

"Nothing earth-shaking. Atkins loaned me out to a crappy hospital, Northpark General, for several months. When he died the man who took over temporarily brought me back into the normal training program. But then Conway took over the chairmanship and had me doing useless clerical work instead of the clinical training rotation I should have been on. His death got me out of that dead-end."

"You didn't care much for either of them, that about it?"

"If you'd write that in capitals, I'll sign it."

"I didn't kill them either," he says in mock seriousness. "I'm saying that, because I, too, thought they were both first-class assholes."

"Really?" I'm surprised. Surprised by his opinion and by the fact that he'd state it.

"Yeah, and when I read about their deaths, I was pleased like one is always pleased when a bully gets what's coming to him. Not that they had violent death coming to them, but if that's what the good Lord meted out, who am I to object.

"You have set yourself the task of finding out who may have wanted to kill them. I don't know who that would be. I'm sure a lot of people were pleased just as I was, but that's a long way from murder. I'm confused about one thing, I thought Atkins was accidentally killed by a hit-and-run driver."

"The police have reason to think it wasn't accidental."

"I see. Well, back to your original question—why were they expelled? That was a case of someone being angry enough with them to blow the whistle to the headmaster about a scheme of theirs. They were stealing exams from the school printing department prior to exam times and selling copies to other students. None of the students knew that Atkins and Conway were the ones stealing the exams. They paid a kid who worked for Building Maintenance to handle the actual sale. I learned about the details years later. My uncle was on the school's Board of Governors and he spilled the beans one night over a snifter of brandy. The better students, as you can imagine, were angry, because the poorer students were buying the exams and getting an advantage. The whole operation could have had a quick death if one of the good students had gone to the Headmaster, but one of those strange social situations developed wherein it would have been regarded bad form to blow the whistle. The better students' answer was to also buy the exams in order to level out the playing field. For a while, you had to be really stupid to fail any class. The school administration talked of it as a 'golden age of academics' at St. Paul's." Beeman laughs. "My uncle told me there was much embarrassment when they learned the truth. They managed to hush it up pretty well, but it did leak out that it had been a student who had squealed, only no one knew who it was. My uncle drew the line there and wouldn't tell me either—even after I'd refilled his brandy glass.

"And they were both expelled?" I ask.

"Indeed. We were very surprised. From the students' and alumni's priorities, everyone couldn't understand how the Headmaster would dare. Hockey was king at St. Paul's, and Atkins and Conway were the stars of the team. They were called 'The Mason and Dickson Line.' But viewing it now, I'd say the punishment was logical. The school's priority was its reputation as a place that dished out excellent teaching and built fine moral character—just look at me," he says smiling, "So they were obliged to expel those two."

I remind myself of my purpose here and ask, "There must have been speculation about who might have turned them in: can you remember any names?"

"Isn't that contradictory? I mean, being turned in to the school authorities might give Atkins and Conway a motive to get even, but how would having blown the whistle give that person a motive for murder?"

"Beats me. This news about whistle-blowing is new to me and I haven't had time to think about it."

We stare at each other for a moment. I wonder about Beeman's seeming interest and willing involvement in the topic. I can't think of a reason why I shouldn't trust it, so I continue as if this really was a common problem we were discussing.

"It's slim, and maybe this incident from so long ago was forgotten by all concerned. Being expelled, however, must have made a huge problem for both of them at the time. From the little I've learned about their family backgrounds, it suggests they would have gone on to one of the big Ivy League schools had it not been for this very black mark that was now on their records. Would you agree?"

"Without a doubt." He nods emphatically.

"Could it have been that they did do something to get even with the person who blew the whistle, and murder was this person's response?"

"In other words, the name you want is that of a person in my class whom I think capable of murder in order to even the score?"

The words might suggest that Beeman is offended, but his blue eyes are twinkling. He is enjoying the game.

"Yes."

He shakes his head. "Sorry."

Beeman glances at his watch. "I've got to get over to the Lake Street screening room. I'm not putting you off, Brahms—are you by any chance related?"

"Yes, distantly."

"Really? Well, as I was saying, I'm interested in the problem but I haven't anything worthwhile to contribute. Maybe something will occur to me while I'm watching one of the films I have to see this evening. I do some of my most creative thinking while watching bad movies."

He is on his feet and holding out his hand while moving both of us toward the door.

"How do I get hold of you?" he asks.

"I'm in the book, David Brahms, M. D.

22

The good reception I'd just had pushes another earlier idea forward in my mind. It was one that I'd put aside, because I thought it was almost certain she wouldn't agree to see me. The person most likely to know about Atkins and Conway's relationship is Atkins's sister—Conway's wife, Lenore. I'd had little hope that Dunstan Beeman would do otherwise than order me out of his office the moment I opened his door, but it turned out he wasn't that kind of person. Maybe Lenore Conway isn't either. First I need her address and phone number, so after saying goodbye to Beeman on the sidewalk in front of the Tribune Building, I do a pivot and go right back inside to ask the guard, who had quizzed me earlier, if he has a telephone book.

"I saw you walk out with Beeman," he says when I walk up. "He must not have wanted your film." He gestures toward my box of filters.

"As soon as I look up a number in the phone book, I gotta take the film over to Lake Street to the screening room for him."

He shakes his head in sympathy. "Big shot can't carry it himself, eh." He laughs, "An' you bein' a CEO, an' all."

He pulls the white pages book from under the counter and drops it on top. I pull it over to me and open it. I will Dickson Conway to be listed, but once again reality wins over wishing. It's unlisted.

I walk a few paces away and take out my cell phone and call the surgery office where the department secretary answers.

"Hi Cynthia, this is David Brahms. I'm lucky I caught you before you left for the day. I just realized I have a book of Dr. Conway's that I should return to Mrs. Conway. Would you look up the phone number and street address for me? Sure, I'll wait."

The guard becomes involved in some business with another *Trib* employee. I help myself to notepaper lying on his desk and write down the information the secretary gives me.

I wave a thanks and a goodbye to the guard, and he interrupts his conversation to return it.

Standing on the busy sidewalk outside the Tribune Building, I try to place the street that I wrote down, 205 W. Bellevue. I know I've seen the street sign, but I can't remember where. The two hundred block means it's close to the lake. I wait for the light to change at the Michigan Avenue and Illinois intersection so I can cross. When it does, the first car in the line is a taxi. I walk up to his window.

"205 East Bellevue. Can you tell me where that is?"

"Hop in, I'll take you there."

"I don't want to go there right now," I say.

"Four blocks south of Division, off Rush," he says and turns to his radio to answer a dispatcher.

"Thanks, friend," I throw out even though he has already shifted his attention.

I hurry back to the sidewalk before the light changes. I retrace my steps to the Intercontinental Hotel, which has a quiet lobby where I can sit and collect myself before calling Conway's widow.

The hotel was created by the transformation of Chicago's former Masonic Temple, and the grandiose fantasy that was the Masonic movement in its heyday is evident in the remnants of a décor that still hints at oriental mysteries known only to the anointed few. It's difficult for me, an unequivocal rationalist, to imagine how grown men could have taken so seriously the childish pleasure of belonging to a secret club, replete with magical symbols, solemn oaths and special handshakes known only to the initiated and protected from revelation by the certain knowledge of excommunication.

I remind myself that in by-gone days the medical "fraternity" bore a close resemblance to the Masons and that our political parties and corporate "families" today demand the same blind loyalty, regarding outsiders to be undeserving of honesty. Only the secret handshake has been dispensed with.

The lobby is indeed quiet and the deep armchairs soothing. I begin to consider what sort of woman Mrs. Conway might be. Is she deeply grieving? Will a lofty patrician confront me, who considers me beneath her notice and my problem not worthy of her concern? Or might I find a surprise awaiting me as I had with Dunstan Beeman? What quality can I put in my voice that might cause her to listen a moment longer than it takes to say, "Thank you, but I gave at the office." I decide that I can't know any of these answers ahead of time, but at least taking the time to consider the possibilities may prepare me to react as needed.

I get out my cell phone and make the call.

"Hello." A young girl, a teenager, answers.

"Hi, I'd like to speak to Mrs. Conway. My name is Dr. David Brahms."

"Just a minute."

A guy in a business suit comes into the lounge, sits opposite me and takes out his phone and punches a memory button. He greets the person who answers with a booming voice as if he were making a transatlantic call in the forties. His voice registers disappointment. The person he wants isn't there. Thank God!

"Yes, this is Mrs. Conway."

I'm so immersed in annoyance with my neighbor that

I'm surprised when she speaks and I don't start off on the right foot. I stumble into an explanation of being a resident at Northwestern Hospital. She interrupts and asks how she can help me.

I don't want to say that I'm suspected of killing her husband. At the same time I don't want to present a problem that will prompt her to refer me back to university authorities.

"I may know something about the person who killed both Dr. Conway and Dr. Atkins—I worked in your husband's lab. I need to talk to you before I can go to the police." Wow, where did that come from?

"What do you need to talk to me about?"

"It's something that, when you hear what it is, I'm sure you'll agree shouldn't be talked about over the phone."

I say that because I've heard that phrase said many times before. But just what is it that shouldn't be talked about over the phone? Is she wondering the same thing?

"Well all right, if you can come here now. My granddaughter and I have plans for later."

"Yes I can."

"Do you know my address?"

I read from the note I hold and she confirms it. The location, as described by the taxi driver, is very near to the Intercontinental. I can walk there in fifteen minutes but I judge that this would seem too rushed. I tell her that I'll be there in half an hour and after I hang up I go straight to the bar in the small lounge and order a neat Grey Goose, the breathless drink..

As soon as I get to Bellevue, I remember the area. I had walked along these attractive streets a couple of years back and thought that if I were ever very, very rich I would want one of these elegant old homes. What a perfect place: quiet, tree-lined and easy walking distance to the action of the Magnificent Mile. The Conway home is smaller than the mansions on either side, but what it lacks in size it more than makes up in style. Maybe one of the nineteenth century giants of Chicago architecture designed it—Louis Sullivan, Wellborn Root?

I press the doorbell and soon I see a pert face check me out through a narrow window beside the door.

The door swings open. She is about five-eight, wearing a pair of those hip-huggers that are held up by about one centimeter of purchase on her butt, above this, bare abdomen to her rib cage. Her body says sixteen, but her hesitant awareness of her sexuality says thirteen—that is, thirteen in an isolated and sheltered girls' school.

"I'm Doctor Brahms. I have an . . . "

"Yeah, C'mon in."

I follow her through a large foyer and along a hallway covered with framed etchings. We come out into an octagonal room with large windows overlooking a back garden. Above each of these windows is a semi-circular pane of stained glass. My mother dragged me into enough antique shops when I was a kid for me to recognize Louis Comfort Tiffany. Here they all are, the lamps I'd seen in those stores, done here as windows. I can still name them: geranium, iris, peony, poppy and tulip. The effect is stunning. I doubt if there is a room in all of Chicago that can compare with this one.

"They are beautiful aren't they?" I swing around in the direction of the voice. She has just entered from another room. She's wearing a gray dress that complements her slightly lighter gray hair. She is smiling because she is enjoying my reaction to the windows. It is a very friendly, outgoing smile. I think I'm in luck.

"They are . . . they're magical," I answer.

She is a handsome woman. Not surprising, since her brother was a very handsome man. There is none of his self-adoration in her attitude however. In spite of the smile, I detect sadness. Is it grief or something else?

"We bought the house, my husband and I, from the

estate of the lady for whom the house and the windows were made. She was one hundred and five when she died. I believe she hung on that long, because she couldn't think of leaving this room."

I laugh out loud. It's a great notion.

"Please sit down, Doctor Brahms."

My peripheral vision catches movement, and I turn to glimpse the granddaughter leaving the room.

When I look back at Mrs. Conway, she is smiling.

"These clothing fads, where will it end?"

I return the smile, but don't say what I'm thinking—that I'm eager to find out.

"Now what is this about knowing who killed my husband?"

"First, I must tell you that I have a personal motive in coming here. Incredible as it is to me, the police lieutenant in charge of the investigation, Lieutenant Gemiano, believes that I had strong enough motives to be the person to kill both your brother and your husband."

Saying this has clearly shocked her. Her gray eyes begin taking a new appraisal of this stranger whom she has admitted to her home.

"I didn't do it, of course," I hurry to say and her expression says I had better explain myself, so I relate the whole story of my experience with Drs. Atkins and Conway and of the circumstantial facts that would seem to give me opportunity to be the killer. When I finish she looks perplexed.

"Are you sure that this policeman—he interviewed me by the way—seriously suspects you? I mean, you have described a frustrating experience, but it hardly adds up to a motive for murder."

I nod agreement. "I believe Lieutenant Gemiano would have said so too before the next murder."

"Next murder?"

She has stepped back into cautiousness, but is still

listening, so I hurry on into the history of my relationship with Fahra and the events leading up to my finding Ahmad's body. Throughout my telling her this story, I'm aware that I have a reason to be here with her, and that I need to change the direction from one of confession to one of inquiry.

"The murder of this man has nothing to do with the deaths of your brother and husband. It is only linked in Lieutenant Gemiano's mind because of my involvement. If in fact Dr. Atkins *was* murdered, then I'm inclined to think Gemiano is right in thinking the same person is responsible for your husband's death. The question is, who had a motive—and an opportunity."

"Besides yourself."

She's not easily deterred. "Yes, besides me."

"I'm confused. On the phone you told me that you knew something about the person who killed Dickson and Mason. Did you only say that to get me to agree to see you?"

"No, it wasn't a lie. But I don't know just how relevant the information I have is. I figured this person had a very strong grudge. To have a grudge against both men suggests that it was formed at a time in their lives when they and the murderer were in close contact."

I look to her for affirmation of the logic of my reasoning.

"Yes, I see your point."

"I know of one incident from an earlier time, which I'll tell you about. I came here hoping that you might know more about that incident, or of other times that your brother and husband were associated in a setting where they could have made an enemy."

I can read an alert anticipation in her face, as if she's wondering how much I know of a family secret. Past her silence, I hear rock music coming from a distant part of the house.

I break the silence. "St. Paul's School. Your brother and husband were expelled for stealing and selling copies of school examinations. Someone squealed on them. It's possible that this person was retaliating for some injury done him. This is the incident I know about."

My mentioning the expulsion affects her enough to cause her to stand and walk slowly to one of the windows overlooking the garden. She turns back to me.

"That was a long time ago," she says.

"I know. But perhaps you remember something more about it."

"Something just occurred to me. I'm a little slow. I understand, now, your motive in coming here. It's not that you have information about my husband's killer that you came, but that you want to find some other person with a possible motive in order to undermine Lieutenant Gemiano's suspicion of you." She puts the flat of her hand to her cheek as an expression of her embarrassment at being obtuse.

"Exactly," I say. "Wouldn't you?"

She thinks about it. "Yes, of course I would, but I didn't see this at first." She puts that aside and returns to my question about St. Paul's. "It's so old . . . I mean . . . I mean I have sympathy for the situation you're in, but this direction is . . . pathetic. You're wasting your time. Can't you see that this thing at St. Paul's is too old to provoke someone to commit murder today?"

"Perhaps you know of something that's stronger."

She returns to her chair, sits and looks at me in a way an adult might do when suggesting an obvious solution to a child with a problem.

"Your plan would work better if you could identify someone with a better motive than yours for killing this Ahmad. Young surgical residents don't usually kill rivals."

"Not usually. But I know nothing about the world he moved in and I'm such an outsider that no one in his world will talk to me any more than they would talk to the police. It will be the old story of a minority group closing ranks. No one heard anything and no one saw anything."

Stymied, she doesn't offer a rebuttal, so I guide the focus back to my former chiefs. "I must learn who had a motive to kill your brother and husband."

I've always been fascinated by the phenomenon of critical moments, wherein a determined point of view changes, almost unnoticed, to a different, and frequently opposite position. These unexpected changes create sudden alterations in the course of history, and I've always thought the consequences of these altered points of view are never fully examined. Such a process of revision occurs this moment in Lenore Conway. I can recognize it taking place in her body. Her shoulders face me more squarely, she leans forward a bit and her expression says that I am to become a confidante.

"I believe that both Dickson and my brother made many enemies over the years. They knew it and enjoyed the fact. My husband's favorite saying was that one had to break eggs to make an omelet. You don't have a very high opinion of them, suffering as you did from their high-handedness, but they were both very brilliant men. Fortune endowed them with superior intellects, energy and forceful personalities." She sighs. "And they knew it and regarded us average beings with arrogance.

"What I'm saying is that coming to know about all the people they have offended is as difficult a task as getting inside this Ahmad's group."

I had not expected anything like this to happen when I rang the doorbell. She is saying that looking for someone with a motive was going to be hard, because there are so many to sort through, but I believe her attitude has shifted from her earlier desire to direct my attention elsewhere, to a willingness to help me look at her own family.

"There may have been many with resentments," I say,

"Such as my own—but there must have been some person who harbored more than resentment. I think it's likely that either your husband or your brother spoke of them in a different way, fumed about them, or laughed sadistically at them. Can you remember someone who stood out?"

She concentrates inwardly, scanning her memory. She shakes her head. "You have to understand that my husband didn't discuss everything he was doing with me. Neither did Mason. Early on an unspoken understanding was arrived at wherein we knew the areas in each of our lives that were off-limits. It happens I believe in every relationship. If a relationship is to be maintained this kind of unconscious compromise occurs. Both of them knew that I did not approve of ruthless pursuit of self-advancement. Consequently, I was not privy to the details of whom they stepped on to get to their goals. At the same time I had my own projects that I didn't talk about, nor was I asked about."

"You knew your husband for a long time," I state, not knowing what prompted the remark.

"Yes, my whole life. Why do you say that?"

"I don't know."

"Perhaps the question arises out of curiosity about how we came to marry, since we had basically different attitudes."

I start to protest that I am not trying to pry, but she waves this aside.

"No, it's true, we were opposites. You see he was my brother's best friend since they were in kindergarten together. My brother is—was—seven years older than I. He was my glorious older brother and he had a handsome, glorious friend. I fell in love with Dickson the moment it first entered a young girl's mind to fall in love. Of course, he barely knew I existed, but in my fantasies I knew he would one day discover me and I would be waiting. He finally did when I was eighteen. I never for a moment considered that our views were at opposite poles. I think I considered any differences we had—where my brother was concerned, also—to be a manifestation of the differences in our ages and our sex."

"And by the time you married, it would have been an established behavior to keep things from the little sister," I add.

"Yes, and especially those things you knew would anger her."

Great. Together we have agreed upon the rationale for her knowing nothing that can help me. My desperation causes me to press one more time.

"I understand clearly what you're saying, but still in a moment of fury or fear, either of them might have let go with an expletive towards someone with whom they'd had a particularly nasty clash."

I see that she is considering my suggestion once again, and before she can give a negative reply—the reply that closes the door of memory—I add the specific instance.

"Being expelled from St. Paul's must have created an explosion in your family."

"That it did. Nothing like it had ever happened in our family, or so my father kept saying. And then the fireworks were re-ignited with each Ivy League rejection."

"You didn't hear your brother name some person that he blamed for causing the trouble. After all, someone did go to the Headmaster and report what he and your husband had been up to."

"Heavens, I was only ten years old."

"Ten-year-olds have very good memories."

She visibly emerges from participation with me. I watch her re-establish a position of reserve. She becomes a dignified elder.

"I'm sorry, I know what you want to find—another suspect beside yourself—and I do think you are innocent. I know you realize that I would never be talking to you, now, if I had not intuitively decided that you were not a killer. But I can't supply you with the name you want." She laughs lightly. "Years ago when it was very fashionable, I was in psychoanalysis. It was surprising the kind of things one remembers in free-association. You, however, are in need of a more rapid answer."

"Yes, free-association can't be rushed. I know, I've been in analysis for almost a year."

"Is that so. May I ask with whom? Maybe it's with my old analyst."

"Mordecai Steiner."

She shakes her head. "No. My analyst is probably retired by now . . . or dead."

It is apparent that our meeting is over. I'm glad I came even if I've gained nothing that will help me with Gemiano. I feel like I've made a friend. She walks with me back to the front door. In the foyer the rock music flows down the stairwell with greater force. She glances up the stairs and then gives me a smile that says she is bonded to a loved but alien being.

I'm on the steps leading off the front stoop when she calls after me and asks where she should call if she happens to remember anything.

"I'm in the book, David Brahms, M.D.

23

I begin walking back toward the hospital not knowing what I'm going to do next. Just having mentioned Dr. Steiner, I think of him now. It was comfortable to be able to go into his office and spill my guts and have him listen to me. If psychoanalysis had no other efficacy, it at least afforded you the illusion that you weren't alone. You believe the person who is listening to you is a valid judge of human worth and the fact that he or she is continuing to see you is proof that you are basically a good guy. A temporarily screwed-up guy, but at the core OK, and given time you'd get your act together. Fahra's loving me is validating, but there's a difference. Where she's concerned, I feel that I have to be more than just a good guy. I can't expect, nor do I want, her to tolerate me as someone who is flawed, but potentially repairable.

I'm walking down Rush Street, when I decide to call Jeff and tell him I'm on the way back to the hospital. He'd agreed to cover for me so I could make my attempt to see Dunstan Beeman. I'd stretched that time to pay the call on Lenore Conway.

I text him. "Jff, cmng 10 mn Dv."

I get a message back. "Stop! I call."

I do what he commands; I stop walking and wait. About five minutes pass. He must be moving to a location where he can talk freely. My phone rings and I switch it on.

"What's up?" I ask.

"I was just taking my phone out to call you when you called. The cops were just here to arrest you and haul your butt off the ward. I told them that you were feeling sick and had gone home. You're not there are you?" he asks anxiously.

"No, I'm on Rush. How do you know they intended to arrest me?"

"Let's see, the conversation went like this. 'Where's David Brahms?' 'Why?' 'Because, we're here to arrest him.' 'Oh. He went home sick.' 'Sick?' 'Sick.'"

"And then they left?"

"Yeah, they just left the ward, but one of them is probably downstairs in case you come back."

"Damn, I'm on call."

"I'll do your shift. Just don't come near this place."

"Where can I go? I can't go to Fahra's. They know about us and they're sure to know her address by now. How about your place?"

"Sure, only the apartment is locked and the key is in my pocket."

"You could meet me someplace—the Starbuck's near the hospital."

"I don't think so. I was more than a little surly when they came up here. If I were one of them and I saw me leave the building, I'd follow."

I think of his asking another resident to bring the key to me at Starbuck's, but it occurs to me that I'd be dragging others into an obstruction of justice.

"OK, I have an idea, but I won't tell you so you can go on truthfully saying you don't know."

"Thanks, Brahms. Maintaining a spotless conscience is my goal in life."

"Which life is that?" I say in our habitual joking manner, but I don't feel so jocular.

I hang up and dial Marty Frumin's office number.

"Martin Frumin," he answers.

"Marty, this is . . . "

"I know. I'll probably stop off someplace and then go

on home." He hangs up.

"Uh . . . OK," I say to a dead phone.

What was that all about? Slowly, the meaning comes together. He cut me off as if he didn't want to give me a chance to say my name. That could only mean that if his line is tapped there would be no proof that he knew he was talking to me. That's weird. That means Marty suspects a wiretap, and why would Gemiano do that? He can't think I'm hiding; it's too early for that. I remember what Marty said at the end, "Stop off someplace and then go on home." Can he be saying that he's going to John's Place and wants to meet me there? I guess I'll go and find out.

Next, I call Fahra's office—gone for the day. I call her apartment and get the machine. I don't know what message to leave. Before I hear the beep that ends the recording, I hurry and say, "I'm OK. I'll get in touch." I call Alifa's gallery—closed. I call her apartment and score.

After the opening greetings, she tells me that she's heard about my experience last night and sympathizes.

"The situation has gotten worse," I say. "I guess I'm officially a fugitive. There is a warrant out for my arrest for murder, and the cops are looking for me."

"Where are you?"

"It's better that you don't know. The less you know the less trouble you're likely to get into."

"I'm not afraid of that."

"Still. What I'd like you to do for me is to contact Fahra in case she has a message for me. I don't think she should talk to me on the phone. My lawyer thinks it's possible that the police have tapped his phone, so why not Fahra's. Keep that in mind when you talk to her. She's not at home right now. I'll call you again later tonight."

"OK, I'll do what I can," she says.

"Thanks, friend."

"*De nada*, friend."

I dig into my pocket for the paper on which I wrote the

number for the Harbor Lodge. I dial it again and the same guy answers. I ask for Mike. His response is the same, "No answer."

"Where is your hotel located?"

He has hung up.

It has started to rain. I begin walking toward the Chicago Street El station.

Marty is in the rear booth that has the high back, the one that John calls "the snug." I call out a Guinness to John and slide into the booth.

"Gemiano came to my office," Marty says. "I know about the warrant."

"Am I right in thinking that you believe they might have a tap on your phone? So soon?"

"Yes, probably too soon, but I'd rather be safe than sorry. Gemiano's attitude was very hostile. He spoke to me as if he were sure I was conspiring to help you avoid him. He reminded me—the prick—that as an attorney, I am an officer of the law."

This is all very unbelievable. How can I, David Brahms, who doesn't even have an overdue library book be sitting and hearing that I'm a fugitive wanted for murder?

"Gemiano had me brought to his office this morning," I say, "where he warned me not to leave the city. I thought that meant I'd have a few more days, at least, before they decided to issue a warrant."

"Yeah, It surprised me too. It's not going to be in your interest, you know, to remain a fugitive for long. We've probably got a few hours in which Gemiano has to allow for the fact that you might have done something like go to the movies."

"He knows that I'm scheduled to be on duty at the hospital tonight. A friend of mine explained that my absence was due to sickness."

"But since you're not home in bed, Gemiano will

conclude you're not sick and, therefore, hiding—that's not good. Have you found anything in your research into Atkins and Conway that helps us?"

"A little." I tell Marty of Beeman's story about the theft of exams and of my visit to Lenore Conway and how neither of them knew the whistle-blower's name.

John brings the Guinness over to the booth himself.

"Neither of you guys is here if anyone calls; am I right about that?"

Marty laughs. "Right on. How'd you know?"

"This is the first time you've gone back here to the snug when there were other seats available."

John leaves and Marty says, "My research is promising, but getting this kind of information takes time. I have uncovered a lawsuit by a doctor at the National Institute of Health, who claims that Dickson Conway took credit for research that he had done. The case hasn't come to trial."

"Interesting. It jibes with what his wife alluded to."

"Unfortunately, there is no motive for murder there, since I believe the guy would be waiting for his revenge and compensation in court."

"Yeah, I see what you mean," I agree in a leaden tone.

"But finding this case is promising. I'm willing to bet my membership in the John's Place Club that I'll find other legal actions against one or both of them."

We sit looking at our drinks. On both our minds is the fact that none of Marty's research will prevent me from occupying a jail cell before morning.

My cell phone buzzes. I'm surprised that it's Ralph Springer.

"Hi David, I heard that you went home sick. I was wondering if it's anything serious, or just a bug. In other words, will you be in tomorrow or will someone have to cover your patients?"

"Nothing serious, Dr. Springer. Only a petty virus, you know, the trots, but there's a good chance I won't be coming in tomorrow. Jeff Richards is taking my shift tonight."

As I'm saying this, I'm also thinking that something is wrong here. My chief resident, Mike Hawthorne, would be interested in my immediate state of health and ward coverage, not the Chief of Surgery.

"Don't worry, David, I'll take care of everything. Where are you, by the way? Sounds like a bar."

I laugh, "Not a bar, but the Starbuck's near the hospital."

"Get better. I'll see you later."

Very weird. "Just another minute, if you don't mind, Marty," I say and dial Jeff's cell.

He answers and I ask, "You on my ward?"

"Yeah, why?"

"Go to the window at the south end of the hall and see if there's any action around Starbuck's and call me back."

Marty is looking a question at me.

"I hope what I fear isn't true. I'll know in a few minutes."

It is two and a half minutes later that my phone buzzes.

"Yeah?"

"Buck's must have announced they're giving prizes to the first ten cops to enter their door. Three squad cars just pulled up and the guys dashed inside."

"Thanks. I'll explain later." I hang up.

I'm not having a good feeling. I look at Marty. "I just found out that one of my heroes has clay feet. That was Ralph Springer, the acting Chief. He turned me in to the cops—tried to anyway."

"He must have heard that there was a warrant for your arrest."

"Right. But, he didn't have to join in the posse. I guess I crossed that line and became persona non grata in his book."

This incident has served to reawaken the urgency for

action. I get back to our earlier topic.

"I have a piece of information that could be very important in identifying Conway's killer. Very important. It involves a friend, however, and I need to talk to him before I tell you the details. Do you understand?"

"Sort of, but I gotta remind you that you are no longer in a position to afford any fancy discretion. Do *you* understand?"

"I'll keep calling him. What are your plans for the evening?" I say with mock cheerfulness.

"Dinner, watch the news and then I'll stay up to be ready to drive downtown to protect a certain client's rights."

"Sounds like surgeons' hours."

Marty leaves. I could continue to sit here and make my calls to the Harbor Lodge, but I'd rather make them from home. It's entirely possible that Gemiano has my apartment staked out, but I reason I can risk walking that way to see if I can spot a police car. The cops to whom Gemiano may have given the assignment can't have any sure idea of what I look like. They will either be in my place, out in the hallway or in the lobby waiting for my return. Most likely they'll choose the comfort of their patrol car and a thermos of coffee.

It's raining a little harder when I leave the bar. The tail end of rush hour traffic is splashing along beside me on Fullerton. My apartment building is now a block ahead of me, across the street and on the corner. I scan both sides of Fullerton. No patrol car. If I were doing this stakeout, I'd park down the side street and across Fullerton from the building, where I'd have a view of the entrance, while I'd be in a place where the target of the stakeout wouldn't be likely to spot me before I saw him. Thinking this causes me to stop walking. I am near the corner and only a few paces from stepping into view of the side street to my right. I am like Caesar at the Rubicon. A few steps farther and a new phase of my life may be introduced, but unlike Caesar's, mine won't lead on to glory.

From where I stand, I can look across Fullerton and down the side street adjacent to my apartment. No patrol car there either. I can just feel the car's presence, parked in the side street around the corner of the building I'm standing in front of. I could chance a peep around the corner of the building but the streetlight is bright and my head would stand out like that of an actor peeking through the curtain at the "house." I back away from taking that chance.

I retrace my steps back along Fullerton and make a wide detouring loop of several blocks, so I can cross the side street behind any car that might be facing my building.

Successfully, I reach the alley behind my place and the back stairs. Fortunately I'm not such a high priority fugitive yet to warrant a stakeout at the back of the building. No one greets me when I open the back stairway door to my floor. I carefully try the doorknob to my apartment. It's still locked. I insert the key and open the door. The lights don't snap on revealing Gemiano sitting there waiting for me, smiling smugly like Sidney Greenstreet in *The Maltese Falcon*. I take a few deep breaths, then shake off the rain. Standing back a couple of yards from the window in the dark living room I can see across Fullerton and down the side street to the spot where I figured the patrol car would be parked. I don't spot an easily identifiable blue and white. And then, three cars back from the corner, I make out two guys in the front seat of a dark sedan. Of course, Gemiano would send detectives.

I go to the phone in the kitchen and notice that I have two messages. They will keep. First I have to try once more to get in touch with Moran. By the light coming in the kitchen window I read the number off the note I'd made earlier and dial it.

"Harbor Lodge."

"I want to talk . . . "

"Yeah, I know. He's here, just came in."

I hear the ring and then Mike answers.

I plunge right in. "Mike, this is David Brahms. I'm calling because the police think I killed Dickson Conway and unless you can convince me I shouldn't, I'm going to have to tell them that you were up there in my office that night and dropped your flashlight right under the fire extinguisher that was used to kill Conway."

It was a mouthful. He doesn't say anything for a few seconds. "You haven't told them about the penlight?" he says.

"No."

"You mean you were planning on letting me get away with it?"

So he did it! I don't know what to say.

He laughs. "I don't know whether I should be deeply grateful or whether I should be worried about your soul, old friend. You were prepared to let a murderer go unpunished when a word from you would have brought the villain to justice."

His tone is mocking. It changes. 'Hell David, I'm grateful. Really. Keeping that to yourself was a *very* friendly thing to do. But I'm afraid I can't return the favor and be guilty. What I have to tell you won't help you with your immediate problem of clearing yourself. *I didn't kill Conway.* I was up there as you say, but when I left him he was very much alive." He pauses and we are both silent. He says, "OK, you're thinking, 'Why should I believe that?' Am I right?"

"Something like that. What happened that night, Mike?"

"You know about that extra month causing me to lose the fellowship at Hopkins. Of course, I was furious and all I did at first was curse Conway to myself for almost a month. My girlfriend finally convinced me to go and talk to him. I was standing nearby when I heard him tell Ralph Springer that he was going to be working late that night in the lab. I figured this would be a good time and place to approach him. Nobody would be around and there would be no interruptions. I went up there at eight o'clock. As I approached his office I could hear him on the phone, so I waited in your space until he ended his conversation. That must be when I dropped the penlight. His door was open, so I went in and asked if I could talk to him. Surprisingly, he was friendly and open. I told him about the fellowship I'd lost and he said that he had no idea this had happened; no one had told him. He agreed with me that it was unfair. He told me he was going to call the Chief of Surgery at Hopkins, Ferguson, and explain what had happened. You can't imagine my surprise. I couldn't believe he was the same man. I thanked him and left, but I didn't trust him to make the call. That must have been about eight-thirty."

I've begun thinking that this is all very easy for him to say. After all, Conway isn't around to support or refute Mike's story.

"So you're saying he must have been killed after eight-thirty."

"It was later than that."

"Why do you say that?"

"Because it would have been after he made the call to Ferguson."

"How do you know he made a call to Ferguson?"

"Because Ferguson called me the next morning and said that Conway had phoned and explained what had happened and had asked him as a personal favor to reinstate me in their program. Ferguson then told me to come immediately to Baltimore."

"He did? And you went there?"

"That's right. I'm staying in this crummy hotel until I can find a decent apartment."

I had a thought. "That phone call that Conway made to

Ferguson; the police could check the time—they should be told."

"They were. I told the lieutenant in charge after I got the call from Ferguson. The call was made to Baltimore shortly after I left him, at the time I was sitting with my girlfriend and her sister in the hospital cafeteria."

"So Gemiano has known that all along."

"Yeah, that was the detective's name."

I'm washed out. I get myself together enough to say, "Thanks Mike. I'm glad you're in the clear, and it's good news about your fellowship, but you're right, you didn't return the favor."

"Yeah, sorry about that. "

I hang up, numb with disappointment and fear. I now have no further plan to prevent being arrested and indicted for murder. I look down at the number 2 shining at me from my answering machine. I tap the button.

"You have two messages," the very odd Donald Duck voice on my machine announces. "First message, sent today at 4:10 p.m." A voice I recognize immediately as Gemiano's says, "Doctor Brahms, I want you to call me as soon as you get this message." He tells me his phone number.

"Second message, sent today at 6:31 p.m." This time it is a woman. "Doctor Brahms, this is Lenore Conway. I can't see that this will be of any help to you, but as you were leaving my house you mentioned the name of your psychoanalyst, Mordecai Steiner. That name stirred a memory of that time when Mason was expelled from St. Paul's. Maybe I'm wrong, and I wouldn't want to cause any trouble through an error of memory, but I believe it was Mordecai Steiner, or some name very like it that I heard my brother say to my father. He was very angry and I remember our father saying that he was going to demand an explanation of why the Headmaster accepted this other boy's word instead of my brother's. Well, that's all and as I said before, I think this is very old and of no relevance to my husband's death, but I thought I should tell you anyway. Goodbye."

Mordecai Steiner? No way! I know what happened. My saying his name probably caused a faulty synapse in her aging brain. If I had said Zubin Mehta, that's the name she would have remembered. Still, the idea bothers me.

I can check the class roster. The computer is in the living room, but any light from the monitor might tell those who are watching that I'm at home. I get a blanket from the bedroom for a makeshift tent. I put it over the computer and crawl under it and fire up the engine. It takes an agonizingly long time to get logged in, but finally I get to the St. Paul's School site and type in "bowwow" and go to the class of '57. I scroll through the roster to the s's. I sit paralyzed, unable to breathe. There it is, Mordecai Steiner. Can this be my Mordecai Steiner? But again, how many Mordecai Steiners can there be? About as many as there are Dunstan Beemans. I recover and realize the answer to my question must be right here on this site. There must be a list of alumni addresses. I back up to the alumni home page and see the link and click. Then, I scroll to . . . "Mordecai Steiner, M.D. Home address, 150 S. Forest, Evanston, IL. Office address, 1405 122 S. Michigan Ave. Chicago, IL."

Son-of-a-bitch! Steiner went to school with Atkins and Conway and at no time did he give me a hint of having known them. Even though I have accepted his stance of keeping his personal life and views out of my sessions, I feel his silence about knowing them amounts to betrayal. Now a more important truth steps front and center; Steiner was the student who blew the whistle. He must have been. I feel emptied. Steiner should have told me he knew them. I really think he should have, but that's another issue, one having to do with my treatment. The larger disappointment at this moment is the loss of my hope that finding out who had snitched to the Headmaster at St. Paul's School would lead me to the name I could give to Gemiano. That hope is dead. Steiner is definitely not the murderer. Looking back, I clearly remember that Steiner didn't know Atkins had been hit by a van, and he seemed genuinely startled to learn Conway had been murdered.

I shut down the computer and stand looking out the window at the detectives in the dark sedan parked like two cats waiting for a mouse. I stir myself. Steiner. I have to talk to him. Maybe, just maybe, now that ours is no longer a therapy relationship, he will tell me something about those two guys. This is the least that he owes me. I have no other leads and only a few hours to work with at most. It is a quarter to eight. He's certain to still be up. A phone call is not a good idea. He can put me off too easily and I need ideas, and I need them now. I open a drawer beneath the phone and take out my city map. I can't see to read the fine print in the dark, so I shove the map in my back pocket, knowing I have to take the red line north to Evanston, anyway, and I can find Forest Street on the map once I'm in the train. I walk to the living room and then return to the kitchen—to get a banana. I'm starving.

24

I leave by the back door and walk a detour—west to Sheffield, north to Wrightwood, south to Fullerton—to the Fullerton El station: Rain continues a light, but steady drenching and the wind is blowing it under the sheltering roof of the station. Luckily, a train is approaching when I walk onto the platform. The car that stops in front of me is nearly empty. The few passengers look me over when I sit down, then look away. I bring out the map and unfold it and, as usual, the section I want is on the other side. I work at refolding it until I've isolated the Evanston area. I find Forest Street without trouble; it runs north and south only three blocks from the South Boulevard station, midway between the station and Lake Michigan.

Now that I've determined how I'm going to get to Steiner's house, what am I going to say to him when I ring the bell and he opens his door? Even though I'm no longer an active patient, going to his house and meeting him in a setting outside of his office carries the same sort of unnatural feeling that seeing one's teacher in a bathing suit at the beach had for us when we were children. The present circumstance is completely different too. He can't remain mute while I wrestle with the meaning that my questions have for me. I'm determined to accept only real answers to my questions.

I climb down the stairs of the station at South Boulevard with three other passengers. The heavy cloud has made the night very dark. The rain swallows the light from the streetlights, confining it to a scintillating cone around each

post. At the intersection with Forest, Steiner's street, I find
I had not read the map carefully. I thought Forest began at
South Blvd. and ran north with a large cemetery lying on
the south side of the boulevard. I see now there is a short
block of Forest running south into the cemetery. Since it's
the first block, number 150 must be there and I head in
that direction. The few houses are large, built in the style
of the early part of the twentieth century and with ample
grounds. I find 150. Two huge spruce trees stand on each
side of the walk, obscuring a good view of the house from
the sidewalk. It isn't until I have walked past the trees that
I see light shining through the leaded glass of the front
downstairs windows. So he's at home.

I stand at the door and feel for the doorbell. I find it,
but before I press it, I push the hood of my windbreaker
back off my head and give my hair a rough combing with
my hands. I take and exhale a deep breath and push the
doorbell. Soon, I hear someone approaching the door and
see an outline through the opaque glass next to the door.
The porch light goes on then the door opens.

"Doctor Brahms." There is mild surprise in his voice.

"I'm sorry to have to bother you, sir, but I have to ask
you some questions."

"Indeed? Please come in."

Steiner closes the door and turns, holding out his hand
to take my soaked windbreaker, which he hangs on a
hook.

"We had better go inside and sit down," he says.

Steiner leads the way into a living room that looks as if
it had been furnished many years ago in an eclectic
collection of styles and incongruous elements, such as the
bronze Victorian lamp base in the form of a nude wood
nymph. He is wearing loose-fitting camp pants and a khaki
T-shirt. Seen without his usual jacket and tie, he appears
thinner. He motions me toward an overstuffed leather
chair.

Steiner settles back in the mate to my chair and studies me for a long moment as if I'm a tourist who has strayed beyond the velvet rope that marks the boundary between the public area and the private wing of the castle.

"Yes, Doctor Brahms, what is it you want to see me about?"

The easy course is to slip into the familiar form of our relationship, he listening, I presenting my thoughts. I fight this.

"I came to ask you some questions and I'd like direct answers."

He regards me calmly, waiting.

"I learned today that you were in the same class as Mason Atkins and Dickson Conway. Mrs. Conway told me she believes you were the person who turned them in to the school's headmaster for stealing exams."

This statement causes no visible reaction.

"Is that true, Doctor Steiner?"

"Yes, it is. Your source is correct."

"But you let me believe that you didn't know them, just as you did with Ahmad."

"You never asked me, Doctor Brahms."

I'm feeling very frustrated—angry. "Come on, damn it, it's the usual thing to acknowledge—without being asked—if one knows the answer to a question that a friend is trying to understand. How could you let me talk about them as much as I did without contributing what you knew?"

He thinks about this for some moments, forming a reply. He looks weary, as if he were about to try once again to explain a concept to a slow student without any hope that this attempt will succeed where other attempts had failed.

"It is really no different than the situation with Ahmad, don't you see. How would your knowing of my past association with these men have helped you understand your reaction to them? Most assuredly it would have had the opposite effect. We could have begun sharing our complaints about them while any appreciation you may have been able to gain about your personal reaction to people in their position would have been lost to you. As you know, the analytic situation is not the same as that which exists between two friends."

A familiar theme. I can't be satisfied with this psychoanalytic nostrum. It may be true in general, but this was a different case.

"You knew that I was working to find out as much as I could about them. You let me waste my time."

He nods agreement. At least I had penetrated his professional stance enough for an agreement on a current reality.

He says with resignation, "Yes, but I thought . . . I hoped that you would quickly give up that line of inquiry, just as I had hoped that Mason Atkins would quickly tire of tormenting you. A misjudgment in both cases. At any rate, I agree that it can do no harm now to tell you about my dealings with them."

I see him relax his formal stance.

"It was my misfortune," he begins, "to be one of those children who, plagued by frequent illness and possessing less than normal strength and stamina, becomes the designated scapegoat for those boys who needed one. While the number of active bullies in the average childhood group is usually small, those who enjoy the sport as spectators are many. Added to this was the fact that I was Jewish and my parents chose to live in a predominantly gentile neighborhood and to send me to a prep school which, especially back when I attended, was the same. I'm explaining this to you to make my experience with Mason Atkins and Dickson Conway understandable.

"Almost from the first hours at St. Paul's School they marked me as the target for their sadism. I have long thought that this perverse impulse was the main element in their uncommonly strong bond." He smiles ruefully. "As you are aware, today there is a saying, 'Get a life.' It nicely exposes the fact that a person is externalizing their inner conflicts. The bully is forced to back off or risk being seen by all as the one with the problem. What a handy tool—too bad we didn't have it back then. I credit psychoanalysis with making such unconscious mechanisms as the externalizing of internal conflict so universally recognized that such a useful tool as 'Get a life' now exists."

Steiner smiles at himself. "I digress. The point was that for the first three years at St. Paul's their torment of me was endless. They had been engaged in stealing and selling exams since early in the junior year, but it was after a particularly nasty trick which they played on me that embarrassed me greatly in front of a young woman whom I cared for, that I decided to take action and report them to the school authorities."

Steiner interrupts his story to adjust the cushion in his chair. He visibly pulls his energy together to continue. "Since I did not trust the Headmaster, although a good man in many ways, to act against the strong wishes of the many for whom Atkins and Conway represented a hockey championship, I wrote letters containing irrefutable evidence to all of the members of the Board of Governors.

"As you know, small groups may conspire to hide information that works contrary to their vested interests—a President and his advisors for instance. But when information becomes too widely known to hide, the action that has to be taken by those in authority must follow the larger group's ethical guidelines. I knew, when I mailed those letters, that both of them would be expelled. I also anticipated the ethical course that would be forced upon the admissions directors of the Ivy League schools when they asked for and got the report from St. Paul's. I had repaid Atkins and Conroy in full." He unfolds and refolds his hands. "That's the story."

I'm enthralled with his story. I picture what it must have been like to be the misfit who is the brunt of a school hero's derision. I'm not satisfied, however. Steiner has termed his not telling all of this earlier a misjudgment. Is this the only apology he's offering? I'm angry, but at the same time I don't want to sully the parting sentiments I felt about him and my treatment. I shrug. I can see that I'm really only wanting to find a substitute injustice for the greater one I'm facing.

"It really doesn't matter any more anyway," I say dismally. "You see, Doctor, today the police issued an arrest warrant. Hell, I'm a fugitive at this very moment wanted for murder."

Steiner registers surprise and outrage. "You're not serious! They have gone that far?"

"I have trouble believing it, but it's true."

He stares at me long enough for me to become uncomfortable, but Steiner seems to have receded into himself. His eyes move, but they are not focused on anything in the room. A mental chessboard has his attention and I can feel him arriving at the next move.

Emerging from this introspection, he says, "I shouldn't worry about the problem with the police if I were you. I believe I can help you."

"No shit . . . I mean, really?"

"Yes, but it's best if I leave an explanation till later." He moves in his seat and begins slowly to rise, so I get up as well.

Steiner holds out his hand and I take it, like we've just made a deal.

"Good night, Doctor Brahms."

"Good night, sir." This seems to be it—meeting adjourned.

He leads me back to the front door where I take my windbreaker off a hook. I look to him for some further parting remark, but he is apparently not intending one. He opens the door and stands aside. It's raining harder.

Once I reach the shelter of the El station, I call Alifa. She answers immediately, as if she's waiting for my call.

"I talked to Fahra," she tells me. "She's at home now. I remembered the name of the woman who lives in the first floor flat, a friend of Fahra's. I asked her to go upstairs and get Fahra to come down to her phone."

"Smart. Alifa, I'd like to come to Fahra's apartment. The police may be watching the main entrance to her building, so I'd like her to unlock the back door and leave the lights off in the back stairwell. I'm calling from Evanston, so it will take at least forty-five minutes for me to get there."

"I'll see that she gets the message. Anything else I can do?" she asks.

"I just talked to my and Fahra's analyst, who said there was something he could do to help. Keep your fingers crossed that he wasn't just talking through his hat."

"They're crossed."

As I'd calculated, three quarters of later I get to Fahra's place. I hadn't planned it this way, but it happens that I'm wearing dark clothing, so it is only a dark shadow that sneaks from the alley, across the backyard and into the back door of her flat. She has heard me climb the stairs and opens the door to the dark kitchen before I can knock.

Without a word we are in each other's arms.

Still holding her tightly, I begin telling her what I'd learned. "I told you that Ralph Springer said that both Atkins and Conway were kicked out of St. Paul's School. I found out that it was for stealing exam papers and it was Doctor Steiner who turned them in."

"Doctor Steiner?" she gasps.

Sitting in the darkness of her dining room, I run through the details of all that had happened since I'd last been able to talk to her.

"And Doctor Steiner didn't give you any idea of how he was going to help you?" she asked when I had finished my story.

"I figure he must know someone with clout in the city government, someone who has the power to tell Gemiano to cool it unless he has absolute proof of my guilt. Maybe the Police Commissioner is a former patient."

Fahra laughs. "That's really not very far out."

"We'll have to wait and see. In the meantime I'd like to stay here tonight. The cops are sitting in front of my apartment and may decide to enter it at any time."

"Of course you'll stay here."

We go to bed and I fall asleep almost immediately in Fahra's arms, completely spent. I have a pleasant, protected feeling, Fahra's warm body and Papa Steiner solving my problems.

25

We awake to the sound of the doorbell ringing . . . and ringing. Fahra puts on a robe and goes down. Moments later I hear voices in the flat and Fahra comes to the bedroom door.

"It's the police, David—a detective. He says you're to go with him to Police Headquarters. The detective said he was to tell you that you are no longer under arrest; the warrant has been dropped." She's smiling. "I think it's the truth."

Fantastic! Steiner did it.

I dress quickly and Fahra makes a bagel with lox for me to take along.

"Call me at the office as soon as you can. I'll tell Celeste, who'll answer the phone, to be your call straight through to me." She kisses me.

My mood is high during the drive to Headquarters. Steiner came through for me. Like the saying goes, "It's not what you know, it's who you know."

Gemiano is certainly in a different mood than I've known before. He has coffee brought in immediately. Once I've got the coffee and we're settled in our chairs he becomes serious.

"I'm afraid I have bad news." His manner is that of the police officer appearing at the door to tell a family that one of their loved ones has been killed.

"Last night your analyst, Doctor Steiner, called here. I'd gone home, but when he said he had information about the murderer of Mason Atkins and Dickson Conway, the sergeant on duty got me on the line. Steiner said that if I met him at his house he could identify the killer. I had another detective pick me up and we went there immediately. When we arrived we found the front door ajar and when we didn't get an answer to ringing the bell, we went in. We found Steiner dead in his study. He had injected himself with something."

Gemiano looks at me for my reaction. What he sees is total shock. I'm speechless.

Gemiano watches me until he's sure I'm with him again. "Steiner left a suicide note. In it he confesses to killing the two doctors, Atkins and Conway. The note. . ."

"What?" explodes from me.

"Yeah, that's what the note says. He claims he killed the two doctors for past injuries done to him while he was a student."

"That's crazy," I burst out.

Gemiano is nodding. "Yes, yes, I'm sorry." When I've recovered a bit, he adds, "There was another sealed letter marked 'confidential' addressed to you and 'Miss Fahra Esma,'" He looks at me. "It tells the true story, the story of why he did what he did. In it he also confesses to killing Ahmad Basir—that's not in the suicide note."

"He said he killed Ahmad?" I say in total disbelief.

"Yeah, he said that, but before I get to that, there are some details in the suicide note I want to mention. Your doctor describes in detail how each person was killed. Of particular interest to me is his description of using the fire extinguisher to hit Nixon Conway and then wiping the fingerprints off the handle. This is something that had confused me and made me have some doubt about your guilt. It was obvious that the handle had been wiped, but I figured that knowing you had handled the extinguisher at an earlier time, as you'd told me, you would have taken care to wipe the entire extinguisher clean. I know I would have."

I've been listening, but it's like hearing someone tearing down one of my friends. I feel like saying, "Oh, shut up!" I control my feelings enough to ask, "Lieutenant, what about this *other* letter?"

"Yeah, OK. As I said, 'confidential' was written on the envelope. You understand, of course, that I had to read it. He must certainly have known that too. This alerted me, however, to it being a good idea to read the letter when I was alone. And I *am* the only one who has read it. The suicide note doesn't mention you, but this other letter makes it clear that the murders had everything to do with you."

"With me?" With me?

Gemiano goes on. "Yes, but it's like this, I believe the suicide note is sufficient for the DA's purpose, especially since it includes details that only we, the police, know about. The suicide note does not mention Ahmad Basir, only the letter written to you does. I've said nothing about this letter to anyone except you. The detective who was with me never saw it. He was busy calling the Evanston police. Now, I'm not planning to include this confidential letter as evidence. That means that the killing of Ahmad Basir will officially remain unexplained, and no doubt be consigned eventually to the stack of unsolved, probably drug-related murders. I've made a copy of this 'confidential' letter for myself, but I'm going to give the original to you. I'm giving it to you and saying nothing about it, because I was wrong to get the arrest warrant when I did. "

At this point Gemiano pauses to assess how much of what he's just said I've digested and how I'm taking it.

He goes on. "I think you can appreciate that I'm sticking my neck *way* out. Technically, I'll be withholding evidence in a capital crime. I'm not withholding evidence, however, which would lead to the arrest and conviction of Basir's murderer. That's why I'm willing to take the risk. What I'm saying is that it's important to me that you and your girlfriend say nothing about the letter or what's in it—ever." Gemiano looks at me and I nod. He takes an envelope out of his desk drawer and hands it to me. It is a sealed Chicago Police Department envelope.

I realize that a favor is being done for me, but not having read the letter, I'm unsure just what I'm agreeing to. I thank him, nevertheless.

Gemiano gets up. I can see that he wants to bring this interview to an end— wants to get me and Steiner's letter out of the building. He opens his office door and shuts it quickly when I leave.

Outside on the sidewalk, I dial Fahra's number and am put through easily.

"What happened?" she asks. "How did Dr. Steiner do it?"

"I have some horrible news. It's way too much to understand, but the way he got the warrant dropped was . . . " I freeze up. I can't say the words.

"Yes?"

"Fahra, Dr. Steiner wrote a note confessing that he killed both Atkins and Conway. . . and Ahmad."

I hear her gasp and then silence follows. I know the disbelief she must be experiencing.

"Did you understand what I said?" I ask.

"No. No I don't understand. Are you saying he made a false confession in order to satisfy the police, so they would leave you alone?"

"No, I'm saying he really did commit the murders." I then explain as much as Gemiano did to me.

"Gemiano says that everything is explained in a letter Steiner addressed to the two of us. Do you want me to read it now?"

She doesn't answer and I can hear her sobbing. I wait a while, then prompt, "Fahra?"

"No. No, I'm not ready for any more. You can read it if you want to, but I don't want to hear more right now."

"It's addressed to both of us. I don't want to read it without you."

"If you can wait, let's meet after work and we can read it together."

So we decide to meet at the Grand Street El stop after work and return to the site of our first date: The Anatolian Kebab.

Next I call Marty and his secretary answers.

"He's right here, Dr. Brahms, waiting for your call."

When Marty comes on the line, I tell him everything that happened last night and the experience I'd just had in Gemiano's office, leaving out any mention of the letter I have in my pocket. I need to read the letter before I make a decision there. Marty is shocked as one would expect. He has questions but he also recognizes my need to digest this by myself. He says we'd go over it all again later. He begins ending the conversation.

"Marty," I interrupt, "you realize that this fulfills your part of our professional services deal. Your medical consultant is now on call."

He laughs. "So long for now, Dr. Brahms."

When I get to the hospital, I find Jeff and retell the events of last evening and this morning. He listens carefully and inquires about many of the details. What comes through is the compassionate friend that lies beneath the cool and quipping façade. I promise to call him later as soon as Fahra and I read Steiner's letter. I have no doubt that I'll tell him everything that's in it. I trust him to honor Gemiano's —and now my—request for silence.

I'm aware throughout the day of the presence of the letter in my hip pocket. I want to take it out and read it, but I also want Fahra to be there.

Finally, I'm able to leave the hospital and jog to the El station. I meet Fahra and we kiss and hold each other for a long moment before boarding the Brown Line train to Western.

This huge event in our lives, the unexplained suicide of Dr. Steiner, is not known or cared about by the many people on the train or on the streets and I'm offended. How can they go about their lives so blithely, when this horrendous thing has happened? I then remind myself that daily, and unaware, totally occupied with my own concerns, I must pass so many others who are suffering some tragedy in their lives.

We are early and the restaurant is empty. Sonya is there, of course, with her enigmatic smile. We wait until she's taken our order. I take the envelope from my pocket, tear it open and lay the letter on the table. There appear to be half-a-dozen or more handwritten pages.

"Ready?"

I see that she's tense, but she says, "Yes."

I start to read, a squawk comes out and I clear my throat.

"Dear Ms. Esma and Dr. Brahms,

It is difficult for me to write this letter, since it will be an account of incredibly poor judgment and unspeakable viciousness on my part. Although I do not intend to excuse myself by it, there has been a factor that has affected my ability to think clearly. I scourge myself with the idea that I possessed sufficient self-awareness to have sought help, but didn't, especially early on. What's done is done, however, and now I leave the judgment of my actions to you and others and I will simply tell the story. It seems that I am experiencing an interval of rational thinking at this moment and, therefore, I hope the narrative will be rational also. At the same time, I'm cognizant that to a disturbed mind, the irrational can seem quite rational.

I ended my account, Dr. Brahms, when you were just here, by saying that I had repaid my two tormentors in full. They were removed from my life and our paths would never cross again in such a way that they could retaliate for what I had done to them. That was true until many years later when Mason Atkins learned that you were my patient.

Although I don't know this for certain, I think it likely that when you fainted in the ER, Atkins heard of it and inquired about the incident and was possibly reassured by your nurse friend, or her husband, that you had been referred to Dr. Mordecai Steiner for treatment.

Atkins's native sadism and wish to get even with me led him to send you to that despicable Northpark General Hospital to languish. He knew that I would figure out you were being punished because of me. I thought of terminating your treatment and sending you to a colleague, but I realized that would not necessarily affect what he would do where your training was concerned. He could continue to punish you knowing that I would know it was because of your association with me. I, also, considered calling him and confronting him, but this is what he wanted me to do, of course, and might have resulted in his need to find additional ways to hurt you if he thought I was not sufficiently suffering his retaliation. I elected, instead, to work with you to help you resolve the issues you had with your father and authority figures like Atkins. I thought he would eventually have to let you continue with the standard training or else have it become apparent that he was acting in an unusual and unacceptable way where you were concerned.

Now I have to relate another circumstance that was developing in my life. Not long after your treatment with me began, I discovered that I had acute myeloid leukemia. I began chemotherapy with a poor prognosis. The effects of the condition were insidious, manifested chiefly by easy fatigue, irritability and impatience, but the effect of chemotherapy was more taxing, causing intense nausea and despair. It happened that as I left a conference I was attending at Northwestern Hospital, I impulsively decided to go to Atkins's office to talk to him about the situation. He, as I had earlier thought he might, took the opportunity to mock me and bait me about the problems he would cause for you. He was very clever. He had made an intuitive psychological guess—which he gloated over— that I had made an emotional association between you and my son, who had died some years ago.

I left his office enraged. It was several days later, after attending another long and exhausting meeting at the hospital, and suffering the acute effects of the chemotherapy I had received the day before, that I saw him crossing the deserted street ahead of me on that snowy night. Would I have accelerated and aimed my car at him if I were not influenced by my illness and the effects of the chemotherapy? I don't know. I have to admit that I thoroughly hated the man. Perhaps at this time it makes no real difference. History will only record a murderer and a victim.

After this I should certainly have sought help. That would have meant, of course, admitting to a colleague that I had committed murder. Besides, my deranged mind began telling me that Atkins had deserved to die. At any rate, I believed the problem was no more. Then Dickson Conway turned up and it was clear that Atkins had talked to him about you and his retaliatory program.

I couldn't tolerate standing by passively and watching your career be damaged more, so I went to see Conway in his research office. Perhaps he would not be as vicious as his friend. Often, in the absence of the co-sadist, one member of a duo becomes impotent to act. This didn't prove to be the case. He was worse, if that is possible. I was in a blind rage. I left him and started down the hall and then I saw the fire extinguisher on the wall in one of the rooms and took it from its wall-mount and returned to his office. He was sitting with his back to me. I hit him with all of my strength. I believe he died instantly. It was difficult for me to do, but I managed to drag his body to the stairwell, hoping that it would look like he'd fallen accidentally.

A curious thing was happening to me mentally. These

two murders made me feel powerful. I believe they compensated for the repressed awareness that I was losing my power—that I was in fact dying. I had become the sword of God. There remained one further obstacle in your path and by removing it I could make up for some of the harm already done to you. I could kill Ahmad. I told myself—and maybe I was correct—that it was the only way to guarantee that you and Miss Esma would be rid of this menace.

I had hired a private detective once in the past to locate a person who owed me money. I called him and said I had another similar situation. He called me after several days with Ahmad's address. I went there carrying a gun I'd had since the army and not traceable to me. I waited in the back stairway of Ahmad's apartment building for him to come home. As he was opening his apartment door I came up behind him and forced him to enter the apartment and sit down. I then shot him and left by the rear stairway. I had no way, of course, of knowing that you intended to be there that night. It is very important to me that you understand and believe that you had no part in any of my actions. What I did was all about me— and my illness—as I prefer to believe. My decision to end my life follows my conclusion that I have no option. I am going to die soon anyway, and I don't want my final days to be days of public disgrace suffered in prison.

This is the whole story. I have an urge to add many disclaimers to cast myself in a better light. I guess most people who are about to die feel the same.

My best wishes to you both,.
Mordecai Steiner, M.D."

I look up to see that there are tears running down Fahra's cheeks. She says nothing, only shakes her head.

I fold the letter and return it to the envelope. I have feelings rushing in all directions: shock, disbelief, profound empathy, dismay and affection. They seem to cancel each other out as in an algebraic equation, leaving a residual sadness.

Sonya glides to our table with our order. She hesitates for a moment until she has my eye. This time there's soft sympathy in her smile, almost as if she's known the story all along. Fahra wipes her eyes with her napkin and manages a faint smile. I put my hand out to her and she takes it and squeezes it. For a few moments we look into each other's eyes and then, as if on a signal, we turn our attention to a damned good Turkish meal.

Book for MAY

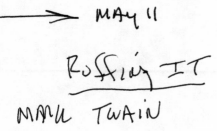 MAY 11

Roffing IT

MARK TWAIN

JUNE

The Reluctant Fundimentalist

MOSin HAMid

LaVergne, TN USA
10 February 2010
172684LV00002B/125/P